I0668919

RUINED…

With him, Eliza felt safe. She could pretend she was just a regular girl on a date with a handsome man.

Vince pressed his lips to her ear and whispered, "Holding you feels so good, I might never let you go."

Tingles swept through her stomach, and she closed her eyes against a rush of tears. This wasn't right, wasn't wise. Being near Vince only made her realize all she could never have. Why torture herself like this? She tensed and put some space between their bodies.

He frowned. "Are you all right?"

"I—I'm fine. I just…" She glanced over her shoulder. Was Oscar watching? If so, he would be displeased to say the least.

"Are you worried about Oscar?" His tone hardened. "Because you're working tonight?"

PRECARIOUS…

"I'm okay," Iris whispered.

Dante gave a low growl. "I'm not." His voice was husky, and the meaning was unmistakable.

What was happening between them? She'd loved him since she was a child, and if she were truthful, she was far from over her crush. But he'd never treated her with anything but brotherly affection. And, while she didn't have a brother, she was pretty sure they didn't look at their sisters like he was looking at her.

Her gaze dropped to his lips. Would they be firm, soft? Would they press against hers with raging passion, or tenderness? "Dante…" Mercy me. She wanted him to kiss her. Wanted it like she wanted her next breath. What kind of woman did that make her? She was *engaged…*

The Martini Club 4 series consists of a total of eight stories by four different authors. They are intertwined and take place somewhat simultaneously, but they are best read in the following order:

Martini Club 4: The 1920s Stories:

Rebellious by Amanda McCabe
Ruined by Alicia Dean
Reckless by Kathy L Wheeler
Runaway by Krysta Scott

Martini Club 4: The 1940s Stories:

Pampered by Kathy L Wheeler
Priceless by Krysta Scott
Perilous by Amanda McCabe
Precarious by Alicia Dean

We hope you enjoy!

Martini Club 4:

Ruined: The 1920s
Precarious: The 1940s

by

Alicia Dean

This is a work of fiction. Names, characters, places, and incidents are either the product of the author's imagination or are used fictitiously, and any resemblance to actual persons living or dead, business establishments, events, or locales, is entirely coincidental.

Martini Club 4: Ruined and Precarious

Contact Information: info@thewildrosepress.com

Cover Art by *Lisa Dawn MacDonald.*

The Wild Rose Press, Inc.
PO Box 708
Adams Basin, NY 14410-0708
Visit us at www.thewildrosepress.com

Publishing History
First Edition, 2021
Trade Paperback ISBN 978-1-5092-3680-0
Digital ISBN 978-1-5092-3679-4
Previously Self-Published

Martini Club 4: Ruined and Precarious
Published in the United States of America

Dedication

To the amazing staff of the Martini Lounge in Edmond, Oklahoma: Candace, Chase, Evan, Ashley, Danielle, Britton, and all the others. Thank you for enhancing our enjoyment at your lovely establishment by being completely awesome.

Acknowledgments

I can't imagine what could be more fun than sharing my passion of writing with a group of ladies that I love so dearly. The journey from the idea to the completion has been incredibly fun, between the weekly Martini Club outings, the weekend retreats, and the laughter and drinks. I'm looking forward to more of the same in the future. I would like to sincerely thank J. Lynn McKay for beta reading our stories, and a special thank you to our honorary MC4 member, Cindy Sorenson, for her friendship and for her read-through and input on our stories. You rock, my friend!

Martini Club 4:
The 1920s

Ruined

Martini Club 4, Book #1

Chapter One

The Earl of Goodwin's Country Estate, Abbots Langley, England, 1924

You must flee, my child." Maud's gaze darted around the kitchen of the main house, then returned to Eliza. "T'isn't safe for you here."

Eliza Gilbert gently patted Maud's arthritic hands. "Please don't fret, Maud. I can take care of myself." The woman had been like a mother to her since her own mum passed away just over a year ago. Maud had no husband, no children. Eliza was the closest to family she had. "I don't want to leave you. Besides, I have nowhere to go." Eliza tried to keep the hitch out of her voice. She didn't wish to upset Maud further, but the awful truth was, she *truly* had nowhere else to go. Was she destined to be a housemaid like her mum for the rest of her life? *Or worse…*

Worry over Eliza deepened the grooves in Maud's worn features. "But Lord Renwald will be home soon. You promised your mum, God rest her soul, that once the old Earl passed, you would leave." She flitted her free hand to her heart. "The Earl, God rest his soul, was the only thing standing betwixt you and the lord's lechery."

Lord Renwald had been leering at Eliza since she'd turned twelve and started to develop breasts. When she was fifteen, he'd cornered her in the stable, and no telling what might have happened if James, the stable boy, hadn't come to her rescue. Even now, a knot of revulsion clogged her throat at the memory of Lord Renwald's greedy hands on her body. After that, the Earl had kept a close eye on his son when the viscount was home from Oxford. But now the Earl was gone, along with her protection.

Eliza offered Maud a reassuring smile. "I can take care of myself. Rest assured, I'll be no man's tart."

"When Lord Renwald arrives, I'm afraid you won't have a choice." Maud glanced around the kitchen again before lowering her voice. "I've packed a valise for you should you need to leave in a rush. You'll find it in the cubby beneath the stairs. I've also tucked a few pounds in the pocket." Tears surfaced in her kind brown eyes. "I hope it never comes to that, but should you need to flee, you take that and run. And never look back."

Eliza pushed aside the worry Maud's words evoked. Granted, the man had been a plague on her life since childhood, but surely he would not be so bold as to force the issue. She would simply make it clear that she intended to remain on as part of the staff. Anything more was out of the question.

"I will, I promise. As I said, I can handle him." She wished she were as confident as she proclaimed but worrying Maud would not help matters. "Now, let's see to polishing the staircase banister shall we?"

****

Two days later, Lord Renwald returned to the estate. He hadn't troubled to attend his father's funeral, but he was back to claim his inheritance. With Maud's help, Eliza succeeded in staying out of his way the entire day. She breathed a sigh of relief when suppertime came and went and she hadn't run into him. Once her tasks were completed, she headed to her room in the attic. Just before she reached the top of the stairs, Miles, one of the footmen, approached.

"Eliza, the master has requested your presence in the study." Miles' features showed concern, but his tone remained level.

Eliza swallowed the apprehensive flutter that darted from her heart to her throat. "Why does he wish to see me?"

"I am afraid I do not know." But his failure to look her in the eyes indicated he did, just as she did.

Eliza nodded. "Thank you, Miles."

With lead feet, she made her way to the study. She smoothed her dull brown uniform skirt with trembling fingers, then knocked timidly, a foolish part of her hoping he wouldn't hear.

"Come in."

She drew in a fortifying breath and opened the door. Lord Renwald stood in front of the fireplace, a snifter of dark amber liquid in his hand, one booted foot propped on the marble hearth. He was tall and thin, reminding her of an ostrich the way he always strutted around with his chin jutted forward.

"You wished to see me, my lord?"

The viscount stretched his thick lips into a self-satisfied grin. "Yes, do come in. Close the door."

She hesitated for a moment, then did as he bade.

His gaze ran over her body. "No sense beating around the bush. I believe you've been aware of my…interest in you for quite some time."

She crossed her hands in front of her and tightened

her lips but didn't respond.

"I have a new position for you. You will no longer toil as a housemaid. Instead, I shall take you as my mistress." His tone indicated he'd offered her a rare gift.

She refrained from releasing the mocking laughter bubbling inside. "Thank you for the offer, my lord, but I respectfully decline."

His eyes widened. "Decline, do you? Perhaps you misunderstood. My statement was not a request. You *will* become my mistress." He stalked toward her, and Eliza took a step back.

"No, I will not. I shall leave my employment here altogether before I agree to become your mistress."

He threw his head back and laughed. "While I find your coyness delightful, my patience is wearing thin." He finished off his drink and slammed the glass down on a nearby table with a sharp crack like a gunshot. He strode to her and grabbed her shoulders. Yanking her against his body, he pressed wet, thick lips on her mouth.

Bile surfaced in her throat, and she gagged, jerking away from him and wiping her mouth.

He glared down at her. His muddy brown eyes sparked fire just before he slapped her cheek so hard, her ears rang.

Tears sprang to her eyes, but she turned back to him, lifting her chin and staring into his hateful face. "Release me this instant." In spite of the stinging in her cheek and her fear of what else he might be capable of, she forced bravado into her tone. "I hereby resign."

Rage suffused his narrow cheeks with red. "You stupid chit. You dare to defy *me*?" He gripped a handful of her hair and jerked her head back. "I shall have you. And when I am finished, you will be out on the streets. But not until I say, do you understand?" Without giving her a chance to respond, he once more forced his mouth on hers. His grip on her hair brought fresh tears in her eyes and set her scalp on fire. He grabbed the front of her uniform blouse and yanked. Cool air hit her exposed breasts. Panic threatened to choke her.

He was going to rape her. If she didn't do something now, he was going to have his way with her. Nausea and terror clamped her stomach. A haze filled her mind, and all she could think was, *I'm going to die, I'm going to die…*

Desperation spurring her, she reached out to the side table. Her fingers closed around the neck of a crystal vase. With a cry, she hefted the urn and slammed it into the back of Lord Renwald's head. Flowers spewed into the air, droplets of water sprinkling her face.

Lord Renwald bellowed, then fell to his knees, one hand on his head, blood seeping between his fingers. His mouth gaped like a fish, his eyes wide and agony-filled. He reached his free hand for her and nearly gripped her skirt, but she jumped back, out of his reach. He frowned as if perplexed, then thudded to the floor—still as a corpse.

Eliza stood frozen for a moment. Her entire body trembled. Warm stickiness coated her fingers. She'd killed a man. Not just a man, but an Earl. Dear Heaven, she'd *killed* him. If they caught her, she'd be put to death. The realization jolted her from her trance. She dropped the vase and rushed to the door, flinging it open. She raced down the hallway, to the stairs that led to the lower floor. Nearly flying, she hurried down the steps, past the wide-eyed stares of the other housemaids, and opened the cubby. Just as Maud promised, the valise was inside. Eliza snatched it and rushed to the back door. Her heart ached that she hadn't had a chance to tell Maud goodbye, to thank her. But she'd promised the woman she would run and never look back. She didn't know where she would go, or how she would get there, but she knew she would never return.

Chapter Two

Manhattan, New York, Six Months Later

Eliza buttoned an emerald green jacket over her yellow drop-waist dress. The weather was balmy for October, and she would prefer to shed the jacket altogether, but she couldn't seek employment with the frayed sleeves of her dress showing. She *must* land this position. Her purse held all the money she had in the world—five dollars, her final pay from the garment factory. Two days had passed since she'd been let go, but she hadn't yet found the nerve to tell her flatmates. Jess and Charli and Meggie had done so much for her from the moment they met on the docks, through their travels, and setting up in New York. It was time she stood on her own and repaid them.

She pushed open the diner door, jingling a bell hanging above. The sign outside stated they had need of a counter girl. The position probably did not pay as much as the factory, but she had to find employment—soon.

The smell of frying meat filled the air, making her stomach rumble. She approached the counter. A middle-aged man with a receding hairline and a cigar stub protruding from his mouth narrowed his eyes at her. The name badge on his stained apron read Frederick. "Can I help you, miss?"

"Yes, please." Her stomach growled again, and her

face warmed. Hopefully, he hadn't heard. She was famished. The last thing she'd eaten was one of Charli's cinnamon scones that morning. Her mouth watered at the thought of the warm, flaky, delicious pastries. Why hadn't she eaten two? She swallowed. "I've come to inquire about the position as counter girl. I'm a hard worker and a fast learner. I'd make you a fine employee."

He frowned. "Sorry, the position is filled." His eyes dropped away. He was lying. She'd told enough fibs to recognize when others were doing the same.

"But, sir. Your sign is still up. Are you certain the position has been filled?"

With a grunt, he plucked the cigar from his mouth and pointed it at her. "Okay, truth is, the position's still open. But you ain't getting it. I don't want no dame with a limey accent greetin' my customers."

She blinked in surprise. In all the months she'd been in America, she'd been treated well. Truly believed she'd found the land of opportunity. She'd never forget her first glimpse of the Statue of Liberty. Her heart had swelled with happiness and hope. At that moment, she'd felt anything was possible. This man's prejudice was not indicative of the attitude of most Americans she'd met. She had no desire to work with an oaf such as this, but she was desperate.

"Please, sir. I can disguise my accent." She attempted to erase the British inflection as she said the words, but even to her ears, she was unsuccessful. "I need work, and I promise you won't regret it." Before he could deny her a second time, she rushed on, "Or I can cook. Wash dishes. Anything you need. In London, I was head of the entire kitchen staff." Not quite the truth, but it was unlikely he would check her references all the way in England. Besides, she'd killed her former boss, so there would be no one to give her a poor review. "You won't regret it, I promise."

"Sorry, doll. I only need a counter girl. And you can't disguise your accent. You sound about as American as Mussolini. Now scram. I got work to do."

She drew in a breath, ready to launch into an argument, but the set of his features and the clenching of his fists told her the words would be useless. And she didn't want to make any more of a fool of herself than she already had.

Eyes down, she hurried past the occupants in the diner. Stepping outside, she hiccupped back tears. Dusk was settling over the city, along with the smell of exhaust from the vehicles clogging the streets. She headed down the crowded sidewalk, barely aware of the bleeping horns and chatter of pedestrians. Her brain fogged with worry. What now?

How much longer could she pretend to leave for work each morning, while in reality walking the streets of New York City, searching for a job? She would certainly have to confess the truth to her friends when her meager funds ran out.

She pulled out her clutch and unlatched the clasp. The paltry five dollars inside mocked her. Three of that would be taken by her share of the rent, due tomorrow. Only two dollars left to last until she not only found a position but received her first week's pay. And judging from her job search the past few days, it was certain to be a while before something surfaced. If it ever did. She suppressed the urge to weep. What would she do?

Just as she clasped the latch on her purse, a force

jarred her from behind, slamming her to the walk. She fell to her knee, instinctively thrusting her hands in front of her. Her clutch skittered away. Cement scraped the flesh on her palms, and stinging agony shot through her wrists to her shoulders. She choked back a sob and came to her feet just in time to see a man in a brown shirt, fedora low over his eyes snatch up her clutch and take off running.

"Hey!" She started after him, but the pain in her knee impeded her progress. A few passersby shot curious looks but moved on without offering assistance. The thief disappeared around a corner. She halted, breathing heavily. "Bloody fig!" The words came out more as a sob than the angry insult she intended. She stomped her foot, causing another wave of pain to shoot through her body. Holding out her bleeding, scraped hands, she assessed the damage. Her palms throbbed like hell, but she was so angry she was certain she wasn't feeling the pain as much as she would when her adrenaline ebbed.

"Bloody horsefeathers. *Damn, damn, damnation.*"

Her mother would have told her maybe the poor bloke needed it worse than she did, but her mother was addle-brained if she believed that, God rest her soul. The chances he needed it more than she did were slim. Even if he did, that was of no consequence. It was *her* money. She'd sweated and poked her fingers with those bloody sewing needles for a solid week to earn that. And now look at her. Where had it gotten her? Was her fate in Abbots Langley more desirable than the one she now faced?

No, no it wasn't. Not only would she have been at Lord Renwald's lecherous mercy, in Abbots Langley she had no one other than Maud. And Maud was getting on in years. Eliza had lost her mum and the Earl. Once Maud was gone, she would have no one. In New York, she had friends—sisters, really.

At the thought of the girls, panic leapt to her throat. That was all the cash she had. Rent was due. She had no job. How would she face her flatmates? More than just flatmates, they were her friends. They'd found her on the docks, included her on their journey to America on the *Empress of India*—they'd *saved* her. She'd posed as their lady's maid, and the ship's steward had allowed all four girls to board without raising a brow. They'd all been running from something, though none of them from a murder they'd committed, as was she. She hadn't confessed the incident with Lord Renwald. She'd only told the girls she was leaving the employ of a tyrant boss. It was the partial truth at least, and thank Heaven, they'd believed her. Trusted her. *What a bunch of saps*. If they knew the real her…

No matter how much she tried, she wasn't like the other girls. They'd come from wealthy, loving homes. They had already found opportunity here in the land of the free. And she had been nothing but a failure.

"Hey, Miss, are you okay?"

She whirled at the sound of a male voice, for one second foolishly believing her attacker had suffered a bout of conscience and come to return the money. But this man was not the one who had mugged her. The crook had been slight of build. The man standing in front of her was tall and wide. He wore a brown pinstriped suit with a dark gold vest underneath. His stomach protruded through a gap between the buttons. His brown hair was sparse on top, combed to the side to try and take advantage of the small amount he still possessed. She frowned. The man looked familiar. Where had she seen him before?

She wasn't certain, but she had more important things on her mind at the moment. She had to find a way to come up with money—fast. And find a job—immediately. Yeah, fat chance of either of those happening. She drew in a deep breath and wiped the back of her hand over her brow. "I'm fine. Just a little scuffed up. That…cad…stole my pocket book."

"Yes, I heard your…*opinion* of the thief." Amusement lit his eyes.

Heat flooded her cheeks. So he'd heard her swearing like a fishwife? "Yes, well—"

"Don't worry. I don't blame you. In your position, I might have said worse."

She cast her eyes down. "It's just that…I only this moment…obtained a job at the diner. I needed that money to get by until I received my pay."

"You're saying you were hired at the diner?"

She lifted her head. Something in his expression told her he knew she was lying. How? Then it dawned on her. He looked familiar because he'd been one of the customers inside. *Horsefeathers*. He'd heard her humiliation with the owner, and now this?

"Yes. Um, I really must be getting home now. If you'll pardon me." She started down the sidewalk, but his voice stopped her.

"Wait. You're hurt. Let me take you to the hospital."

She paused and looked back at him. "No, thank you. It's only a few scrapes. I'm almost home." In truth, she was quite a distance from home. She'd traveled over fifteen blocks in her job search. She didn't relish the idea of walking back on an injured knee. But she also didn't relish the thought of being accosted by a bounder.

He offered a smile. "I understand why you wouldn't trust me. You don't know me. But I've seen you before. At The Globe Theater, right?"

She nodded slowly. "My friend, Meggie, is an actress who performs there."

"Lady Margaret, of course. My name is Oscar Cummings. I have a regular box at the theater."

Ah, yes. She'd seen him there a few times. But she was also certain he'd been in the diner. "Right. Mr. Cummings. I remember. Nice to see you again, but really, I must be going."

"Please." He took her arm in a gentle grip. "My car is right here." He pointed to a black sedan. "I live nearby. If you won't go to the hospital, at least let me take you to my apartment where I have salve and bandages to treat your wounds. You shouldn't walk home in this condition."

He was right. Her hands stung as though fire ants feasted on her flesh. Her knees throbbed, and it took every ounce of willpower not to burst into tears. A ride in an automobile sounded so much more appealing than limping fifteen blocks home. But going to the apartment of a strange man? No, not wise. She'd learned her lesson from Lord Renwald.

She shook her head. "No need. I'm not far from home. Thank you for your kind offer."

"Of course." He bowed at the waist. "If you're certain you're okay, I'll leave you. However, I fear my gentlemanly conscience will be sorely vexed." He wiped at his eyes. Were those…tears? He gave an embarrassed laugh. "Forgive me my sentimentality. You remind me of my niece, and the thought of her wandering the streets injured, unattended…"

She stood indecisively. He most definitely seemed harmless. And he was so concerned. He was a regular at the theater…

And Lord Renwald had been the son of a kind man she knew and trusted. Yet she couldn't trust *him* as far as she could toss him.

"Thank you, but no." She turned her back and took two steps. Pain shot from her knee to her thigh, her leg crumpled, and she nearly fell again. Blast! Frustrated tears fought to surface, but she would not cry…

"Miss, please. Let me help you."

Her knee hurt too badly to think clearly. Making it home in this condition would be painful, if not impossible. Her instincts had sharpened during her time on the streets before she'd met the girls. She knew in her gut, this man was not a blackguard. He was more like the Earl than Lord Renwald. Biting her lip to stem the tears, she nodded. "On second thought, your help would be appreciated, Mr. Cummings."

Worry melted from his face, replaced by relief. "Splendid." He held the door open for her, and she slipped inside, then settled against the seat.

He climbed into the driver's side, and the vehicle bumped along the streets, passing pedestrians at nearly ten times their speed. Eliza let out a contented sigh. This was the only way to get around. Someday, maybe she would have one of her own.

"What kind of automobile is this?" She tried to keep the envy out of her voice.

"A Jordan Brougham. I own a Nash as well, but I prefer the Jordan. It's a much smoother ride."

"It's beautiful."

He shot her a smile and, in a few moments, pulled next to a curb in front of a building that was at least twenty floors high. Inside, he escorted her across a mosaic-patterned carpet in black and gray tones that was as plush as cotton.

They stepped off the elevator on the twentieth floor. Nervously, she followed. She hadn't seen anything this fancy since the estate in Abbots Langley. And there she'd been a mere servant. Here, she was a guest. Her stomach no longer rumbled with hunger, it was too filled with apprehension.

He stopped before double wooden doors and fitted his key in the lock, then swung the door open. She remained rooted in the hallway until he said, "Please, come in. It's fine."

With a hesitant step, she was inside. She looked around, unable to stop a small gasp from escaping her lips. The room was as opulent as any at the Earl's estate. Rich golden draperies hung over floor length windows. In the center of the room sat a sofa with a matching settee and chair covered in ivory satin and trimmed in gold. The décor was elegant and luxurious without being vulgar.

"Your home is lovely."

Mr. Cummings smiled. "Thank you. Have a seat, and I'll get some salve and bandages."

Eliza eyed the sofa warily. She would not sit on such a glorious item and make a mess of it. "I can stand."

"Nonsense. Sit." He prodded with a gentle hand to

her back until she lowered gingerly onto the edge of the sofa. "I'll be right back."

In moments, he returned, carrying a first aid kit and a glass of water. He sat next to her and placed the kit on the gleaming oak coffee table. Retrieving a bottle of aspirin, he shook out two and handed them to her, along with the water. She swallowed the aspirin, and he took the glass from her, setting it on a side table. He removed bandages and antiseptic salve. "Give me your hands." She did, and he rested them, palms up, on his knees. He offered a reassuring smile. "This won't hurt much, I promise."

She released the breath she'd had pent up in her chest. He was so kind, just the type of man she imagined her father would have been had he lived. He'd died in a farming accident when she was an infant. She had no recollection of him at all—only the locket with a small photo of his mustached, smiling image she wore around her neck—but when she was small, she'd fantasized about what he was like. Oscar Cummings was so close to a fantasy father, it was eerie.

"There, all done."

She blinked and looked down. Her hands were bandaged, the pain had ebbed, and she'd barely been aware of his ministrations.

"Thank you. Really. You're much too kind."

He chuckled. "Nonsense, my dear. I'm pleased I could help."

She rose from the sofa, unsure of what to do next. She couldn't very well ask him for a ride home after all his kindness, but his penthouse was five miles or so from The Gables Boardinghouse where she lived. She couldn't walk that distance in the dark. And she hadn't the funds for a taxi. Letting him know of her troubles was out of the question. He'd heard enough of her complaints. With an uncertain laugh, she said, "Now, I must be off. Thank you again."

"Let me see you home. You can't go wandering the streets after dark."

Relief swept through her. "That's very kind of you."

He narrowed his eyes as if in thought and put a finger to his lips. "Now that I think about it, perhaps I can offer you something more than a bandage and a ride home."

Her interest piqued, she lifted her brows. "Such as?"

"I am aware you…uh…just landed a new job, but I might have a position for you. Something I think you'll enjoy more. One that pays *much* better."

Hope lit inside her, but she attempted not to appear too anxious. "What kind of position would that be?"

"I need a hostess. Someone to help me with parties."

"Parties?" A position that paid for assisting with parties? Who'd ever heard of such a thing? "You would like to hire me to plan parties?"

"Not plan parties. More like a hostess. I need someone to help me by mingling with my guests. The job pays twenty-five dollars a week."

She nearly gasped aloud. Had she heard him correctly? Surely she was in a dream. Her salary at the factory had been five dollars per week, but once they deducted monies as reimbursement for what they considered mistakes—a crooked stitch, a bent needle, or any other minor misstep—she was lucky to come home with half that. “You would pay me to attend parties?”

“Yes. People love to have fun, and they enjoy having beautiful girls around them at parties. And you are quite beautiful.”

Her cheeks warmed at the compliment. Excitement brimmed at his proposal. Everything in her screamed, *‘Take the job, you ninny. What possible chance will you ever have for such an opportunity?’* But another part of her acknowledged the warning bells. Her mum always said if something seemed too good to be true, it probably was. This most definitely reeked of ‘too good to be true.’ But what if it wasn’t? Mr. Cummings seemed one of the nicest men she’d ever met. Had he wanted to harm her, mightn’t he have already done so?

She surveyed the lavish surroundings, decision made. Too good to be true, be damned. With no position at all, she would be a fool to turn down such an offer.

“Thank you. Yes, I accept.” Her heart swelled with happiness. To go from sweaty, back-breaking, potentially life-threatening work in the Garment District to a party hostess in a place like this was a dream come true.

Mr. Cummings smiled and patted her shoulder. “I’m very pleased. I think you will enjoy working for me.” A mischievous smile touched his mouth. “I hope the gentleman at the diner won’t mind too much that you’ve changed your mind.”

She dropped her eyes and shook her head. “I doubt he’ll give it a second thought.”

“Wonderful.” He reached into his breast pocket and retrieved his wallet. He pulled out two twenty dollar bills and held them out. “Here is an advance.”

She jerked her gaze to his. “Advance? But, I haven’t yet lifted a finger. Why would you pay me an advance?”

“You need evening dresses. I’m sure you wouldn’t want to wear your own nice things to work in. And you were robbed, remember? You will need some pocket money before your salary begins.” He pushed the bills into her injured hand and gently closed her fingertips over the cash. “I provide an advance for all my girls. It’s part of the contract.”

“Contract?”

“Yes. Just a small detail to get out of the way. Come, and we’ll be set.” She followed him to a small desk where he opened a drawer and withdrew a few sheets of paper, then handed them to her.

She squinted at the document, cheeks burning. Her reading skills were limited at best. She could make out most of the words but didn’t understand exactly what they meant. “Um, this part here. Where I will per-perform any tasks you dee-deem appro—”

“Appropriate?” he coaxed gently.

“Yes, deem appropriate. What does that mean exactly?”

He favored her with another of those fatherly smiles. “It simply means that, as your employer, I determine the tasks you perform. Such as, serving drinks, chatting with partygoers. Perhaps once in a while, I will ask you to dance with a gentleman. The usual sort of thing.”

Those things didn’t sound all that unpleasant. Was he being forthright with her? “Those are common tasks one might expect to perform at a party?”

"Precisely." He shared another smile and handed her a fountain pen. "Once you sign the contract, I'll take you home."

She frowned down at the paper once more. "This states that I must stay for two years. If I choose to leave your employ, I'll be required to pay a fee of…" She looked up at him. "Does this say one thousand dollars?" Even with the generous salary Oscar was offering, it would take years to save that amount.

"Yes, but that's simply standard language in the agreement. It protects my investment and assures that my employees do not take the advance and then up and disappear on me."

That made sense. He had to cover his investments. Besides, why wouldn't she want to do this for two years? It sounded divine. "This is all very generous."

"Would you be able to start, say, two nights from now? I'm hosting a party, and I would love your assistance."

He seemed sincere. Nothing at all like Lord Renwald. She'd learned to recognize lechery in a man's gaze. She nodded, still not quite believing the luck that had turned her way. "I am absolutely available two nights from now. Where do I sign?"

Chapter Three

Eliza let herself into the boardinghouse, bubbling with excitement to tell her flatmates her good news. Of course, they didn't know she'd lost her former position. She would have to admit she'd been keeping it from them.

No matter, she had found employment, wonderful, thrilling employment. Her friends would be happy for her.

She fit her key in the lock and swung the door open. Jessica sat at their small, chipped kitchen table reading the *New York World.* She wrote for the newspaper and always had her nose stuck in some rag or another.

"Jess! I have the most splendid news!"

Jess grinned and leaned back in her chair, her reddish-blonde bob swinging with the motion. "Something certainly has you hopped up. So, dish."

Eliza shrugged out of her jacket and draped it on the back of a chair. Jess's gaze dropped to her hands. "What happened?"

"Oh, this? It's nothing. Just a few scrapes." Why worry her friends? The aspirin and salve had eased the pain considerably. Everything was fine now, and she could pay her own way. "Before I give you my news, I must confess, I haven't been completely honest with you and the other girls."

Jess raised her brows. “Why doesn’t that surprise me?”

Eliza ignored her droll tone. “I lost my job at the garment factory two days ago.”

“Oh, darling, why didn’t you tell us?” Concern replaced her playful expression. “We could have helped you. Maybe I can check at the paper and see if they have an opening.”

She settled on the chair next to Jess. “I appreciate that, but you and Meggie and Charli have already done so much for me. I didn’t want to be a burden.” She took Jess’s hands in hers, wincing at the slight sting in her palms. “But none of that matters now, because I found a new position. A fabulous one! Do you know Oscar Cummings? He’s a regular at The Globe. Tall, big belly, booming laugh.”

“I don’t know the name, but I believe I’ve seen him at the theater.”

Eliza explained how she’d run into Oscar, leaving out the part about the mugging. “I have enough rent money to cover the next few weeks. That’s not even the best part. He gave me an advance to purchase new dresses. Isn’t that the bee’s knees?”

Jess frowned. “Are you certain Oscar is on the level?” Jess was a reporter, so she was naturally suspicious. Always trying to sniff out a juicy story.

“I admit I was hesitant, but he was so kind. He brought me to his apartment and saw to my injuries, personally. Had he wanted to do anything…vile…I mean, wasn’t that the perfect opportunity?” Her thoughts flashed to Lord Renwald. What would Jess say if Eliza told her the story? That Eliza had a very good reason for knowing what would happen with a cad rather than a gentleman like Mr. Cummings.

"Well, I'm happy for you. But you must be careful. Maybe I should sniff out this Oscar fellow. Make sure he's on the up and up."

"Of course, but you won't find anything shady. He's quite the respectable gentleman." Eliza dug out the bills Oscar had given her and held them out. "Generous, too. He gave me an advance so I could buy something nice to wear to his parties." She grinned, happier than she'd been since before her mum passed. "How would you like to go shopping?"

****

Oscar's apartment was bursting at the edges with smartly dressed men and women. Eliza tried not to gawk at the flappers, but they were terribly exciting, and their dresses were daring and flashy. Her own gown—a bare-backed shimmery gold satin with a feathered hemline—was the nicest she'd ever owned. She'd never felt more fancy—or more exposed—in all her life. She'd purchased the dress at B. Altman's but had barely worked up the nerve to enter the elegant shop. She'd been out of her element, just as she was now.

She shoved away the worry. Tonight was too special…too fabulous to let anything spoil it. So many interesting people and Oscar was *paying* her to chat with them, drink with them. She'd danced with a few blokes, which had made her feel slightly uncomfortable, but she was having *fun*. Sometimes she almost forgot she was working.

She sipped from her wine goblet, trying not to gape like a ninny, but everything was just so…grand. This was the second of Oscar's parties she'd attended and she'd never dreamed a position could be so easy.

Soft jazz music played on the phonograph, and Oscar's elegant guests laughed and chatted. A cool breeze drifted in from the open balcony door.

Oscar approached, looking debonair in a double-breasted black tuxedo. "How are you, my dear? Enjoying yourself?"

"Oh yes, a bundle. Isn't there something more I should do? I feel so..." She searched for the right word—lucky? Pampered? "Useless. I don't wish to take advantage of your kindness."

"Nonsense. You are doing exactly what I'm paying you to do—looking beautiful and entertaining my guests."

"Yes, Mr. Cummings."

"I've told you before, it's Oscar." He pointed his cigar toward a group of three gentlemen standing near the fireplace. "Why don't you go chat with those men, introduce yourself, charm them."

Her face warmed. She had no idea how to charm men, but she wasn't going to let Oscar down now. He might release her, and she fervently wanted to maintain her position. She'd played many roles since fleeing Abbots Langley. She'd had to in order to survive on the streets. Playing the role of charming hostess? No effort at all.

The three men looked up and smiled when she approached. Two of them were of medium build, wearing similar plaid suits with waistcoats. One had slicked down hair, the other was nearly bald. The third man was taller with a pencil thin mustache.

"Good evening, gentlemen, I'm Eliza. I hope you're enjoying yourselves."

The tall one bent at the waist in a bow. "I must say I'm enjoying myself much more now that you've joined us. My name is Clifford." He gestured toward the balding chap, then the other gent in turn. "Harold and Les."

She shook hands with each man and smiled. From their conversations, she learned one was a judge, and the other two were bankers. She made appropriately impressed noises and asked what she hoped were halfway intelligent questions.

The three men puffed out their chests and attempted to talk over one another. Eliza made a concentrated effort to appear interested, but everything they said was so…boring. It was, however, scads better than working in the dark, dirty factory, jabbing her fingers until they were bleeding and raw, heading home so knackered she could barely move.

A cry of distress caught her attention, and she swung around. A young woman—bright red hair sticking out in haphazard pieces from a glittery headband, lovely ivory gown crumpled and falling off her shoulders—was trying to tug her hand out of Oscar's.

"No!" Her shrill voice carried across the room. "I won't. You can't make me. Not anymore."

Oscar released her hand and slipped his arm around her shoulders, speaking quietly into her ear. He then scanned the room, smiling at his guests, although his smile seemed a bit strained. "Please, ladies and gentlemen, do not be alarmed. The young lady is a little overwrought, but she just needs a good night's rest. Go back to having a good time, and I'll make sure she's taken care of."

“Excuse me,” Eliza said to her companions. She moved quickly to Oscar’s side. The girl buried her face in her hands, and her shoulders shook with sobs. “Is there anything I can do to help?”

“No, thank you, Eliza. I’ll see her home. I’m certain she’ll be fine in the morning.” He glanced around and his voice lowered. “The girl is one of my employees. She recently had somewhat of a…breakdown. She’s still—”

“Liar!” The girl lifted her face from her hands, her expression twisted in hate. Black make up was smeared around her desperate-looking eyes. “You know that’s not true.” She raised her chin and faced Oscar squarely.

Eliza glanced around the room. Some of the partygoers’ gazes were riveted on the scene, their expressions a mixture of discomfort and curiosity.

“Please, my dear.” Oscar shook his head regretfully and said to Eliza, “She’s mentally unstable. I’m afraid my hopes that she’d improved were a bit optimistic. I should have seen she wasn’t ready to go out in public quite yet.”

His words sounded comforting, but in the girl’s blue eyes, Eliza saw panic. Was that part of her instability, or was there more going on?

“Are you okay?” Eliza asked softly.

The girl shook her head. “I—I’m finished. I can’t do this anymore.”

Oscar’s lips thinned, and his fleshy jowls quivered. “Now, now, you’re getting balled up over nothing.” He put his arm around the girl and led her away. “There, there, my dear. You just need some rest.”

“I can’t—I just can’t. Not any longer. I quit. I don’t care about the…”

Her voice faded as she and Oscar moved farther away.

Half an hour later, Oscar returned, smiling, moving among the guests, the incident with the young woman apparently forgotten.

The rest of the evening held a pall. Eliza laughed and drank as she had before, but the image of black-smeared, haunted eyes never left her mind.

Chapter Four

Two days later: Philadelphia, Taggart's Gym

Vince Taggart held the heavy bag while Gianni worked it over. With each punch, grunts and droplets of sweat flew. The man had the makings of a champ if he could just show some self-discipline. He spent his nights drinking and carousing with women. If a guy didn't train hard and forego the party life, he'd never make it in the boxing world. You were either all in or not in at all. And Gianni was definitely not all in.

The more the guy sweated, the more Vince could smell last night's booze. "Okay, champ, that's enough. Why don't you hit the showers and come back tomorrow."

Gianni nodded, breathing heavily. "Yeah, I don't feel so good."

"Maybe tonight, you take it easy, stay home, kick up your feet, get a good night's rest."

Gianni lifted his gloved hands. "What you think I been doing every night?"

Vince shrugged. "Jack Daniels and good looking dames?"

Gianni's face reddened. "Yeah, well. I guess I could cut back a little."

Vince tossed him a towel. He caught it and dabbed sweat from his face and chest. "If you want to make it in this game, kid, you better cut back more than a little."

Gianni nodded and headed to the locker room. Vince shook his head. No way was the kid gonna listen. He'd had to have it pounded in his head over and over before he got it. Vince knew the score. He'd had his own ass pounded a few times before the message was driven home.

Speaking of home, Cynthia still hadn't made it back. His gut told him something was wrong. He intended to find out.

He found Smiley, his right hand man, oiling a heavy bag.

"Hey, Smiley, got a second?"

"Sure, boss. What's up?"

"Can you watch the place for a few days?"

Smiley's forehead wrinkled with his perpetual frown. "Sure." He spat a stream of tobacco juice into the cup he held. "You got a beauty parlor appointment or somethin'?" He chuckled, but the frown never left his face. No matter how happy or how angry he was, his expression never changed.

"How about I lay one right in your kisser?"

Smiley grunted. "You haven't laid one in anyone's kisser in a long time."

Vince scowled. Smiley had been razzing him ever since he'd hung up his gloves. Even though he knew as well as anyone why he quit boxing.

"Not since Benito," Smiley added.

The name punched Vince in the gut. He would never hear that name again that he didn't turn to ice inside. He'd never close his eyes again without seeing the kid's face. Vince drew in a deep breath and let it out slowly. The guilt wasn't so easy to release. "I've told you a thousand times not to bring that up."

"It wasn't your fault. That's a risk these palookas take when they step in the ring."

"Thanks to me, he's a cripple."

Smiley rubbed a gnarled hand over his gray whiskers. With cauliflower ears, a flat nose with no cartilage left, and a patchwork of scars on his mug, he was the ugliest man Vince had ever seen. But he was also Vince's best friend. Ever since '19 when they'd fought in Chicago.

Smiley'd had Vince on the ropes, could have finished him off, but he didn't. His gaze connected with Vince's, and something changed in his demeanor. He'd dropped his hands, stepped back, and motioned with the gloves for Vince to come on. Vince finished him off, knowing the entire time Smiley was throwing the fight, but not knowing why.

They'd had a beer later that night, and Smiley had explained. He was on his way out of the boxing game, and Vince was just starting. He saw something in him that made him want to give Vince a leg up. Besides, his manager was a crook, and he wanted him to get a share of the loser's purse rather than the winner's. Unbeknownst to both of them, Vince's career would end two years later. But he'd made enough to buy this gym, and Smiley had worked for him since he opened.

Smiley spat again and wiped his mouth with the back of his hand. "You gotta let that go."

Easy for Smiley to say. Not so easy to do. Smiley knew that as well as anyone.

"So can you watch the place for me or not? I haven't heard from Cynthia since last week."

"You mean when she called and said she was

coming back? You told her you two was through, didn't ya'?"

"I did, but I also told her if she'd come home, we could talk about it. She should have been here by now."

"You think something happened to her?"

"Got a gut feeling. I can't rest til I know. This isn't like her." But then, what of her recent actions had been? He'd broken off their engagement when her three-day trip to New York had stretched out to two months. He didn't know what she'd gotten mixed up in, but she hadn't sounded like his Cynthia, the girl he'd grown up with, the girl he'd always known he'd end up marrying. She'd sounded more—worldly, colder. She told him she wasn't sure if she ever wanted to come back to Philly.

Then, out of the blue, she called last week, in tears, said she was ready to come back. He was pretty sure he didn't want to marry her now—that he'd never look at her the same, like the kind of woman he wanted raising his kids. When he married, he wanted it to be to someone he could trust. He'd thought that woman was Cynthia. Now he knew different, but he cared about her and didn't want her to wind up in trouble, so far from home. So, he'd pretended like there was still a chance for them—he had to do something to get her home where she'd be safe.

"I hope there ain't nothin' wrong." Smiley was fond of Cynthia. He didn't like that she'd done Vince wrong, but his expression said he was worried, too.

"I tried to reach her at the Starlight hotel where she was staying, but they said she took off, without checking out. Left all her stuff there."

He grunted. "Doesn't sound like she was headin'

back. She'da packed up and brought her things. Sounds troublin' all right."

Even though Vince had already been concerned, Smiley's words increased the tension in his gut. "That's why I gotta go check on her." He didn't like New York City—too noisy, too crowded. He hadn't been since May when he'd watched the Yankees slaughter the Philadelphia Athletics six to zip. The Babe had knocked two out of the park that game, and Vince had left in a lather. He hadn't planned on returning any time soon, but Cynthia needed him.

"Sure, I'll watch the place. When you find her, you gonna take her back?"

"Not planning on it." Vince shrugged. "I can't think about that right now. First thing I gotta do is find her."

Alive, he silently prayed.

****

Eliza sat on a barstool at Club 501, her legs crossed, sipping a White Lady. The joint was wall to wall people. There weren't many places as nice as Club 501 that sold liquor. Most were seedy, dangerous. Club 501 had opened a few days ago. The two level speakeasy was as luxurious as a palace with its rich gold and mauve tones, velvet upholstery, and long oak bar.

Meggie was on stage singing "Crazy Blues." She wore a one-shoulder peach calf-length gown with a scalloped hemline trimmed in shimmery silver braid. Her eyes were half closed, blonde curls glistening beneath the spotlight.

Eliza closed her eyes and let the loveliness of Meggie's voice soothe her. Uncanny how she could sing without the hint of an accent.

In the worst of times, Eliza used a mind trick where she traveled to another place and removed herself from whatever was happening. She'd had to use the trick many times as a scullery maid, and when Lord Renwald had trapped her in the barn, but the night he'd nearly raped her, that had been something altogether different. Rather than using a mind trick, she'd fully escaped. Meggie's voice brought her that kind of escape. She was transported to another place.

The song ended, and Eliza opened her eyes, clapping more loudly than anyone else in the place. Meggie winked and curtsied, then went into her next number. Someday, she was going to make it big, Eliza just knew it.

"Need anything else?" Charli appeared at her shoulder, holding a tray full of empty glasses at shoulder level. She wore the Club 501 uniform—a mauve dress that came to mid-thigh with sheer voile that fell to her ankles. She'd acquired a position as cocktail waitress a few days after Meggie had been hired as a singer.

"No, thank you. Last night was a late one. I ought to take it slowly."

Charli wrinkled her pert nose. "What a sweet deal you landed, while I'm stuck in this dive slinging booze."

Eliza pursed her lips. "Now, Charli, this is hardly a dive. Serving drinks here might not be the wealthy lifestyle you're accustomed to, but things could be worse—much worse."

Sympathy shone in Charli's brown eyes. "I know, luv. Selfish of me. I know what you've been through, how awful things were for you before we found you on the docks, then again when you arrived and had to take a position at that ghastly old factory." She let out a sigh. "It's just that I had such high hopes. I wanted so much to start a great life doing what I love most."

Eliza squeezed her friend's hand. "You'll get your bakery, I know you will. You keep schmoozing Mrs. Carter, and you're a shoo in." Mrs. Carter was a successful businesswoman who owned a string of department stores. Charli all but panted after the woman.

Charli giggled and playfully slapped Eliza's knee. "I do not schmooze her. I just find her interesting." She glanced over her shoulder. "Sorry, gotta run. These blokes might perish if I don't keep the hooch flowing." She cocked an impish grin. "See ya, luv."

Eliza scanned the crowd. Jess was supposed to come in, but so far, Eliza hadn't seen her. She was feeling slightly abandoned. At least Oscar wasn't present. Now that he was her employer, she could barely relax when he was at Club 501. She always felt she was on the clock.

Her gaze bounced over a man, then zeroed back. The bloke was looking directly at her. She caught her breath. He was leaning on the bar a few stools down, talking to Charli. He had this…magnetism, some kind of forceful presence that made it impossible to look away.

He was broad, muscular and dressed like a dock worker with brown suspenders over a yellow shirt and a newsboy cap over his dark blond hair, but what caught her attention right off was his smile. His white teeth flashed, and a dimple creased the right side of his face.

Charli moved away, and the man looked up and caught Eliza staring at him. His grin widened. His eyes were so blue—so electrifying, that Eliza could feel their allure even in the dimly lit, smoky bar.

He winked and gave her a finger salute off the brim of his cap.

A tingle ran from her toes, all the way through her body, making her head swim. *My, but he was a fresh one.* With superhuman effort, she dragged her attention away, but it didn't keep her heart from racing faster than a thoroughbred at Churchill Downs.

She swallowed and took a deep breath, fingering the pendant at her neck, trying to slow her heart rate. What on earth was wrong with her? She met plenty of handsome men—men more pleasing to the eye than he with his workmen clothing and slightly crooked nose. But never had any man sent her blood rushing through her veins like this.

She gulped from her glass. *Get ahold of yourself.* She was not the kind of girl to pick up strange men in bars—even if they did have a devil of a smile and eyes like an angel.

Chapter Five

Vince stared at the stiff, but lovely spine of the woman at the bar. He grinned. The dame was trying to pretend they hadn't had a moment, that something hadn't passed between them in those brief seconds her eyes had met his. Playing it cool as a cucumber, while he was sweating beneath the brim of his cap. He'd never reacted to a woman that way before. What was so special about her? She was a looker, sure, but so were half the bims in the joint.

Had he been here for any other reason, he would approach the babe and turn on the Taggart charm until he had her eating out of his hands. And, since he was now a free man, he could taste those pouty lips, slide his hands beneath that satiny green dress, run them all over her soft, porcelain skin. But there was no time for such pleasures tonight. He was even more worried about Cynthia than he had been before. He'd booked a room at the Starlight, and the desk manager had confirmed, Cynthia just…disappeared. Without checking out. Without taking her things. Why would she do that? She wouldn't. Not willingly.

The clerk had told Vince she'd started hanging out at a new juice joint called Club 501, and here he was. Not a sign of Cynthia, but he hadn't expected there to be.

He pulled his attention away from the sexy

brunette.

"Hey, buddy, I know you."

Vince turned to find a chubby fellow a few inches taller than him sitting on a stool, a big smile on his big, dumb face. "Taggart, right?"

Vince shook his head. "You got me mixed up with someone else."

"Nah, nah, I know that mug." He snapped his fat fingers next to his skull as if trying to jump start his brain. "Vincent somethin' or other. They called you…the Fist. That's it. Vincent The Fist Taggart. I know youse the guy." He chuckled and shook his head. "I saw you fight at the garden. When I first seen you, I thought you was the next big thing. But after your bout with Luis Benito, you turned yellow as your shirt. Guess you ain't nothin' but a Palooka."

Anger pounded at Vince's temples, and spots danced in front of his eyes. The room shrunk away until it was no bigger than a playing card. But the guy's big fat mouth was the Grand Canyon, opening so wide, Vince could fit his fist through it and rip out his larynx. In no more than half a second, the guy would be laid out flat…

He tightened his jaw and drew a deep breath in through his mouth, started counting backward from ten. When he got to one, he only half wanted to mangle the louse. He forced calm through his body and shrugged. "Yeah, that's right. A palooka."

"Whassa matter? You afraid? Don't worry, pal, I won't hurt ya. I don't fight dames." He let out a boisterous laugh and slapped the bar. A few men around him laughed too, but not as loudly. Apparently, the boob was his own biggest fan.

A slow boil simmered through Vince's blood, but he bit back the urge to plow one right into the guy's fat kisser. He scooped some peanuts out of a bowl on the bar and tilted his head back, feeding them into his mouth. He chewed slowly, looking the guy over, not speaking.

"You fell a long way down from bein' Mr. Tough Guy. We all thought you was heading for the heavyweight title. Turns out you're just another bum."

Don't let him get to you. Think of Cynthia. "Let me ask you something, you a regular here?"

The guy frowned. "Place just opened up a few days ago, but I been here every night. Why?" His tone held suspicion.

"I was just thinking, how about I buy you a drink and we talk about something besides boxing?"

The man blinked and darted a look around, as if he wasn't sure Vince was talking to him. "You want to buy me a drink?"

"Sure. No reason we can't have a nice, civil conversation, now that we got the whole thing about what a coward I am out of the way."

He blinked again, several times, and licked his lips. "You—you sure? No hard feelings, then, huh?"

"No hard feelings." Vince stuck out his hand. "You know my name, but I'm afraid I don't know yours."

The man placed his too-soft hand in Vince's and they shook. "Timothy. Reiker. Tim."

"Well, Timothy. Reiker. Tim. What'll you have?"

"Uh, whisky."

"Couple belts of your finest whisky over here," Vince called to the bartender, a short, dark-haired guy with squinty eyes and a dopey smile.

The bartender slid the hooch in front of them. Vince took a sip, surprised to find the whisky smooth and full-bodied, not like the coffin varnish normally served in juice joints. He turned to his new friend. "You know a girl named Cynthia who hangs out here?" He withdrew his wallet and pulled out the small photo of Cynthia—hands on hips, making a kissy face at the camera—taken last year at the neighborhood barbecue.

Tim swigged the whisky and squinted at the photo. "Huh, Cynthia... Can't really place her...wait. I think she's one of Oscar's girls."

Something unpleasant shifted in Vince's chest. "Oscar's *girls*? What's that supposed to mean?"

"A short skirt." The guy shrugged. "Oscar is...you might say...a...professional party host. He throws these bashes at his place and lines up gorgeous dolls to, you know, entertain the clientele. I never been to one myself, too rich for my blood. But word gets around, ya know?"

Fury pumped through Vince's veins. His fingers tightened around the photo. *Not Cynthia...* "You must have her mixed up with someone else."

"Don't think so." He pointed at the beauty Vince had been eyeballing earlier. "Ask Eliza. She works for Oscar too."

An illogical wave of disappointment washed over him. He didn't even know the dame, why should he care if she was a party girl?

He stood and threw a few bills on the bar. "See you around, pal. A little tip, though." He slapped Tim on the back hard enough that he coughed and nearly spit out his drink. "You might not want to razz any other former prizefighters you happen to meet." He winked. "Not all of them are as much of a pussycat as I am."

Tim's face paled, and he gave a jerky nod. "Sure yeah, thanks for the drink. Take it easy."

Vince wound through the crowd until he reached the stool where the broad was sitting. She looked up at him, golden eyes rimmed by black make up, pouty pink lips made for kissing.

But then, that's what those lips got paid for—kissing and a whole lot more.

"Can I help you?" Her voice was just as he imagined, sweet with an underlying husky tone, but he hadn't predicted the English accent.

"Mind if I have a seat?"

She inclined her head. "Free country."

"Yeah, but not everything is free, am I right?" He slid onto a barstool next to hers.

She raised a brow, a faint hint of amusement hovering on her lovely mouth. "You're quite astute, Mr…?"

"Taggart, Vince Taggart. And you are?"

"Eliza Gilbert. Is there something I can do for you?"

Instinct told him coming on too strong with the interrogation would make her clam up. Something about her made him think she would scare easily. She had a wary look, but at the same time, there was a hint of toughness behind the pretty façade. As if she was waiting for, expecting, an attack and when it came, she'd strike back like a wounded tigress.

"I saw you sitting here all alone, thought I'd stop by and say hi."

She nodded. "My friend, Meggie…Lady Margaret…is the singer. I came to watch her show."

"She's very good." He glanced around nonchalantly. "Draws quite a crowd. Of course, the booze doesn't hurt anything. It's good to find a nice place to knock a few back."

"You're not from here, are you?"

He grinned. "No, what was it, the accent?"

"Precisely."

"Of course, with your accent, you're definitely a local."

She laughed, an unexpected and delightful sound that he felt clear in his chest. "Right, a Yank through and through." Her eyes twinkled. "Where are you from?"

"Philly, Philadelphia. I'm in town looking for someone. A girl. Her name's Cynthia Yost." He showed her the photo. "Do you know her?"

Her brows drew together, and she shook her head. "She doesn't look familiar. She isn't in trouble, is she?"

"I'm afraid she might be. I haven't heard from her in days, and she was supposed to come home a week ago."

"I'm sorry. I hope she's okay, but no, I don't know her."

He didn't detect dishonesty in her response, but then, she was a pro. Maybe she was good at lying. He wouldn't push her tonight, but he'd be back and push a little harder next time. For now, he might as well play nice. "Can I buy you a drink?"

She favored him with another of those head spinning smiles. "That would be marvelous, thank you."

Chapter Six

Vince finished his coffee and wolfed down the remainder of the scrambled eggs and sausage, then paid his check and headed out of the diner. He needed to find Oscar Cummings, and the first place he'd look was Club 501. The joint was in walking distance.

A barefoot negro boy holding a white rag streaked with black polish fell in step beside him. "Shine your shoes, mistah? Only a dime."

"Sorry kid, I'm in a hurry. Maybe later."

"But, suh, yo' shoes is dull as a rusted saxophone." He beamed a white-toothed smile. "Yo' don' want yo' lady to think youse a flat tire, does' ya?"

Vince chuckled and stopped walking. "I guess I got time for a shine. You finish it up real quick, and there's a little something extra in it for you."

"Yessuh, I can finish it up lickety split." The boy led Vince to a rickety chair in front of a barbershop. Vince sat and rested his shoes on an equally rickety stool.

The boy dipped the rag in a tin of polish and snapped it so fast over Vince's wingtips, his hands and the cloth were just a blur.

He jabbered as he worked. "I shines shoes fo' all the gents come along hea. Yessuh, I does such a fine job, I gots a whole passel a regular customahs."

"You ever shine shoes for a man name of Oscar

Cummings?"

The boy paused but didn't look up. "I—I reckon that name don' ring no bells."

But the name *had* run a bell. Vince could see it in the way the boy fell silent. The way his smile was gone when he raised his head. "That be ten cents, mistah."

Vince pulled out his wallet and plucked out a dollar. "You tell me what you know about Oscar Cummings, and I'll give you ten times that amount."

The boy stared at the dollar and licked his lips. He glanced around as if making sure he wasn't overheard. "I heah Mistah Cummins a bad, bad man. I shine his shoes a few times, yeah, but I don' know nuthin' 'bout him. 'Cept he got a place ovah to Fifth Street where he throw pahties. I hear his girls don' listen, Mistah Cummins rough em up. They's this one girl, Miss Eliza. She come down this way a lot. She give me a dime evah time she see me, even though she don' get no shine." He frowned and shook his head, dropping his gaze to the ground. "It be a shame if Mistah Cummins hurt dat nice lady." His head snapped up, and he stared at Vince, eyes wide, as if he'd said too much. He snatched the bill out of Vince's hand. "That's all ah know, 'cept you done, mistah."

Vince rubbed the boy's head. "Thank you. You did a swell job. I can see my face in these shoes."

The boy bobbed his head and scurried away, disappearing into the crowd.

The uneasiness in Vince's gut grew. If Cynthia had worked for Cummings, and she'd wanted to leave, what might the 'bad man' have done to stop her?

****

"Carolina Shout" played on the phonograph, a song

Eliza liked, but right now, it was too loud. She had a headache—a guilt headache if she were honest. She couldn't stop thinking about Mr. Taggart or the girl he'd been asking about. She looked vaguely like the girl at Oscar's party, but Eliza was sure it wasn't the same person. They only slightly resembled, and besides, Oscar said that girl had gone home. If Mr. Taggart's friend was home, he wouldn't be looking for her. Maybe she should ask Oscar if he knew Cynthia Yost…

No, she shouldn't get involved. The least attention she brought to herself, the better.

Pushing Mr. Taggart from her mind, Eliza smiled at Gregor Ackerman—a man at Oscar's party she'd been instructed to 'be nice' to—trying to focus on his lengthy story about his executive position with the Hudson and Manhattan Railroad. How many stories could one tell about being superintendent of a railroad? Apparently plenty. His hair was greased down, parted in the middle, and flipped up on either side of the part. As hard as she tried to be polite, her attention kept wandering to the way he continually caressed his mustache as if it were a lover.

"Well, are you?"

Eliza blinked. In all the ramblings, she'd apparently missed a question. "Am I what?"

"Ready to hit the road?"

"Wh—where are we going?"

"A little joint I know in Harlem."

"Oh, no. I'm sorry. I can't leave the party. I'm working for Oscar."

He stopped stroking his mustache long enough to throw his head back and laugh. "Of course you are, and I've purchased you for the evening."

A sick feeling twisted her stomach. "I beg your pardon. I'm sure I don't know what you're talking about."

"Ah, you're new. You don't know the score."

The *score*? She searched the sea of people until she spotted Oscar. "Excuse me." She wove through the crowd to Oscar's side. "Oscar, can I speak with you?"

He broke off in the midst of a conversation with two gentlemen and a woman. "Excuse me," he said to his companions. He took Eliza's arm and led her a few feet away. "Yes, Eliza?" He smiled, but she detected irritation beneath the surface.

"This man…Gregor…is trying to get me to leave with him. He said he *purchased* me."

Oscar gave a condescending smile. "Yes, dear. That's correct."

"But, I—I don't want to go with him. I don't even know him."

"That's part of your job, Eliza. Entertaining clients. Accompanying them when they want a pretty girl on their arm."

"Yes, at your parties."

A hard glint entered his brown eyes. "Or anything I deem appropriate, as your contract states."

Chills washed through her. "But, Oscar—"

"No buts. Go with the man. You'll have a good time." His mouth tightened, and she sensed a warning in his tone. A flash of fear skittered over her flesh. His eyes held a threat similar to the one in Lord Renwald's gaze. "But mostly, make sure that *he* has a good time."

He turned his back on her and rejoined the group.

Her stomach did somersaults, and Champagne sloshed sickeningly up to her throat.

Gregor appeared at her side. "I presume we straightened out our little misunderstanding. Shall we go now?"

She nodded numbly and followed him out the door and downstairs where he helped her into the passenger seat of a Rolls Royce. What if he was like Lord Renwald? What if he expected her to…?

She shuddered. No, absolutely not. Oscar would not send her with some cad who would take advantage of her. She forced a smile, sitting stiffly in the seat next to Gregor.

Gregor nattered on during the entire ride, and Eliza pretended to listen, all the while focusing her gaze outside the window. Although it was close to midnight, the city was teeming with vehicles and pedestrians.

In spite of her fear, she gave a small smile when they passed the Strand Theater where *Hot Water* was playing. She and her friends had splurged and attended the movie a few weeks ago. They'd had a nifty time and laughed so hard their sides hurt. With her new position and the other girls' busy lives, would they ever share an outing like that again?

Her attention was drawn to a large billboard advertisement for Lucky Strike cigarettes. She concentrated on the word 'Lucky' and hoped that was an omen for her evening. That this man sitting next to her would not be another Lord Renwald.

The drive to Harlem didn't take as long as she'd hoped. In no time, Gregor was opening her door and offering his hand. She took it, hoping he couldn't feel the trembling.

Inside, The Jubilee Jumper was loud and smoky. Colored people danced on a small floor, sweat gleaming on their ebony skin.

Gregor led her to a table where another couple sat with drinks in front of them. He introduced her to Betty and Carl. The woman was several years older than Eliza with red lips and a glittery purple feathered headband seated tightly on her blonde bob.

Gregor threw an arm around Eliza and planted a wet kiss on her mouth. She shuddered.

"Be right back, doll."

Betty must have sensed her discomfort. She leaned over, "What'sa matter, hon? You look like you lost your best friend."

Eliza blinked and darted a glance around. No one seemed to be paying them any mind. "He—he's pawing all over me."

Raucous laughter burst from her. "Honey, you don't have to worry about Gregor. He's a three letter man."

"A…what?"

"He wants a doll on his arm, but when it comes to…relations, he prefers men."

"He…" Shock rendered her silent. She'd heard about things like that but didn't believe it was real. Perhaps it was. No matter how aghast she was, how foreign the thought, all she could feel was relief. If all Oscar's customers were like Gregor, her job would be a cakewalk.

Chapter Seven

All four girls were home at the same time. A rare occasion indeed. Between Eliza's position with Oscar, Jessica chasing newspaper stories, and Meggie and Charli working at the club, they were seldom together anymore. Eliza missed her friends. They hadn't known one another that long, but they were the most important people in the world. Well, next to Maud, but she would probably never see the kind woman again. Sadness pierced her heart. She wished she could at least write to her, let her know how much she appreciated her, and how sorry she was that she had to run off. She swallowed back a knot in her throat. She couldn't think about that right now or she'd weep like a baby.

Her flatmates were discussing the upcoming party that would be held at the Plaza, once the winner of the United States Presidency election was announced. Even though women had won the right to vote, she couldn't participate since she wasn't an American citizen, and she wasn't all that familiar with either of the candidates. But she had a feeling, based on the talk she'd heard and the abundance of 'Keep Cool with Coolidge' signs she'd seen since arriving in America, Mr. Coolidge would be the victor. Oscar was forcing her to attend the event, but she really didn't mind. Meggie would be performing, and Jessica would be there. Eliza had convinced Charli to go as well, and a night out with the girls would be fun.

Eliza bit into a buttery peach scone and chewed, then swallowed a mouthful of tea. She glanced at the article Jessica was reading, a write up of the speakeasy. "Mr. Markov has made quite a success of Club 501."

A pretty flush crept over Jess's face. Eliza suspected she was sweet on Mr. Markov, but she hadn't admitted it. Apparently, Eliza wasn't the *only* one who kept secrets.

"Nonsense." Jess's haughty declaration didn't fool Eliza for one moment. "Eliza, you work for Oscar Cummings, so I'm sure you know. I understand they're questioning some of his employees about a missing girl. Her family in Iowa has been looking for her, and they traced her here."

Eliza's chest squeezed. "Why would they question Oscar's employees?"

Jessica lifted her slender shoulders. "I think she was seen hanging around."

Her mind went to Vince Taggart. He was also looking for a missing girl, someone who might have worked for Oscar. If anything were to happen, if the police were to come sniffing around Oscar's, might they find out what she did to Lord Renwald? A lump rose to her throat.

Of course, the constables had to be searching for her. They would know she was the last one who saw him…

"Is there something wrong with your scone?" Charli planted her hands on her hips and scrunched her pert nose.

"No, no, not at all. It's delicious." Eliza forced another bite into her mouth, but it could have been sawdust for all the enjoyment it now gave her. She'd come so far, had gone to great lengths to flee, to remain free. But with even a hint of trouble, that could all come crashing down.

****

The next night at Oscar's party, Eliza tried to put the missing girls out of her mind. The penthouse was filled with people; everyone seemed to be in an exceptionally good mood.

She meandered around the room and chatted with Oscar's guests. Her enthusiasm for the position had dimmed, but really, she'd overreacted at the Jubilee. Betty and her husband had been nice people. The music and dancing were incredible. She'd never seen people move like that. Other than some uncomfortable pawing, Betty had been right, Gregor hadn't made a pass at her. She could do this. The money was fabulous, and employment was not easy to find—especially for a female immigrant.

She forced herself to relax and enjoy the party. She'd been here for three hours, and Oscar hadn't asked her—correction, *insisted*—that she leave with anyone. Maybe this would be like the other nights and she could just mingle and drink and entertain guests—here, under Oscar's roof.

Tonight, she wore the last of her new gowns, a black, figure hugging knee-length with fringe along the hem that went down to her ankles. She felt daring…pretty, even. She'd have to go shopping if she didn't want to start rotating the same dresses all over again. At least she had plenty of funds to buy new things. Oscar had been more than generous. His many moods confused her. He could scare the bloody daylights out of her one moment, then become kind and giving in the next.

Oscar and a tall man with thick, dark hair approached. "Eliza, my dear, I would like you to meet Thomas Killman."

She took his hand. He was handsome, if a little fleshy. "How do you do."

"Delighted, my dear." He bent and placed a wet kiss on the back of her hand. She resisted the urge to rub the saliva off on her dress.

"I would like you to be Mr. Killman's companion for the evening."

Eliza smiled. At least she wouldn't have to leave the party. "Of course. It will be my pleasure."

His brows lifted, and a broad smile spread over his face. "Indeed?"

Oscar took her arm and led her a few paces away, out of Mr. Killman's earshot. "This is going to be a little different arrangement tonight. You'll have to be extra nice to him."

"I'm always nice, Oscar. Always polite. I will be his escort for the entire evening. As late as he wants."

"That's fine. But he's going to want more than an escort." He narrowed his eyes. "Much more."

"More?" Her heart thudded madly. "I—I don't understand."

"Eliza, please. You aren't really that naïve, are you? You will have sex with him."

The room spun and her ears rang. She must not have heard him correctly. "Wh—what did you say?" The words came out in a squeak from her strangled throat.

"I believe you know exactly what I said."

The world dropped out from under her. She would not do something so, so depraved.

"No!" She'd meant to keep her voice low, but when heads turned her way, she realized she'd shouted the word.

All pretense of civility left Oscar's features. He tightened his lips and gripped her arm. "You heard me. You'll have to sleep with him. All the other girls do that sort of thing. You've just managed to avoid it so far. But he picked you."

This was the reason she left England. Her mother warned her on her deathbed that once the Earl was gone, she needed to run. Lord Renwald would make her his whore. She'd run, but not far enough. "No, I can't. I absolutely won't." Her voice rose with each word.

Oscar looked over her shoulder and nodded toward Mr. Killman and held up a finger as if to say one more moment. He tightened his grasp on her upper arm and pulled her farther from Killman. "Keep your voice down. Don't you dare embarrass me." His brown eyes turned almost black with anger, and his tone became low, deadly. "I repeat, you don't have a choice. I'm not asking, I'm telling. You signed a contract."

The words of the agreement came flooding back. "You're saying you deem this appropriate?"

"That's exactly what I'm saying."

Tears knotted in her throat and surfaced in her eyes. For a moment, she couldn't speak, couldn't breathe. Then, she managed to choke out, "No, Oscar, please. Please don't make me, I can't do this. I'll do anything else, anything at all, but please don't make me do this."

His fingers bit into her arm, and she cried out. "I

own you. You'll do exactly as I say."

Own her? No one owned her. Panic quickly turned into fury. She jerked her arm from his grasp. "Bugger off!" She spun and headed through the crowd toward the front door. She didn't spare a glance for Thomas Killman. She could care less what he thought. The repulsive man deserved to be humiliated.

She'd just made it into the hallway when Oscar caught up to her. He closed the door with a decisive click, and they were alone in the corridor.

"Now you listen to me, girlie—"

"I will not! You can go to the devil. I quit."

She whirled to leave, but he grabbed her once more by the arm and yanked her to him until they were nose to nose. The stench of garlic and whisky almost made her retch. "You will do exactly as I say, you understand?"

"Let me go," she gritted through clenched teeth.

He yanked her closer, and she spat on him. Spittle landed on the bridge of his nose. He flinched, his expression darkening like a black cloud. He rubbed the saliva off on the arm of his suit. Lifting a beefy hand, he slapped her across the mouth. Her head jerked, and she stumbled to the floor, finally free of his hold. The coppery taste of blood filled her mouth. Her lips at first felt numb, then began stinging and burning like they were on fire.

"Oh my God, you…you…" She lifted a hand and touched her lip. Blood seeped onto her fingers.

Oscar's expression became contrite. "Now, I'm sorry. I didn't want to have to do that." He removed a handkerchief from his pocket and stepped forward. Squatting to help her to her feet, he dabbed at her lip.

"But you must do as I say."

She tugged away, tears trembling on her lashes. "I will not. I'll go to the police."

He laughed. "And tell them what? You been prostituting but you decided to stop? You could get prison time just for what you done so far. What do you think your friends would say to that? You would lose them. You'd have nothing. You're stuck. Might as well make the best of it." He reached up once more and gently wiped her mouth. "I didn't want to hurt you, doll, but you gotta understand how this works. Here on out, you don't give me guff. You savvy?"

Realization rippled through her body, and she sagged with the weight of it. He was right. She really didn't have a choice. If Oscar were to contact the authorities about her breach of contract, they might open an investigation into her past. They'd surely learn what had happened in England.

She took the handkerchief from his hand and held it to her mouth. Without looking at him, she brushed by and went inside the apartment. Heart heavy, she found Mr, Killman and smiled. "Are you ready?" The words were dragged from her like butter from a churn.

He slipped an arm around her waist. "I have a hotel room just down the street. Let's get out of here. You and me gonna have a ball."

Chapter Eight

The room was dark and quiet, except for the sound of Thomas Killman's snores. Eliza's body trembled so furiously, she was afraid she'd wake him. He'd been surprised she was a virgin. She'd hoped telling him would make him change his mind. He'd paused, like he was considering it. Then, he'd pulled her to him, covered her mouth with his thin, papery lips. Shoved his sharp, skinny tongue in her mouth. She'd felt like she was swallowing a garter snake. And then…then…

Her trembling increased. She eased out of bed so as not to wake the snoring lout. She crawled gingerly from the bed and stumbled into the loo. She soaped the cloth with a bar of Jersey Cream and scrubbed her skin. Over and over, she scrubbed. Every inch of her body. She did her best to rinse the suds, but with only the faucet at her disposal, she did a poor job. No matter, she'd rather her skin be matted with dried soap than have his…touch, his sliminess on her. She attempted to blot the water with a small hand towel. Shivering, she pulled her dress over her still damp skin.

She lifted her head and stared at herself in the mirror. Her lip was puffy from Oscar's blow. Makeup was smeared over her pale flesh. The eyes that stared back at her were hollow…empty. In the reflection, she saw what she'd become.

Exactly what Lord Renwald tried to make her.

****

The taxi driver dropped Eliza off at the Gables. She handed him some coins and climbed out. As quietly as she could, she slipped her key in the knob and turned. *Please let the girls be asleep...*

She couldn't face them right now. Surely they would see what she'd seen when she looked in the mirror…a whore. What would her sweet Maud think of her now? She would be ashamed to her very core. For the first time since leaving Abbots Langley, Eliza was glad Maud was not around.

She stepped inside the flat, and her heart dropped into her stomach. Shame flooded her cheeks. Meggie sat on the sofa wearing a pale blue dressing gown, legs crossed, one bare foot swinging furiously. She glared at Eliza. "Where the bloody hell have you been?"

"A…party. At Oscar's."

Meggie gave an unladylike snort. "Tell it to Sweeney, 'cause I'm not buying it."

Eliza usually found Meggie's adoption of American phrases amusing. But right now, it only infuriated her. "You don't know what you are saying, *Lady* Margaret."

She flinched as if Eliza had slapped her. Immediately, a pang of guilt sliced through her. Meggie had been nothing but kind to her, had never lorded her status over her. Hurting her feelings was the last thing Eliza wanted to do.

"Eliza, it's after three in the morning, and you have a split lip. I only want to help."

Eliza turned her back and paced the tiny living room. God, what would her friends say if they knew what had happened tonight? What she'd done? They would all hate her. And she couldn't blame them. She bit her lip and tried to keep her voice steady. "You don't understand, Meggie. I can't let you help. This is *my* predicament, and the cost is too much." She glanced toward the window. Outside, lights were scattered in the night sky. Somewhere out there was Thomas Killman, the man she'd given herself to. Her mum would be so ashamed…

Meggie pushed to her feet and came over to clasp Eliza's hands. "What is it? I'm certain we can help."

Eliza's heart thudded in fear. Meggie wouldn't tell the others…? "No! You mustn't say anything. To anyone. Promise me, Meggie."

She gave a sympathetic smile. "Of course, I promise. Nothing can be so dire to warrant this sort of distress. You must tell me what happened."

Tugging loose from her hold, Eliza moved to stare out the window. She couldn't face her friend while she told the lie. "I-I fell."

"Blast it, Eliza! If you don't tell me the truth right this minute then I shall call the constable."

Fear zipped through her veins. "You wouldn't."

"I would. Now, spill."

Eliza turned to face Meggie. Tears crowded her throat and rose to her eyes. Maybe a half-truth would satisfy her friend. "Th-the job with Oscar isn't quite as…as grand as I first believed." Even that small confession felt good. How lovely it would be to completely unburden herself. But she mustn't. For all their sakes.

"Is he the one who hurt you?"

The sympathy in her friend's gaze left her unable to speak.

"Oh, darling, he is, isn't he? Please tell me what's going on. I can't help if I don't know." Meggie took her arm and lowered her to the sofa, then settled next to her.

Eliza picked up her pocketbook and played with the clasp, not meeting Meggie's eyes. "It's fine, truly. I just thought it would be…"

"What, Eliza? You never answered my question. Did he hurt you?"

"No, it's just as I said. I f-fell. I just believed the work would be a little more…glamorous. Truly, Meggie. I'm fine. It really is a grand opportunity."

"But?"

She shrugged. "I didn't realize I would be expected to…" Revulsion overwhelmed her as she recalled the feel of Thomas Killman's sweaty body, the image of his hideous face above hers… She shuddered. "…to…date…some of the guests."

"Date… Eliza, you're not…what I mean is…" She paused and visible swallowed. "…you aren't…you haven't been…" Her face paled, and she seemed to have difficulty breathing. "…are you *prostituting* yourself?"

Anger shot through her—unwarranted anger, since Meggie was spot on, but she couldn't help but be miffed. She rose to her feet and turned on her friend. "Of course not! How dare you suggest such a thing." A light thump brought her attention to the floor where she'd dropped her purse. Cash fluttered from the opening. She quickly bent to thrust it back inside. Before Meggie could question her, she rushed to explain, "It—it's my pay for last week."

"Oh, Eliza." Meggie stood and once more held her

hands. "I know there is much more going on than you are sharing. You must leave his employ immediately. We'll help you, all of us, Charli, Jess, and I, until you find some other position."

"You've done so much for me already. I'm the daughter of a *housekeeper,* Meggie. The three of you—you're ladies." Unbelievable that they'd even become friends. Eliza was so far below their class. "You've taken me in, helped pay my way. How can I bear not doing my part?" She wiped tears from her cheeks and took a deep breath. "Besides, I-I can't just…leave any time I choose."

"Don't be ridiculous. Of course you can. He doesn't *own* you."

Eliza pulled from her grip and dabbed at her cheeks. "Actually, he does. I…I signed a contract. I'm obligated to remain for two years. Unless I can pay the termination fee."

"That's bunk, Eliza. The man is treating you like a slave. It's probably less trouble to just pay his damned extortion fees. All of us will chip in, and with the funds you have there…" Meggie indicated the cash Eliza had shoved back into her clutch. "How much is the scoundrel demanding?"

Eliza clenched her jaw until her teeth ached. Meggie was in for a shock. "One thousand dollars."

Meggie's eyes rounded, and she dropped onto the sofa as if her legs could no longer hold her upright. "A-a thousand?"

"Yes, a fortune, I'm afraid." Eliza would have laughed at her own stupidity if it weren't so unfunny. "I'm stuck with Oscar for the next two years." Provided, that is, she survived the degradation.

****

Vince felt out of sorts in his new suit. The bow tie was strangling him. He wasn't used to dressing fancy, and didn't like it, not one bit. But, if he wanted to fit in with the classy crowd at Cummings' party, he had to play along. He wasn't sure exactly what his next move would be, but Cummings' name had come up too often in his search for Cynthia. And, if she had truly worked for the man, Vince needed to learn more about him.

He eyeballed a waiter with a serving tray coming his way. Glasses of booze and bite-sized sandwiches filled the tray. The sandwiches, they could keep. But he wouldn't say no to a shot of whisky to wet his whistle and calm his nerves.

Vince chose a glass and tipped the whisky to his lips, drinking deeply. Getting an invite to Cummings' party hadn't been as hard as he thought it would be. Cost him half a dozen double shots of booze, but his pal, Timothy, had fixed him up.

Now he just had to gather some information. He'd gone to the police station, but while Detective Mulligan had been pleased to meet one of his favorite prizefighters, he hadn't been all that concerned about Cynthia. Vince could tell the guy thought he was overreacting. Although he did promise to check into it, it was obvious Vince was on his own in the investigation.

His gaze searched the crowded room. He clenched his jaw when he realized what he was searching for. Or, more accurately, who. The dame from Club 501. He hadn't seen her since that night. Hadn't had a chance to talk to her again. He tried to convince himself he only wanted to see her to find out if she knew anything about

Cynthia. But even he wasn't buying it.

A heavyset man with a wide, phony smile approached and stuck out his hand. "Good evening, sir. Oscar Cummings. Welcome. You're Mr. Taggart, is that correct?"

So, this was Cummings. Vince narrowed his eyes, trying to read the man. He was nothing other than gracious host on the surface, but what lay underneath those beady eyes? "Yeah." Vince shook his hand.

"I believe you're new to the scene, aren't you?"

"Yeah, my first time." Vince forced a smile past stiff lips. This fat bastard was whoring out young women and getting rich off of them. And he might be doing worse than that. Like murder.

Oscar waved an arm around the room. "What's your pleasure? Is there anything…special you're interested in?"

"Special?" Vince realized he sounded like an owl repeating everything the man said. He'd better appear more worldly if he didn't want to raise suspicions. "Yeah, I might be interested in something special. Any recommendations?"

Oscar let out a belly laugh. "I recommend you choose one of these pretty girls and have yourself a real good time. It'll cost you, but trust me, worth every penny. Just pick one out. Your choice."

The whole idea sickened him. What kind of pathetic excuse for a man would have to *buy* a woman's company? In spite of the bad taste the situation left in his mouth, he tried to appear interested and impressed. He scanned the room. His heart gave a little bump when he spotted Eliza from Club 501.

He tilted his glass toward her. "What about that

one?" He hoped his voice sounded more casual than he felt. The idea of spending a night of passion with a dame like her… Nah, he needed to waylay those kinds of thoughts. He wasn't the type to buy a prostitute. And he was here for one reason only.

Oscar followed the direction he'd pointed. "Oh yes, good choice. Eliza is a quite a prize. And quite a looker. She's new, but she's a sweet one."

An odd sense of protectiveness rose. At the club, he'd sensed something vulnerable and innocent, even though he'd been told she was one of Oscar's girls. She just didn't seem the type. When their gazes met that first time, he thought some kind of current—some kind of connection had passed between them. But apparently, she was just really good at her job—enticing men.

Vince nodded. "I'll take her."

Cummings guffawed and clapped him on the shoulder. "You won't be sorry."

Was the asshole speaking from experience? The thought tightened his gut. He couldn't imagine the beautiful, graceful woman being with a pig like Cummings. But then, she was a prostitute. He needed to keep reminding himself of the fact. She'd screw anyone.

Chapter Nine

He was here, at Oscar's. The man with the thousand-watt smile and heavenly eyes. But tonight, rather than the clothing of a dock worker, he wore a smart gray suit with a black bow tie. His hat was gone, and his golden hair gleamed with threads of sunlight. What was he doing here? She inwardly snorted. Silly question. He was doing exactly what the other men were doing here. Looking for a good time. Her pulse sped up when he and Oscar headed toward her.

"Eliza, I'd like you to meet someone. Vincent Taggart, Eliza Gilbert."

Eliza inclined her head. She didn't reveal that she'd already met him. She wasn't sure why, but it didn't seem prudent. "How do you do."

Mr. Taggart grinned like they shared a secret. "Very well, thank you."

"Mr. Taggart will be your…date for the evening. You are to accompany him to the silver room."

Eliza's mouth went dry, and she tried to swallow, but couldn't. This man had purchased an evening with her? *Horsefeathers*. Now he knew she was a…

Shame heated the skin on her face until she thought she would burst into flames. But there was nothing to do, no escape. She sucked in a deep breath and steeled herself for the humiliation. It was, after all, part of the deal in her line of work.

Oscar had made her go to dinner earlier this evening with a bloke who accosted her, right out on the street, but it hadn't gone further than repulsive pawing while he had her pinned against his motorcar. The memory of his sweaty hands and moist mouth on hers brought nausea to her throat. Since the time with Killman, she hadn't been required to sexually pleasure any other guests. But it appeared her luck had run out.

He studied her with intense blue eyes. The dimple on the right side of his firm mouth creased with a smile. For the first time, she noticed a scar on his slightly crooked nose. The man was a ruffian, so why did he make her pulse race?

She'd resigned herself to giving her body to whatever slobbering pig came along. She would suffer through it, let her mind go somewhere far, far away.

But this man—how on Earth could she be intimate with him and not feel…*something* decidedly unprofessional.

Nerves fluttered in her stomach. "That sounds lovely." As the words came out, she realized that there was a grain of truth to them. She couldn't imagine this handsome, charming man's attentions being as vile as Killman's. In fact, having his lips on hers, his touch on her skin…

No! He was just like the others. A disgusting pig who had to buy women's favors. Well, he didn't likely have to buy women. He probably had them throwing themselves at him. So why would he engage in such illicit activities? For some kind of depraved thrill?

"Follow me, Mr. Taggart."

"Please, call me Vince."

Excitement had her heart racing while at the same

time, disappointment tugged at her. It was crazy to feel like this—to think he was better than that. That he didn't seem like that type of person. She didn't know the man at all, so where would she get such an idea?

She turned to lead him to the door, and he took hold of her hand. His warm fingers closed around hers, and tingles of delight rippled up her arm to her breasts.

Good Heavens, what was wrong with her? This man did strange things to her that were not at all unpleasant. Nerve-wracking yes, unpleasant, most definitely not.

With a hand resting on her lower back, burning like a coal oven through the thin material of her dress, he led her down the hall to one of the rooms Oscar maintained for the convenience of his guests.

With a turn of the key, she pushed the door open. He followed her inside, and she closed the door behind them. "So…"

Mr. Taggart didn't reply. She waited. Thomas Killman had made all the moves. All she'd had to do was suffer through them. But Mr. Taggart was just looking at her. His arms were crossed over his broad chest that even a suit couldn't disguise. His eyes narrowed, but he said nothing.

She laughed self-consciously and lifted her arms, let them drop to her sides. "Can I…get you anything?" Her voice warbled, and she cleared her throat.

He uncrossed his arms and shoved his hands in his pants pocket. "You seem awful nervous for a pro."

"You've been with a lot of…pros?" The thought that he had done this before, perhaps many times, was oddly disturbing.

He shook his head. "My first time." His tone was

warm, husky, washing over her skin like a lover's caress.

She drew in a fortifying breath and mustered a coy smile. It was time she began acting the part of a vamp. Apparently, that was to be her calling. She sauntered over to him. "Well, you just relax, sugar."

She wound her arms around his neck and pressed her body to his. He was somehow hard and yielding at the same time. Warmth spread through her, settling between her thighs. She locked onto the clear sky of his eyes and stood on her tiptoes. He hadn't spoken. Hadn't moved. So, he was leaving this all up to her. She swallowed hard and touched her lips to his. His only reaction was a sharp intake of breath.

She nibbled on his lower lip, then once more kissed him. His arms went around her, settling on her hips, pulling her into him.

He returned the kiss, and she opened for him. Surprised delight rippled through her when his hot tongue touched hers. His kisses were nothing at all like those of the slobbery, disgusting Killman. She let out a soft moan.

His muscles tensed beneath her hands, and he broke the kiss. He took hold of her arms and pulled them from his neck. "That's not what I want." His voice was hoarse, and he took in short breaths as he stared down at her with hooded eyes.

She suffered a brief moment of relief mixed with disappointment. What else could he want? She'd heard dreadful stories. Men who liked to get mean with the girls. Panic fluttered to her chest. She stepped back quickly.

"I don't do any of that rough stuff. Oscar won't let

anyone hurt me." She didn't know that to be true. In fact, Oscar would probably allow anything for money. But she hoped this man would believe her.

He gave a gentle smile and stepped forward, caressed her cheek with his large, rough hand. "I don't want to hurt you. I just want to talk."

She frowned. "Talk?" Was he going to ask more questions about the girl? She couldn't help him, why didn't he just leave her alone? She swallowed nervously. What if his questions about his friend led to more probing questions about her past? No, they wouldn't. *Just keep calm...he doesn't know anything about you...*

"Sure. I like you. I'd like to get to know you."

She shook her head. "Oscar doesn't want us to get tied up with any one man. We don't have…relationships."

"I'm not looking for a relationship. Can we just talk?"

"About what?"

"Anything. Just get to know one another. Where are you from? From your accent, I'm guessing England?"

Fear made her heart thud in her chest. Was he sent by the constables? Had they traced her here? "I—I'm from Australia. My accent sounds English?"

He narrowed his eyes as if he didn't believe her. Fortunately, he didn't pursue the matter. "Yeah, maybe I got that wrong. So how did you get mixed up with Oscar?"

She fiddled with the pendant, trying to settle her nerves. "He offered me a job when I needed one."

"You like doing this?"

She slid her eyes away from his. "It's a living."

"What would you like to do? What do you want?"

What did she want? She wanted to meet a nice man, marry, and have kids. But that would never happen now. "I don't know. I never really thought about it."

"Everyone thinks about their dreams."

She let out a humorless chuckle. "Not when you're living a nightmare." Her hand flew to her mouth, and she widened her eyes. "I didn't mean that. Please don't tell Oscar. I like my job. He's been good to me."

Mr. Taggart's brows drew in a fierce scowl. "You seem frightened. Does he hurt you?"

She shook her head. "No. I just don't want to upset him. You won't say anything, will you?"

"Of course not. This whole thing will just be between us."

She smiled in relief. "Did you ever find the girl you were looking for?"

He shook his head. "I'm afraid I haven't. Why, have you heard something?"

"No, I don't know anything about her." Would it help his search if she mentioned the girl she'd seen with Oscar? No, she wasn't the same girl, and they probably had no connection. The less she revealed to this man, to anyone, the better. She'd asked Oscar about the girl, and Oscar explained that she'd gone back home. No, mentioning the incident would serve no purpose. "I hope she's okay." She paused, then as casually as she could, said, "Is she your…girlfriend?"

"No. A friend from back home." A shadow passed over his face. "Someone I've known my entire life."

The girl obviously meant a great deal to him. Eliza

hoped he found her. Odd how two girls who worked for Oscar had gone missing. Coincidence? A shudder passed through her. She prayed that was the case.

Chapter Ten

Vince couldn't erase the feel of Eliza Gilbert's soft mouth on his. Even now, his body heated with the urge to taste her lips again. He had to remind himself she was a prostitute. But it was difficult. Her innocent golden eyes didn't fit with her occupation. His body had reacted to her physically, but he'd also felt an odd connection in his soul as well. He tried to take his mind off of her, frowning down at an article in the *World.* A young woman from Iowa, Roxy Gould, had been found murdered in an alley near Club 501.

Suspicion gnawed at his gut. Had the same thing happened to Cynthia?

No, he wouldn't think that. She had to be okay. She was just…missing. She wasn't dead.

He had to find out where she was, what had happened. Earlier, he'd cornered Lady Margaret to see if the singer would be more forthcoming than her friend. But she hadn't been. He rubbed his jaw. As a matter of fact, she'd been almost…hostile. Slapping his mug when he'd dared to doubt her integrity. Well, birds of a feather…

He headed to Club 501, where he spotted Oscar Cummings at a table in the corner. The man downed a drink and signaled for the waitress, the cute red-haired girl Eliza had been speaking with the night he first saw her. The girl brought another drink just as Vince approached Oscar's table. "This seat taken?" He gestured to a chair across the table.

"No, please. Sit."

Vince settled in the chair and set his glass of whisky on the table.

Oscar studied him. "You're the man from the party last night. Mr.…Taggart. Hope everything was…satisfactory." He smiled and took a dainty sip from the glass. "Are you interested in another night with Eliza?"

Interested? His body ached to have another night with her. Only this time, he'd savor those full, soft lips, stroke her smooth pale flesh, ease her gown off her body and…

He shifted in his chair and shook off the mental image of a warm, naked Eliza Gilbert. The woman was a prostitute. He couldn't let her loveliness, her sweet, beguiling eyes make him forget. "Actually, I was hoping for some information. I'm looking for a friend of mine, Cynthia Yost."

An almost imperceptible twitch around the eyes was his only reaction. "I'm afraid I don't know anyone by that name."

"Is that right? Because, I heard she worked for you."

His mouth tightened until a white ring appeared around it, and his eyes went flat. "Did Eliza tell you that?"

She hadn't. He'd given her his room number at The Starlight and asked her to let him know if she thought of anything. He'd hoped he'd hear from her, even if it wasn't about Cynthia. Every time he parted from her, he immediately wanted to see her again. *Damn*. What was he getting himself into? He brought his attention back to Cummings. The bastard would probably knock her around if he thought she'd told him anything. His grip tightened on the glass. "No, I heard it here at Club 501. Eliza and I didn't exactly do a lot of…talking, if you know what I mean." Vince winked.

Oscar's fleshy face smoothed out, and he licked his lips. "I know precisely what you mean. I admit, I'm often tempted by the delectable Eliza myself. If I didn't have a strict rule about not sampling the merchandise…"

Vince released the glass and clenched his fists beneath the table to keep from plowing them into Cummings' fat face. The thought of this pig with his hands on Eliza…

Might as well get used to it, pal. A lot of pigs put their hands on her.

He shook off the thought and focused on the conversation. "See, I'm just sure you know Cynthia. I got it from a pretty good source she was one of your girls." He leaned back in his chair, making sure Cummings got the idea. He wasn't going anywhere until he had some answers. "Cynthia Yost. You sure that doesn't ring a bell?"

Cummings scowled as if deep in thought and lifted the glass, downing the contents in one gulp. "Oh, wait a minute. Cynthia, did you say? Yes, yes. She did work for me. She was a sweet little gal. But she left about a week ago. Said she was going back home."

"Yeah, she was supposed to go home. But she never made it."

"Oh my, that's a shame. I can get my private investigator on it. I did care deeply for the girl."

"I just bet you did." Vince had learned to read people in the ring. He had to know if they were going for the body or the jaw, had to know if they were ready to be finished off, or if they were going in for the kill. This snake thought he had Vince on the ropes, but what he didn't know was, Vince would be the one going in for the kill.

****

Eliza's eyes snapped open. What was that? Jess's shriek carried to her from the other room. That must have been what woke her. She rose from the narrow bed and threw a robe on over her gown. In the kitchen, a burning smell hung in the air. Jess stood at the table, newspaper clenched in her fists. Charli stood next to her, her wan features even more pale, a pan of blackened scones on the counter behind her.

Eliza yawned and moved to the stove to prepare a cup of tea. "What the devil is going on?"

"Meggie! She's truly lost her senses." Jess thrust the paper out.

Eliza took it and squinted at the print. She struggled to make out the words, trying not to show how difficult it was. Her friends suspected her reading limitations but were kind enough not to speak of it. Even with her inadequate abilities, the meaning of the article sunk in, and her knees weakened.

She lifted her gaze to Jess. "Meggie was involved in some kind of…shootout?"

Jess's lips tightened. "It appears so." She snatched the paper back and whirled toward hers and Meggie's room.

Eliza turned to Charli, who had resumed mixing her batter, seemingly lost in a world of her own. "What on Earth was Meggie thinking? How did she even come in contact with *gangsters*?"

Charli hesitated, and Eliza wondered if she'd heard her. She was about to repeat herself when Charli faced her with a grimace. "I haven't the foggiest. We'd best make sure Jess doesn't throttle her."

Charlie headed to Meggie's room, and Eliza followed, arriving at the bedroom door in time to hear Jess murmur, "It *is* true. You reckless girl. You could have been killed. What on earth drove you to do such a thing?"

Instead of responding, Meggie turned a chagrined look toward Charli. "I guess I'm not so perfect after all, am I?"

"I should have never said that, Megs. I'm so sorry." Charli's voice was soft, contrite.

The conversation faded into background noise as a horrific realization struck Eliza. Meggie had risked her life for her. She was trying to come up with the money for the contract. Nausea struck her chest. If Meggie had died…

"I must get ready for work. I'm glad you're okay, Meggie," Charli said.

"Me too." Jess hugged Meggie.

Eliza stepped through the doorway, allowing Jess and Charli to slip out, and moved farther into the room.

"I'm so sorry, Eliza," Meg choked out. "I completely failed you."

"No. No, don't ever say that." Eliza rushed to the bed and wrapped her arms around her, fighting back tears. "I can't believe you did that—*for me*."

Meggie squeezed back, then released her. "Don't you see? It was all for nothing."

God. She couldn't let her friend endanger herself like that. Next time, she might not be so lucky. Meggie had been protecting Eliza since they met on the docks, and now, doing so had almost cost her her life. "No. Please, Meggie." Eliza forced a smile. "I have wonderful news. The contract's been paid. A gentleman I met at one of the parties offered me a position as his housekeeper, and he's buying out my contract. I'm free and clear."

Eliza forced herself to meet Meggie's penetrating gaze. She purposely kept her expression innocent. She was a practiced liar. No reason her friend should sniff out the fib.

Meggie narrowed her eyes. "That sounds quite marvelous. Almost unbelievably so."

With practiced guile, Eliza steadily returned Maggie's stare. "Yes, quite. I was surprised myself, but he's English. He was delighted to come across a Brit with housekeeping experience." To bolster the lie, Eliza added, "You may meet him if you wish."

A few seconds ticked by before Meggie sighed and hugged her again. "Thank God, Eliza. Thank God."

Yes, thank God. Now, Meggie would be safe. And Eliza wouldn't have yet another death on her conscience.

Chapter Eleven

Eliza hurried along the sidewalk, shifting the grocery bag in her arms. She'd gone to the store and purchased more flour and fruit for Charli's scones. Hopefully, making a new batch would put the sparkle back in her lovely green eyes. Something was wrong with her friend, and Eliza had no idea what. She didn't pry though. That might open the door for Charli to pry as well, and she certainly didn't want that.

She'd had to get out of the apartment after lying to Meggie. Not that lying was unusual, but she was afraid if she didn't leave, Meggie would sense she was telling an untruth and might once more do something foolish and risk her life to try to help her. Eliza shook her head. She didn't deserve such good friends, such loyalty. Would Meggie feel the same way, still want to help her if she truly knew what she was? What she'd done?

"Miss Gilbert?"

Eliza's pulse fluttered. Even without looking, she knew that deep, husky voice. She swallowed and turned to find Vince Taggart standing on the sidewalk a few feet away.

"Hello, Mr. Taggart."

"Hello." He stepped forward and reached for the grocery bag. "Let me take that for you."

"No, thank you. I've got it." If he took it, he'd have to accompany her upstairs. She didn't want him to run into her flatmates. Best to keep those two sides of her life totally separate. “It’s not heavy at all.”

“But—”

She rushed on, “If you’re here to ask me more questions about your friend, I’m afraid I don’t have any information. I haven’t learned anything that will be helpful.”

He studied her silently for a few moments. “That’s not why I’m here.”

Something in the intensity of his blue eyes made her heart race. “Then why?”

“I just…” He shrugged and looked away, then back to her. “I just wanted to see you.”

“Why?” She sounded like a parrot, but she couldn’t think of anything else to say.

“Because I couldn’t stop thinking about you. About how much I enjoyed being with you.”

“But we didn’t…” Her cheeks heated, and she dropped her gaze. “I mean, I’m a pro—”

“You’re a beautiful woman I’d like to get to know better.”

She lifted her head, then looked away when she met his eyes. They were just too…striking, too blue. “I’m afraid you’ll have to speak to Oscar. He handles all my transactions.” She could never have a normal outing with a man. A lump of regret rose in her throat. She turned and started up the stairs.

Vince caught up to her in a few steps and grabbed her arm, taking the bag from her at the same time. “That was a lousy thing to say.”

She opened her mouth to accuse him of going around Oscar so he didn’t have to pay. But that was ridiculous. He hadn’t taken what he’d paid for the first time. She lifted a hand and rubbed her forehead. His attention confused her. What was his angle? He didn't want sex. Did he think she was hiding something about Cynthia and if he spent time with her, he could draw it out? "What do you want from me?"

He hesitated slightly, as if weighing whether to answer. "A picnic."

"A what?"

"My family goes on a lot of picnics back home. It's our way to relax, put our cares behind us and just be together. I want to share that with you."

"It's November in New York"

"Yes, and it's close to sixty degrees. Perfect day to spend some time outside."

She wanted to, and his crooked smile made her forget all the reasons she shouldn't. She found herself nodding. "Sounds lovely."

"I hoped you'd say that. I have a lunch packed for us in my Roadster." He turned and pointed down the street to where a blue Packard was parked. "I'll take this up for you then we can go."

She took the bag from him. "I can take this but thank you. Give me five minutes to change. Wait here."

He frowned but nodded. "Okay, yeah. I'll wait here."

****

Why hadn't she wanted him to come up? Was she embarrassed by him? Surely she wasn't ashamed of her living quarters. He wouldn't judge her for that. It wasn't like he lived in a mansion. Maybe she had something to hide. The girl sure seemed to carry a lot of secrets. And still, he couldn't stop thinking about her. About her lips…

He shouldn't be thinking of kissing Eliza Gilbert when Cynthia was missing. He'd gone to the police station after speaking with Oscar, letting them know he'd admitted to knowing her. Detective Mulligan hadn't seemed that confident it meant anything.

But Vince knew in his gut that it did.

He was here to woo Eliza and see what he could find out. But he wasn't lying when he said he wanted to be with her. She wasn't the kind of girl he could marry, but if spending time together made them both happy, why not grab a few moments of pleasure?

His chest tightened when she stepped out the door of the boarding house. She wore a white dress with green trim and matching hat perched at an angle on her dark hair. She looked so fresh, so innocent. His gut ached. The image was only an illusion. How could she look so much like the girl of his dreams yet be so…tarnished?

She smiled as she neared, and the urge to kiss her pink lips nearly overwhelmed him. He tore his gaze away and placed a hand on her lower back, guiding her to his auto and helping her inside.

They drove the short distance to Central Park where he spread out a blanket and began removing items from a basket. "I didn't know what you liked to eat. I should have asked."

"I'm not particular. And right now, I'm famished."

"We have baked ham, cabbage slaw, asparagus, and yellow cake."

"Sounds delicious."

He withdrew the beverages. "Lemonade or ginger beer?"

"Lemonade, please."

He poured her a glass of the tart liquid and opened a beer for himself. As they ate, they talked. She didn't reveal anything of her past but spoke mostly about her roommates. The three women were the most important things in her world, judging from the way she gushed about them.

"Tell me about you." She grinned and popped the last bite of cake into her mouth. "You were a famous prizefighter, I understand. What happened?"

A pall came over the day, the sunlight seeming to dim. He opened his mouth to say that he just got tired of the game, but instead, found the story of the bout with Luis Benito pouring out of him. "It was my last fight on the road to a shot at the heavyweight title." He gave a humorless chuckle. "I was thrilled, although I can't say I was anxious to slug it out with Dempsey. But that was my dream. To win the heavyweight title. Once I did, I'd hang up the gloves. Find a nice girl. Settle down, have a family." The night of the fight came back to him. He could almost smell the sweat, taste the rusty blood, hear the roar of the crowd. "I had Benito on the ropes. I went in to finish him off. I kept pounding and pounding, my juices increasing with every shot. I felt like a machine, invincible. Unstoppable."

He didn't realize he'd fallen silent until Eliza's soft voice said, "Please, go on."

Trying to draw a breath and failing, he continued. "They pulled me off of him. I hadn't even heard the bell ring. The ref lifted my hand. I'd won. I looked back at Benito. Wanted to gloat I guess." An image of the lifeless body rose. He shuddered. He couldn't bring himself to look at Eliza. What would she think of him?

Would she loathe him? Or worse, fear him? He'd come too far now. Whatever the consequences, he wouldn't hold anything back from her. "He was lying there, so still. His head was cocked oddly to the side, eyes staring blankly." His chest heaved. "I thought I'd killed him. Everything inside me turned to ice."

"You…didn't? Kill him, I mean?"

He shook his head, finally meeting her eyes. "Nearly, but no, he survived. He's in a wheelchair for the rest of his life. Because of me."

Her eyes bore into his, sympathy shining in their golden depths. "I'm sorry. I'm sorry for Mr. Benito, but I'm sorry for you too. What a burden that must be."

Vince nodded. His spirit felt lighter after confessing. Smiley was the only other person in the world he'd spoken with about the tragedy. He didn't examine why he'd told Eliza. He was just glad he had. "Yes, it is. I can't close my eyes without seeing him. Every time I start to get angry, I see what I did. I work hard to control my temper now. I'm afraid of what I might do." He took a sip of beer. "Everyone tells me it wasn't my fault, but I know that's not true. I did that to him. Me." He waited for her to argue, to tell him he wasn't to blame.

She placed a gentle hand on his knee. "Of course it was your fault."

He flinched, shooting his gaze to hers. "What?"

"It was your fault that he's crippled, yes. But you didn't do it on purpose. Mr. Benito made the choice to enter the ring with you, so he shares the responsibility. He knew the risks. You are not blameless, but you can't continue to punish yourself. What's done is done. If you could do it over again, I'm sure you would make a different choice. But you can't do it over again, so you have to move past it."

Somehow her insisting he shoulder some of the blame was more freeing than all the well-wishers who'd assured him it hadn't been his fault. It was okay to suffer the guilt, but it was also okay to forgive himself.

Sunlight picked out golden flecks in her eyes, making the breath stall in his chest. He placed his hand around hers where it rested on his knee. She returned his squeeze, and he was utterly lost.

Chapter Twelve

Eliza didn't want to be at the party. Under other circumstances, if she were here for dancing and carefree fun, it would be different. But her carefree days—if she'd ever even had them—were over.

Oscar had insisted all his girls attend the election party at the Plaza. What better opportunity to elicit clients than in a room filled with wealthy, powerful men? At least her friends were here. That made it less unpleasant. She'd insisted Charli accompany her but had lost her in the crowd moments after they arrived. Probably best. If Oscar were to give her an 'assignment,' she didn't want the girls to witness it.

The ballroom was magnificent. Sparkling chandeliers hung from the ceiling like diamonds dripping from the sky. Grecian columns with golden draperies strung between them bordered the entire room. Paul Whiteman's orchestra was performing on a platform stage set within a rectangular alcove at the western end of the room. Meggie would be joining them soon. What a fabulous opportunity for her. All her dreams were coming true.

Why her, and not me? Why can't my dreams come true?

She nearly gasped in horror at the unbidden thought. Her cheeks warmed with shame. How could she be envious of Meggie? She deserved every happiness in the world. Just because Eliza had made poor decisions and ruined her life, it didn't mean she couldn't be happy for her friends. She blinked back tears. She *was* happy for her friends. Really, she was. And Meggie needed an opportunity now more than ever. Club 501 had been raided last night. Eliza hadn't been there, but her three friends had. Jess had gone to *jail*, for Heaven's sake. Thank God they were all right, though Charli and Meggie were now unemployed. Her friends would bounce back, she was certain. And, unlike her, they would do so without stooping to selling their bodies.

She swallowed against the tightness in her throat and clutched a champagne flute in her damp palms, praying she could get through the evening without being forced on a 'date.' Across the enormous dance floor, Oscar stood conversing with two men. *Please don't let either of them choose me…*

If she knew more about American politics, she would know whether or not to be pleased that Mr. Coolidge won the election. From what she gathered, he was the best choice. The people in attendance certainly seemed elated. Excitement buzzed so heavily in the air, she could almost feel the electricity.

She sipped her champagne and glanced around the ballroom. Her gaze landed on a man weaving through the crowd. Directly toward her. Wearing an elegant white tuxedo with a shiny silver bow tie, his dark blond hair neatly combed, except for an errant lock that flopped over his forehead.

Vince Taggart.

She caught her breath. What was he doing here? She hadn't expected him but was inordinately pleased.

She swallowed more champagne as she waited for him to reach her.

He halted a most inappropriate few inches from her trembling body. "Good evening, Eliza. You look beautiful."

She was glad she'd chosen the jade velvet scooped-back gown. The way he looked at her, his eyes glittering like fiery sapphires, she'd chosen well. "Thank you. And you look quite dashing."

His white teeth flashed in a grin, and a dimple creased his jaw. "I don't believe I've ever been called *dashing,* but I like it."

"I wasn't aware you'd be here."

"I didn't plan to be. I was invited because of my, uhm..." His lip curled derisively. "...*celebrity* status. I came because I hoped to see you."

Her pulse rate shot up. Why did he say such flattering things? Things that made her wish the situation were different?

She twisted the chain on her pendant, searching her mind for something to say.

His gaze followed her movements. "Do I make you uncomfortable?"

She dropped the locket and looked away. "Not at all." Another lie. All men made her nervous, but Vince Taggart brought about nerves of a decidedly different sort. She could barely focus, barely breathe when he was around.

He gave a low, soft chuckle. "Then why won't you look at me?" His warm fingers touched her chin and tilted her head up until she was staring into his eyes. "There, that's better." He grinned. "Since you're so comfortable around me, may I have this dance?"

Even the light touch of his fingers on her chin ignited a flame inside her. “Is that a challenge?”

“Whatever it takes to make you say yes.”

Could she ever say no to this man? Not likely. She nodded, and he took the flute from her and placed it on a nearby table.

The orchestra played a song she didn’t recognize, something soft and romantic. She moved into his arms. The warmth of his hands burned through the thick fabric of her dress. She could barely take in a full breath.

He held her close as they moved around the dance floor. Beneath her fingers, his shoulder muscles bunched. He was so strong, so powerful. With him, she felt protected, safe. She could almost pretend that she was just a regular girl on a date with a handsome man.

He pressed his lips to her ear and whispered, “Holding you feels so good, I might never let you go.”

Tingles swept through her stomach, and she closed her eyes against a rush of tears. This wasn’t right, wasn’t wise. Being near Vince only made her realize all she could never have. Why torture herself like this? She tensed and put some space between their bodies.

He frowned. “Are you all right?”

“I—I’m fine. I just…” She glanced over her shoulder. Was Oscar watching? If so, he would be displeased to say the least.

“Are you worried about Oscar?” His tone hardened. “Because you’re working tonight?”

She stiffened her spine and stepped away from his touch. Who did he think he was? He knew she was a prostitute. He had no right to act offended that she was working.

"Yes, I'm working. And I really must get back to it." She turned and hurried across the floor, winding through the crowd of dancers.

The true question was, who did she think *she* was? That she could have a normal dance with a normal man when she was paid to do much more.

As she reached the edge of the dance floor, a hand landed on her wrist. She turned to face Vince, expecting to see anger in his expression. Instead, he looked at her with kindness, sympathy. A knot rose to her throat. Anger would have been easier to deal with.

"Please, let me go."

"Come with me."

Her mind said no, but her heart told her to follow.

He led her into a nearby alcove. Intimacy settled around them, cocooning them in a world where the sound of music grew faint and everyone else faded from existence.

"What—what are you doing?"

He cupped her cheek in his hand. In a husky murmur, he said, "I want to see what it would be like to kiss you when it's not part of your job."

She was drowning in his intense blue eyes. Goosebumps prickled her skin. Her heart lodged in her throat. Somehow finding her voice, she said, "Then kiss me."

His gaze roamed over her face, down to her lips, then back to capture her eyes. He slowly lowered his head. Her heart fluttered like a wild bird as she waited…waited…

His lips touched hers. Firm, warm. Her knees turned to rubber. He left one hand on her face and slipped the other around her waist. Pulled her body to his. Heat licked her flesh. She tilted her head back and he tasted her mouth, devoured it like a meal.

Was this how it felt to be kissed by a lover? She'd never dreamed a mere kiss could completely consume her. She was burning up, yet at the same time drowning.

He released her and pulled away. Took a long, deep breath and let it out slowly, his strong hand still cupping her face. With a rough thumb he stroked her cheek, shooting shivers through her entire body. She was dazed, breathless.

"Your skin feels like silk." His whispered words caressed her just as his hands had.

She swallowed, her mouth so dry it was impossible to form words.

He closed his eyes briefly, shook his head. "I don't know what's happening, but I've never felt this way about another woman. Another person, in my life."

She wanted to say, *Neither have I. Nor will I ever again.* But that would be foolish. Their worlds could never mix. He hadn't said anything about wanting to be with her, and how could he? She wasn't the kind of girl he could ever marry, could ever take home to his family.

She managed to swallow the dryness coating her tongue. Clearing her throat, she stepped back and tugged his hand away from her face. "I'm afraid I must get back to work."

His brows drew together. "Work?"

She forced a brittle smile. "Of course. As I told you, I'm working this evening. If you're interested in my company, you'll need to see Oscar."

Darkness came over his features. His mouth

tightened, and his cobalt eyes shot sparks of anger. "Don't treat me like I'm just one of your clients." He gripped her upper arms. "You know there's more going on between us than that."

Her heart longed to agree, but even if there were something more going on, it could never be. She yanked loose from his hold. "Please, don't manhandle me. Not unless you've paid for my time." Humiliation and regret clogged her chest. She struggled not to cry. "Now if you'll excuse me."

"Don't do this." Vince reached out as if to stop her, but let his hands drop to his sides. "You need to get away from that life. Get away from Oscar."

She lifted the corner of her mouth in a humorless grin. "Why? So you and I can live happily ever after? The prizefighter and the whore?"

"No," he said through gritted teeth. "So you won't wind up dead."

****

Vince sped to the motel, mentally berating himself. What was he thinking? Kissing Eliza Gilbert? All but confessing his love? Why had he let himself get hooked on a dame like her? He was here to look for Cynthia, and that was it. There was no future with Eliza. Maybe when he found Cynthia, he should just go ahead and marry her. Maybe that would get Eliza off his mind. As soon as the thought formed, another one crowded in. *Even if you wanted to, you'll never have a chance to marry Cynthia, she's gone...*

No. She couldn't be. He'd find her, safe, unharmed, and give her the reaming of a lifetime.

When he arrived at The Starlight, Detective Mulligan was waiting on the sidewalk.

"Good evening, Mr. Taggart."

With those simple words, a fist slammed into his gut. Even without the somber expression on the cop's face, Vince would have known something was wrong. He could sense it. "What is it?" he said, not returning the greeting. He knew what the cop would say before he said it.

"I'm afraid we've found the body of a young woman we believe to be Miss Yost. I'd like you to come with me and identify her."

His heart stuttered. For a moment, he couldn't speak, couldn't breathe. "A body? She's…dead?"

Mulligan's mouth turned down at the corners as if he'd tasted something rotten. "We don't have positive ID, but from the description, we're pretty certain it's Miss Yost." He cocked his head toward the curb. "My car's right this way."

Vince's legs barely held him up as he followed the officer to a black Model T with a police emblem on the door.

They drove to a multi-story brick building and through a black gate with the words 'Bellevue Hospital'. In the part of Vince's mind that wasn't consumed with dread and fear, he recalled a news story from a few years earlier about a German spy who'd escaped from the prison ward of Bellevue after pretending to be paralyzed for two years. The press had pummeled the dimwits running the hospital over that one.

All thoughts ceased when the jalopy rolled to a stop in front of large metal doors, and Mulligan climbed out. This was it. In moments he'd learn if the murdered girl was Cynthia. While he didn't wish tragedy on anyone, he found himself hoping she was someone else. That another family would have their world turned upside down.

He and the detective entered a cold, colorless room with grimy windows high up on the wall. A pungent odor of antiseptic and something putrid hung in the air. A dozen or so oval tables were lined up in the long room. Vince tensed when his gaze fell on the hoses hooked to the tables, on the drain underneath. You didn't have to be an Einstein to know what those were for.

A woman lay on the third table. Pale. Blue-mottled skin. The hair was a different color, a bright red. But once he looked into her face, he knew.

"Cynthia!" A hoarse scream left his throat. He scooped her up in his arms and hugged her to him.

The doctor stuck out his hand in a halting gesture. "Sir, I'm afraid you can't—"

Detective Mulligan cut in, "Leave him be, doc."

The doctor looked from the detective to Vince, hesitated, then stepped back.

Vince felt like he'd taken a Dempsey punch to the gut. Cynthia, the girl who'd been almost a sister to him…dead. Her skin was like ice. He eased her back down on the table and slipped off his tuxedo jacket. Gently, he spread it over her upper body.

When they were kids, she would play outside in the cold Philly winters until her nose would be as red as Rudolph's and never complain. They were having too much fun sliding down the hill in his back yard on sheets of cardboard and launching snowballs at one another. Out of all the girls in the neighborhood, she was the toughest. The others would give in to the freezing wind long before Cynthia.

A sob caught in his chest, and he sucked in a lungful of the rancid air. “I’m sorry. So sorry I didn’t stop this. But I promise, I’ll find out who did it. And he’ll pay.”

Chapter Thirteen

The flat was eerily quiet the morning after the Plaza party. For the remainder of the night, Eliza hadn't seen Vince again. He'd probably left after the way she'd treated him. But she had no choice. Keeping her distance was the wise thing to do. He was wrong about Oscar. His concern for his friend made him overly suspicious.

Thank Heavens, Oscar hadn't given her to a client last night. She and Charli had come home together after the party ended. But when she rose this morning, Charli was gone.

She sipped her tea and picked up the *World* off the table. An article in the center of the page caught her attention. Next to the story was a photo of a smiling young woman. She'd seen the face before, but the girl hadn't been smiling. She'd looked terrified, desperate. The eyes had been rimmed in smeared black make up. Not innocent and scrubbed like they were in this photo. Dread crawled up her spine. While this was different from the snapshot Vince had shown her, the girl was one and the same. Her gaze went to the headline.

Body of Cynthia Yost, from Philadelphia, found in Hudson River…

Cynthia Yost.

Dear God…

Her hand shook so violently, she sloshed hot tea on

her fingers. She barely felt the burn.

The girl she'd seen with Oscar was Vince's friend. And now she was dead.

Did Vince know yet? If so, he must be devastated. Tears threatened to spill, but she blinked them away. She pushed to her feet and gulped down the rest of the tea, then hurried down the hall to the loo and bathed. Without questioning why, or what she would say when she saw him, she quickly dressed in a blue linen dress, preparing to go to Vince.

Outside, she hailed a cab—a rare luxury—and asked the driver to take her to The Starlight.

The ride was over in moments, and a bout of nerves consumed her when she stepped to his door. What must the clerk think of a woman visiting a man's room alone, in the middle of the morning?

Immediately following the thought, she inwardly snickered. *You're a strumpet, Eliza, your reputation is the least of your worries.*

She hurriedly rapped her knuckles on the door before she changed her mind.

Several moments of silence passed. She was about to decide Vince wasn't there and leave, when the door slowly swung open.

His hair was mussed, as if he'd been running his fingers through it. The top few buttons of his white shirt were undone, showing a smattering of dark blond chest hairs. His bleak eyes narrowed on her almost as though he didn't recognize her. Then they cleared and he blinked. "Eliza?"

"I—I saw the paper. I'm so sorry."

He nodded and stepped back. "Come in."

She entered, and he closed the door. The room was

small, with two narrow beds and a desk. Somehow, being alone in the motel with him felt even more intimate than the night he'd purchased her services. She cleared her throat and moved farther into the room.

"Have a seat." He gestured toward the straight-backed chair at the desk.

"No, thank you. I won't be long."

"I appreciate you coming."

"Of course. I wanted to tell you how sorry I am about your friend."

He nodded, then let out a long, heartbreaking sigh. "She was more than a friend."

Breathlessly, she waited. Was she his lover…his wife? "More than a friend?"

"We were engaged to be married."

A twinge of jealousy shot through her, followed by guilt. What kind of dreadful person was envious of a dead girl? Still, she couldn't help wonder…what would it be like to have Vince love you so much, he wanted to make you his for eternity? "You must have loved her deeply."

He shrugged. "I loved her, yes. We grew up together. We went together when we were in school. It just seemed the natural thing to marry her." He tightened his jaw and shook his head. "I ended things just before she went missing. She'd gone to New York for a three-day shopping trip that turned into a two-month stay. She called a few weeks ago and said she was coming home, that she wanted another chance. I told her we'd talk about it, even though I knew it was over between us." He lifted his gaze. His eyes were damp. "I just wanted her to come home, to be safe. I would have told her anything."

His pain was like a knife in her heart. She wished she could take it away. "Oh, Vince. I'm so sorry."

He nodded and rubbed his sleeve over his face.

She twisted the locket in her fingers. How angry would he be when she told him? Keeping it from him was not possible. She was living with enough guilt. She couldn't bear it if she didn't come clean.

"It's going to be at least a few days before they release her body so I can take her home." His voice broke, and he drew in a breath. "Home to bury her."

She took a few steps and wrapped her arms around him. He resisted for a moment, then pulled her to him, buried his face in her neck, and sobbed. She brushed her hand over his hair, making soothing noises, telling him she was sorry.

After several moments, he released her and stepped back, thumbing tears from his eyes. "Sorry. Didn't mean to break down like a sissy."

"You aren't a sissy. You're grieving. It's only natural." She couldn't put it off any longer. Gathering her courage, she said, "I have something I need to tell you."

He inclined his head in a nod. "Yes?"

"I saw Cynthia. With Oscar."

His brow furrowed. "You…what?"

"Just before I met you. I saw her. She was at one of Oscar's parties. She was upset. Oscar was helping to calm her."

"You what?" His mouth tightened, and he strode over and grabbed her upper arms in a vise-like grip. His sapphire eyes shot sparks. "You saw her with Oscar? And you lied to me?"

She winced at the pain but didn't pull away. She

deserved it. "I didn't know it was her. She looked different from the picture you showed me. I never heard her name."

His jaw clenched, and he released her abruptly. "Oscar. The son of a bitch. I knew it."

"No, he didn't hurt her. I'm sure. He was concerned for her. He treated her kindly. I asked him about her later, if she was okay, and he said yes, he sent her home."

In a voice as cold as the arctic, he said, "But she didn't go home, did she?"

A lump formed in her throat. "No. She didn't," she whispered.

"Your boss murdered her."

"No, he wouldn't do that. There's a killer, another girl was found. I'm sure it's the same person."

He smirked. "Yeah, a girl who worked for Oscar. I'm sure it's the same person too. Oscar." He shook his head and his mouth tilted in a cruel smile. "You need to wise up. Just because you're a whore, you don't have to be stupid."

A gasp left her before she could stop it. She opened her mouth to protest, but he was right. She was nothing more than a whore. Well, she was a little more than that…she was also a killer.

In a slightly less harsh tone, he said, "I'm sorry. I shouldn't have said that. I'm just upset. Worried. You need to get away from Oscar. Quit. Now."

She closed her eyes. *If only…* "I can't just quit."

"Of course you can. You can find another job. Might not make as much scratch, but you can earn a living." He shook his head. "He's dangerous. It's not safe. You have to leave him." He let out a long sigh.

"I'd like for you to go now. I need to be alone."

She choked back a sob. "I will. But first, there's more I need to say."

The muscles in his shoulders visibly tensed as he waited.

"I thought you should know. The whole truth about me." She drew in a shaky breath. "Not only am I a whore, I'm a killer as well."

His eye twitched, and his jaw clenched, but he didn't speak.

"I left England because I killed a man. My employer."

He snorted a laugh. "You killed a man? Bullshit. What kind of game are you playing?"

She shook her head. "Not a game at all. I thought now was a good time to come clean. You don't like lying, you don't like the kind of person I am, well guess what? I don't blame you. You shouldn't like me. I just thought you should know. You can look it up. Call them and tell them where I am. If you wish to turn me into the constable, I will understand." She'd been free longer than she should have. She was fortunate, actually. "His name was Lord Renwald of Abbots Langley. You can check with Hertfordshire Constabulary. I bashed his head with a vase on the sixteenth of April. Then I ran."

Amusement hovered over his mouth. "And, might I ask why you killed him?"

He found it *funny*? Either that, or he didn't believe her.

She wouldn't tell him the Earl had attacked her. She wouldn't make excuses for what she'd done. She lifted her chin and stared into his eyes. "Because I bloody wanted him dead."

There. That should fix things between them. Forever. Clean. Final.

She took a step back, stalked past him, and strode from the room.

Chapter Fourteen

Eliza, a murderer? That was nuts. But why would she say that? Had she been lying to scare him off? It wouldn't work. He was falling for her. He was angry with her, sure, but he was crazy about her too. They might not have a future together, but he wouldn't see her end up like Cynthia. Somehow, he'd get her away from Oscar. The best way to do that would be to take the piker down. He killed Cynthia. Vince had no doubt about that. He just had to find a way to prove it. The police might help with both his questions.

He used the motel office phone to call Detective Mulligan and relayed the latest about Cummings. The detective assured him they would check into it. Vince then asked him to find out what he could about Lord Renwald.

The detective grunted. "A transcontinental call? That's a lot of mazuma."

"I'll pay for the call. And I'll throw in a pair of signed gloves."

Mulligan's shrill whistle came over the line. "You got yourself a deal. I'll call the hotel when I find out something."

Vince took a walk while he waited on the call. He was gone maybe half an hour and when he returned, a message was waiting for him. He called the detective, gripping the receiver tightly as he listened to Mulligan.

He thanked the detective and hung up the phone. He let out an exasperated grunt. Eliza Gilbert had a lot of explaining to do.

****

Eliza had cleaned the flat end to end to take her mind off her talk with Vince, off his deceased friend. But as small as their living quarters were, it hadn't taken enough time. And, truth be told, she'd thought about nothing else as she cleaned. Would Vince turn her in? She'd thrown the words at him in a moment of upset, but now reality was crowding in. She could possibly go to prison. Possibly be hanged.

A knock on the door made her jump. Was that the constables? They never received visitors at the flat. Her friends wouldn't knock…

She drew in a breath and opened the door.

Vince stood glowering down at her. "You didn't kill him. Why did you lie to me?"

Eliza frowned. "I did kill him. What makes you think I lied?"

"I checked into it. Lord Renwald is very much alive."

"No, that's not true. I hit him. He fell like a stone. There's no way he…" But, it could be true. She had always assumed the blow had killed him. He'd been so bloody, so still… But it was very possible he'd survived. Her knees weakened with relief. She grabbed the doorjamb to keep from falling. She hadn't killed him. She was free of guilt. The full implication of his words registered, and happiness was quickly replaced with disbelief and betrayal. "You…you checked? You really were going to turn me over?"

He nearly growled in frustration. "Of course not. I

just wanted to find out if you were lying to me. As it turns out, you were." He scrubbed a hand over his face. "I don't know why I care about you like I do. I can't trust a word you say."

His words pierced her heart, but he was right. The untruths suddenly weighted her like a thousand boulders. For the first time in a long time, she wanted to come clean. To unburden herself completely. "I didn't meant to fib. I really thought I'd killed him."

"Stop it! Enough of the lies." His shoulders slumped, and he shook his head. "Listen, I don't know what your game is, but I'm done. Please promise me you'll get away from Oscar. That's all I ask. Then I'll leave you to your fantasy world where maybe you've begun to believe your own lies."

She let out a long, slow breath, suddenly knackered, mentally drained. "All right. I realize I haven't been completely truthful with you. But, I'm weary of the deception. Weary of the whole sodden mess." She stepped back and opened the door wider. "If you'll please come in, I'll tell you everything."

He hesitated for just a moment, then removed his cap and stepped through the door. She longed to smooth his unruly blond locks, but kept her fists tightly balled at her sides to prevent it.

"Won't you have a seat?"

"I'll stand."

"Very well." She licked her lips, then began speaking, telling him all the sordid details of Lord Renwald's attack.

His expression darkened, and he crushed the cap between his clenched hands. "I'll kill the bastard myself."

While a faint twinge of fear fluttered through her at the rage she saw in his eyes, some tiny part of her was also moved by his protectiveness. Was it possible he truly cared about her?

"And..." She turned her back to him and paced a few steps, then faced him once more. "And, while I appreciate your concern regarding Oscar, I can't leave his employ. Not for a while, no matter how much I wish I could."

"That's crazy. Why can't you?"

"Because, I signed a contract stating I would stay with him for two years or pay a thousand dollar fee." The enormity of her predicament washed over her. She drew in a shuddering breath. "I—I'm stuck." Tears rose to her throat, but she swallowed them back. "I can't possibly come up with that amount." She thought of the lengths Meggie had gone through to help her. Her friend had nearly gotten herself killed, all because of Eliza's foolish mistake.

"The contract can't be binding. Let me see a copy."

She shook her head. She hated to acknowledge her naivety and stupidity, but she was determined to tell the truth, about everything. "I don't have a copy."

"Son of a bitch." He strode over and took her hands in his. "You can still fight it. He would have to produce a copy, and you can prove it's not legal."

She wanted so desperately to believe him, but an immigrant female who could barely read was no match for Oscar Cummings. "I can't afford a solicitor. And even if I could, it doesn't matter. He's powerful, wealthy. I wouldn't stand a chance."

He brought her hands up to his chest. His body was so warm, comforting. She could almost believe...

"Then I'll buy you out of the contract."

Her eyes widened. "What? No. That's a fortune."

"It's worth it to get you away from that bastard. I'll have the dough wired."

"No, I don't want you to pay. This is my problem."

He shook his head and brushed a thumb down her cheek. "It's my problem too. I'm falling for you."

His touch sent a quiver through her body. She ignored it and tugged loose from his hold, stepping away from him so she could think straight. She shook her head. "You can't fall for me. I'm no good. I'm ruined."

He frowned and closed the distance between them in two strides. "Don't say that. You made some bad choices, but you *are* good."

"You barely know me."

He caressed a lock of her hair between his thumb and forefinger, spoke softly as he gazed at her with the most tender look she'd ever seen. "I know that telling you about Benito gave me a sense of peace I've never felt before. I know that a shoeshine boy told me about the money you've given him, expecting nothing in return. Most people wouldn't do that."

She shrugged, her face heating. "It's nothing."

"Nothing to you, maybe. It's a lot to him. And it shows you have a good heart. Come with me to my hotel. I don't want to let you out of my sight until this is over. I'll call my bank. As soon as the money arrives, I'm taking it to Cummings."

She opened her mouth to reply, but she'd run out of arguments. "You're a stubborn man, Vince Taggart."

He grinned. "Very stubborn."

"If you're going to do this, then I ask one thing.

Please let me take the money to Oscar. I'm afraid of what might happen if you go."

"No. You're never going around him again. While I'll admit, I'd like to tear him to pieces with my bare hands, I plan to let the police handle him. I'll do whatever I can to see he pays for his crimes, but I promise, I'll not fight him."

Crimes. She still didn't believe Oscar was guilty of murder. He was a lot of things—not all of them favorable—but he was not a killer.

In spite of his promise, Vince confronting Oscar was a terrible idea. He believed Oscar murdered his friend. And he had a savage temper that he barely kept under control. If Oscar so much as raised his voice, Vince might kill him. She couldn't let that happen, couldn't let him get in trouble when all he wanted was to make things right.

She had to find a way to keep him from meeting with Oscar, but for now, she would concede. "Fine, then. I appreciate what you're doing for me."

He placed a gentle kiss on her forehead. "I'll just be glad to get you free of him. Grab a few things and let's go. This will all be over tomorrow."

Chapter Fifteen

Eliza lay in the dark, staring at Vince in the other bed. One arm rested over his eyes, and his chest gently rose and fell. The blanket was pulled down to his waist, revealing his broad, bare chest. Faint light shone in from the small window, highlighting golden strands in his dark blond hair. Her breath caught at his flawed, masculine beauty. He hadn't made an attempt to shag her, although if he had, she would have been unable to resist. While her experience with sex had been unpleasant, she somehow knew, with Vince, it would be different. Her skin tingled at his very nearness, burned at his touch. Her pulse jumped like crazy whenever he merely looked at her, and warmth pooled deep in her belly. Yes, sex with him would be something entirely different than what she'd experienced thus far.

Was she falling in love with him? She'd never been in love, she wasn't certain what it felt like. But she did know that being around him made her heart lighter. When she wasn't with him, she thought about him. And, of all the people she'd ever known, he most of all made her wish she was a better person.

His words of affection arose in her mind. He was making a big mistake if he was falling for her. They could never be together. What would he tell his family? That he'd brought a prostitute into their midst? No, it would never work. But, she would be forever grateful for his act of generosity in buying her out of the contract. And somehow, some day, she would pay back every cent.

She worried her lower lip. In spite of Vince's assurance he wouldn't harm Oscar, she couldn't allow him to deliver the money. A confrontation between the two men would surely end in disaster.

Quietly, she slid from beneath the covers and climbed from bed. She paused next to Vince, her fingers itching to run over his taut skin, to trace the faint scars on his chin and jaw. She clenched her hands and turned away. Quietly dressing, she shot quick looks at Vince to make sure he hadn't awakened.

He'd tucked the money into the nightstand drawer. She eased it open, experiencing a twinge of guilt at her deception. She pushed it aside. She wasn't stealing, she was simply doing what he planned to do with the money, although with her method, no one would get hurt.

She slid the money into her reticule and tiptoed to the door. It was near midnight. Was Oscar awake at this hour? He had no parties scheduled until Thursday, choosing to take a break for a few days after the Plaza. Hard to believe the election event had only been last night. So much had happened since then.

Hopefully, Oscar would be awake, and they could settle everything. Vince could go back to Philadelphia and move on with his life. A life without his friend, the poor girl who'd been murdered. *And a life without me too…*

True, she and Vince would never see one another again. But she would not forget him. Not if she lived a hundred years.

The night was cool, and she wrapped her jacket tightly around her body as she hailed a taxi. On the short ride to Oscar's, she questioned the wisdom of her decision. She didn't have a choice, really. Going herself was much wiser than allowing Vince and Oscar to face off.

She paid the taxi and took the elevator to the twentieth floor. Oscar answered a few seconds after her knock, fully dressed. Thank Heavens she hadn't woken him.

His brows rose. "Eliza? What are you doing here? I told you there wouldn't be a party until Thursday, didn't I?"

"Yes, you told me. I'm not here for a party."

"Then what?"

"May I come in?"

He pursed his mouth and hesitated only slightly before giving a curt nod and stepping back to allow her inside. "This is quite unusual. Is everything all right?"

She summoned her courage. No need to be frightened. She and Oscar had an arrangement, and she was holding up her end of the bargain. He would likely be gracious about her decision. "Yes, everything is fine. But I've come here to terminate our contract."

A flash of displeasure crossed his features. "I told you, doll, it will cost you a thousand clams."

She nodded. "I know. I have it." She opened her reticule and pulled out the money.

His face reddened, and his eyes narrowed. "Where did you get that kind of jack? You been working for someone else?"

"No, of course not. A…friend loaned it to me. It

doesn't matter where I got it. I have it." She thrust it toward him. "Here."

He slowly shook his head. "You're right. It doesn't matter. You aren't going anywhere."

Unease trickled through her. "B-but, this lets me out of the contract. You have to let me out."

He took a step toward her, and she backed up. "There's no getting out until I'm ready for you to. The contract is just a piece of paper. You don't even have a copy."

"A deal is a deal. I have the required funds, and you have to set me free."

A burst of laughter bellowed from him. "I don't know who you think you are, but I won't be defied by an ignorant whore."

She drew in a sharp breath. "I don't care what you say, what you call me. I quit." She tossed the money on a side table and turned to leave.

His voice stopped her. "There's only one way out, Eliza. The way Cynthia left."

His words made her freeze. She slowly turned to face him. "Cynthia? You…" Her hand flew to her mouth, and a sob caught in her chest. "Oh my God."

"Yes, that's correct. She tried to double cross me. She paid for her mistake." A malicious grin widened on his fleshy face. "She and Roxy both."

Roxy…? Good God, he was mad.

Although horrified, a part of her was relieved. She would go to the police. They would arrest Oscar, and Vince would finally have closure. And she would finally be free. She just had to find a way to leave Oscar's apartment alive.

As if reading her mind, he said, "If you tell anyone,

they'll never believe you. It's your word against mine. And there is absolutely no proof." His voice turned hard, and his eyes narrowed into tiny slits. "I'm fond of you, Eliza, so I'll give you a chance to be a good girl and forget about all of this. But, believe me when I say, you don't want to fuck with me."

****

Vince's eyes snapped open. His heart raced like crazy. What had woken him? A bad dream? If so, he couldn't recall it. He threw the covers off and shot his gaze around the room. Eliza's bed was empty. Where was she?

The money.

He jumped to his feet and slung open the nightstand drawer. Fear gripped his chest. The dough was gone. Eliza had taken it. She'd stolen from him, when all he'd tried to do was help her.

Another, more disturbing thought took hold. "Son of a bitch." She hadn't stolen the money. She'd taken it to Oscar.

He tugged on a shirt and pants, then stalked out the door. Cold air bit into his skin, and he shivered. How long had Eliza been gone? If Oscar had hurt her…

Pain sliced his heart. If Oscar had hurt her, he'd take him apart, limb by limb. Literally.

He cranked the Packard, jumped in, and headed toward Oscar's at top speed, praying he wasn't too late.

Chapter Sixteen

"You can bloody go to the devil!" Rage scorched through Eliza. How dare he threaten her? He was a murderer and a cheat, and she would *not* be bullied by him. "I am through with you. Maybe the authorities won't believe you killed poor Cynthia, but I can bloody well promise, I'll do all I can to make sure you never hurt another girl."

She had no idea what that would be, nor why she was throwing such foolish words at him when she was at his mercy, but she was bloody tired of being enslaved by the murdering arse.

He started toward her, and she whirled, headed in a dead run to the door. Just before she reached it, Oscar's meaty hand landed on her shoulder and spun her around. He drew back and slapped her across the face. Agony shot through her jaw, and blood spurted from her lip.

He grabbed her hair and tugged. Tears sprang to her eyes. She tried to fight him, but the pain in her head was so severe, she was helpless. He dragged her to the balcony and flung open the doors.

Icy air blasted her. Droplets of freezing rain fell on her face as he yanked her outside.

"Let me go, you bastard." She'd meant the words to be strong, authoritative, but they came out as a sob.

He pulled her to the railing. She reached up and

gripped his wrists, trying to loosen his hold on her hair. She couldn't budge him.

"I could toss you over like a rag doll, you ungrateful bitch."

Beyond the railing, lights glinted like jewels. The automobiles below appeared to be the size of toys. Dizziness assailed her. He was going to kill her…

"No one will ever suspect me. I'll tell them how you showed up, distraught. I tried to console you, but you were out of your mind. You rushed out to the balcony, and the next thing I knew…" His evil chuckle rose in the dark night. "Poor little girl couldn't live with the shame anymore."

He yanked her to her feet and leaned her back over the rail. Terror froze her vocal cords so that she couldn't even scream.

"I don't want to do this, Eliza. Believe it or not, I'm fond of you. But you leave me no choice."

He grabbed her beneath her armpits, but before he could lift her, she brought a knee up and drove it into his groin. He doubled over with a grunt and released her, toppling to the ground.

She found her voice and screamed as loudly as she could, at the same time, circling around him, starting for the terrace door. His hand closed around her ankle and pulled. She slipped and fell, her face landing on the hard concrete. She cried out, but the pain wasn't near as potent as her fear. She kicked against his hold, screaming and flailing her arms. "Let me go! You sodden bastard, let me go!"

He came to his feet and clamped his hands around her shoulders. "You stupid whore," he panted. "I'll be damned if you'll get the best of me." Even out of shape, he was much stronger than she. She fought with all her might, but he managed to drag her back to the railing.

This was it. She was going to die. Despair weighted her heart. Never had life been more precious than at that moment. Vince was right. She was good. Maybe not good enough for him, but she did not deserve to die.

She twisted her head, clamped her teeth on Oscar's finger, and bit down. He let out a guttural cry and released her. She spun to race back toward the door, but he recovered quickly and grabbed her again. Blood dripped from his hand onto the shoulder of her dress. She looked up at him and smiled into his hateful face. "Good luck explaining your blood on my dress, the injury to your hand. Do you really think they'll believe I killed myself?"

"Right now, I don't give a damn." He wrapped an arm around her waist and lifted her toward the balustrade. She clenched the top rail with her hands. Oscar pulled, and her hands began to slip. A whimper left her throat. Fear shrieked through her brain. Hopeless…she was going to die…

She prayed her death would be painless, that her friends, and Vince, would know how much she cared about them. That Oscar wouldn't get away with it, that he'd pay for her murder, for the murders of others…

An inhuman roar sounded, and Oscar's grip loosened. She thumped to the ground, safe…free of Oscar…

She looked up and brushed a curtain of hair from her eyes.

Vince had Oscar by the throat, nearly lifting the heavier man off his feet. His fist slammed into Oscar's face. Blood flew. Over the whine of the wind, the crack of crunching bones sounded. Oscar screamed, his bloody hands scrabbling against Vince's hold. Vince released him, slammed him to the cement, then lunged on top of him.

Over and over, Vince's fists pounded into Oscar, his face, his head, his chest. Eliza climbed to her feet, pausing a moment when dizziness swam in her head. She took a deep breath to steady herself and rushed over to Vince. "Stop, Vince, please!"

As if she hadn't spoken, Vince continued the onslaught. Oscar was no longer screaming, no longer fighting. He lay deathly still. "Vince, please," Eliza sobbed. "You'll kill him! Please stop!"

A noise from the apartment caught her attention. Two men in suits rushed across the room and out onto the balcony. The bigger of the two grabbed Vince's arm. "Come on, Taggart. He's done."

With a tug, the man managed to pull Vince off Oscar's limp form.

The shorter man bent over Oscar and pressed his fingers to his neck. "He's breathing. We better get him to the hospital, though."

Vince's chest rose and fell rapidly. His eyes were wild, unfocused.

She hurried up to him and placed a hand on his cheek. "Are you okay?"

He jerked a nod. "I'm fine." His gaze roved over her body, coming to rest on her face. He narrowed his eyes on her cheek and flinched. "He hit you." He seemed to vibrate, as if his rage was barely under control.

She lifted a hand to her bleeding lip and cheek.

She'd almost forgotten her injuries in her concern for her life, then for Vince's. But now her entire face was starting to burn and throb. But she was *alive*. "I'm fine. It probably looks worse than it is."

He shrugged out of his jacket and wrapped it around her. She hadn't realized until then how cold she was.

"Let's get you inside." They hurried through the balcony door, back into Oscar's living area.

"Mr. Taggart, we'll need to ask you a few questions."

Eliza turned to find the tall man—a cop she presumed, based on the badge attached to his lapel—standing behind her.

"Detective Mulligan," Vince said, slipping an arm around Eliza's waist. "How did you know to come?"

"We been keeping an eye on Cummings. Too many suspicious deaths and disappearances around him. We was driving by and saw your Roadster. Figured we better come up and make sure you wasn't taking the law into your own hands."

Eliza said, "He wasn't. He was rescuing me."

The detective narrowed his eyes on her wounds. "Yeah, I can see he was." He looked at Vince, holding her protectively in his embrace. "We can ask our questions later. Maybe you can come down to the station tomorrow?"

Vince nodded and jerked his head toward Oscar. "Is he gonna make it?" From the expression on his face, he hoped he wouldn't.

"I think so. My partner is calling for a meat wagon." He grimaced a smile. "Ain't gonna get in no hurry, though."

"I'll be down to see you tomorrow," Vince said. "But for now, I'm getting her out of here."

"Yeah, you do that."

Vince led her to the door. On the way, she scooped the money off the table and pressed it into his hand. He grinned. Outside the apartment, he guided her along the hallway until they were several doors down from Oscar's.

He stopped and stared down at her, shaking his head. "What the hell were you thinking, going to see him on your own?"

She snuggled farther into his coat, still warm from his body heat. "I was afraid of what would happen if you went. I thought…I thought he would just take the money and let me go."

"The sorry bastard…he's probably wishing he had."

She chuckled. "I imagine so." The image of an enraged Vince surfaced, and she sobered. "It would have been a bad idea to confront him on your own."

He looked down at the floor and nodded. "Yeah. I was out of control. I almost killed him."

"You can't blame yourself. He murdered the woman you love."

He lifted his head, gazing at her with an expression of deep tenderness. "*Almost* murdered the woman I love."

His meaning registered, and her eyes widened. "What…you love me?"

"Yes, I love you. I knew I cared about you, but I didn't realize how much until I saw Oscar's hands on you. If he'd killed you…" His voice broke, and he shook his head. "I'd have felt like I died too."

"Oh, Vince. I don't know what to say." Except that it could never be. Overwhelming joy mingled with intense sorrow. How could the best thing that had ever happened to her also be the worst?

"Say you care about me too. That you can come to love me in time."

She twisted the locket in her fingers. "I do…care about you. But how can you love me? After all the lies, all the things I've done." Shame washed over her and she dropped her gaze to the floor so he couldn't read it in her expression.

He gently cupped her face in his palms and tilted her head until she was looking at him. "You did what you had to do for survival. And you told me the truth about seeing Oscar with Cynthia. You didn't have to do that. You've had a rough time. Most people would have crumbled under the pressure. You're a fighter." A sad grin appeared. "You're tough, like Cynthia was. You remind me a lot of her. Except I loved her like a sister. I love you with all my heart and soul."

His words sent a shiver of longing down her spine. She couldn't deny it any longer. No matter how hopeless, she felt the same. "I love you too."

A smile lit his face. "I want you to come to Philly with me."

"Oh, no. I couldn't."

"I want my family to meet the woman I'm going to marry."

She gasped with shock. "Oh no, no, Vince. You can't marry me. I'll not make you a proper wife. You need someone good, with a good family. Not a…a…"

"Don't say it," He cut in harshly. "Whatever you're going to call yourself, don't."

Sorrow squeezed her heart, and she tugged loose from him. “But it’s what I am. We can’t deny it. As much as I would love to be the girl of your dreams, I’m not and never can be. Your family would never accept me.”

He let out an exasperated breath. “Dammit, woman. I don’t care what anyone thinks. I love you. You’re perfect in my eyes.”

“Perfect?” She laughed. “Perhaps you took too many blows in the ring.”

He snaked his arm around her waist and pulled her tightly against his chest. “The only kind of ring you and I are going to discuss is a wedding ring.”

She opened her mouth to protest, but he clamped his lips on hers. She gripped his face in her hands and returned the kiss. She’d argue with him later.

Maybe.

Or maybe she’d just let him win this one.

Martini Club 4: The 1940s

Precarious

Martini Club 4

Prologue

Edgartown, Martha's Vineyard, Summer 1941

Iris Taggart paced the wooden walkway, her floor-length skirt swishing around her stockinged legs. She'd dressed carefully for the dance this evening, choosing a shimmering sapphire gown that deepened the color of her light blue eyes. She tugged the puffed sleeves down a few inches, showing more of her shoulders. She put a hand to her middle and inhaled deeply. She'd barely been able to breathe all day, thinking about this evening.

Tonight was the night. She was going to tell Dante that she loved him, before it was too late. He'd enlisted in the armed forces and would be leaving soon. This might be her last chance.

The night air was still, with not even a breeze to relieve the summer heat. The sun had gone down, but still, the air hung heavy with humidity. In the distance, the Harbor Light lighthouse was barely visible against the pinkish blue-black sky.

From several feet away, the sounds of the party carried to her. Although it was faint, she recognized "I'll Never Smile Again"—one of her favorite songs, even though it nearly made her burst into tears each time she heard it. Sophie and Audra loved it, too. They were no doubt dancing to it right now. Had they even noticed she was gone? She hadn't told them she was leaving. They might have tried to talk her out of it. If

Maddie had been here, she definitely would have. Maddie was the oldest of the four girls—friends who'd been inseparable since birth. She was mature, wise. But she was in England, missing their summer at the Vineyard for the first time in years, all because of that blasted war. Fear gripped her heart. What if the United States became involved? Dante would have to fight in a war. He might be killed…

"Iris?"

His voice behind her sent her heart skittering up to her throat. She whirled, clutching a hand to her chest. The half-moon provided little visibility, but the lights along the boardwalk illuminated him, picking up glints in his dark hair and eyes. Each time she saw him, he seemed to be more grown up, more manly, more devastatingly handsome.

"Hello, Dante." Did her voice sound as breathless to him as it did to her? She swallowed and forced strength into her vocal cords. "I didn't expect to see you." That was a complete and utter lie. She'd known this was the time he made his rounds, checking the property, making sure equipment was put away, the residents were safe. She'd known he'd come this way when he was finished.

"What are you doing out here?" He slid a coil of garden hose from his shoulder and dropped it to the ground beside him. The sleeves of his blue-gray shirt were rolled up on his biceps. He looked more dashing in workman's clothes than most men did in the finest suits. "Why aren't you at the party?"

"I-I was, but I needed some fresh air."

He studied her with a scowl. "You seem upset. Is someone bothering you?" He clenched his fists at his sides, and the tendons in his forearms bulged. "Tell me who."

"No, no, it's nothing like that." Dante was always looking out for the four of them, especially her. She'd been a sickly child, had nearly died of pneumonia. He was like a big brother, but she did not think of him as a brother. No, it was much more than that. She didn't want Dante as her protector, she wanted him as her husband. "I was just thinking…about the war. Do you really think America will get involved?"

The anger faded from his face, replaced by sadness. "I'm sure of it."

"Then why did you enlist? Only boys twenty-one or over are required to enlist. You aren't twenty-one." He'd just turned twenty on June fifteenth. She knew almost everything about him. She thought about him all day and night, every day and night.

"I know I didn't have to. I wanted to."

"Why?"

"To serve my country, of course."

"But aren't you scared?"

The side of his mouth lifted in that grin she loved so dearly. "Of course I'm scared, what kind of fool would I be if I wasn't? But that's no excuse to take the coward's way out." He shook his head. "It don't matter anyhow. I got a feeling, before it's all over, none of us fellows will have a choice in the matter."

"The draft, you mean?" Lots of boys were drafted in the last World War. And many of them died. They hadn't had a choice, but Dante did. What on earth was he thinking? "Surely the war won't last all that long?"

He let out a weary sigh. "I'm afraid it's going to last longer than any of us want it to." A faint rumble sounded, and Dante cocked his head to listen. A lock of dark hair fell over his forehead, and her fingers itched to brush it back.

"What was that?" she asked, wanting to draw his attention back to her.

"Simulated gunfire. The U.S. Army is using the Vineyard to practice beach landings and assaults. They've got soldiers posted all around—in the woods and on the Gay Head Cliffs and an observation station at Peaked Hill."

Fear shivered through her, raising bumps on the bare skin of her shoulders, and she wrapped her arms around her middle. Last year, a woman had been murdered, right in her bed, on East Chop in Oak Bluffs. That had frightened Iris, but she was even more frightened now. Life could end in a split second.

Which was why she couldn't wait any longer.

She stepped close to him and rested her hand on his forearm. His muscles were firm beneath her fingers. "Dante, I…" She swallowed, working up the courage to say the words.

"What is it?" His confused gaze dropped to her hand, but he didn't pull away. Good. That was a good sign.

"I-you're going away, and I couldn't let you leave without telling you how I feel about you."

His mouth tightened, and he gently eased her hand off his arm. "Iris, you're just—"

"Don't! Please, don't say it. Let me finish." She peered closely at him. He could never hide his feelings. They always showed in his expressive eyes. "I love you, Dante, I always have."

He grimaced…not the reaction she wanted. Dread

coiled around her heart.

"Look, Iris. I like you a lot. You know I do. But, you're just a kid. You can't really love me."

She gritted her teeth. "I'm not a child. I'll be sixteen in December. I am a woman, Dante Morello. I know how I feel. You care for me, I know you do."

"Of course I care about you." His voice gentled. "But, like a kid sister."

"No, that's not true." She struggled to hold back tears. "I've seen the way you look at me."

He dropped his gaze to the ground and drew in a long, slow breath. He took her hands, his voice low. "I wouldn't hurt you for anything in the world."

"Then don't." Her voice broke. "Tell me you love me."

"I'm sorry, Iris, but you're wrong. I don't love you, not like that. You're just a child."

The music from the party still played in the distance—a different song, but the haunting strains of "I'll Never Smile Again" lingered in her mind. A woman had written the song for her husband, who died only a few months after they married. Iris knew how the woman felt. She was sure she'd never smile again either. Shame burned over her skin. How could she have humiliated herself like that? It was his fault. If he hadn't pretended to care, she never would have thrown herself at him.

She glared up at him. "I hate you, Dante. I hope you never come back from the war. I hope a German blows you to pieces!" She whirled and ran toward the party. She didn't want anyone to see her like this, but she needed to be with her friends. The music grew louder, so she knew she was close to the community center, even though she could barely see through her tears. She halted outside the door, rubbing her eyes, but new tears kept replacing the ones she wiped away. She pulled a handkerchief from her clutch and dabbed at her eyes. Voices carried to her from the back of the dance hall. She recognized those giggles…

"Iris, wait!"

Dante's voice came from a short distance away. He would catch up to her soon, and he would likely look for her inside. To the devil with him.

She hurried around to the back, relieved when she spotted Sophie and Audra. Two boys stood with them. She recognized the Andersen brothers, Waldo and Gregory. She couldn't abide Gregory, but she'd rather be with anyone other than Dante right now.

Sophie spotted her and waved. She wore a golden gown that complemented her beautiful red hair. "Iris! Where have you been?"

Iris shrugged. "I took a walk. I had a headache." She'd tell her friends what happened with Dante later, but she certainly wouldn't share her humiliation with the Andersens.

Gregory held a lit cigarette in her direction. "Here, have a smoke." She took it and put it to her mouth, inhaling until the red tip grew brightly in the dark night. The tobacco had an odd calming effect. Just what she needed. He extended a sliver flask. "Want a shot?"

She'd never drank, nor had she smoked. Momma said it wasn't ladylike, but Dante apparently wasn't interested in ladies, so why bother. She took the flask and tipped it to her mouth. When the liquor reached her throat, she coughed, nearly spewing out the vile liquid. But, it made her feel warm inside, so she took another drink.

Audra plucked the flask from Iris's hand and brought it to her mouth, her blonde curls dancing around her perfect face. "You'll get used to it. It's really quite yummy." She drank, and her eyes watered, but she held it down without gagging.

Gregory slipped his arm around Iris's shoulder, and she cringed at the feel of his damp hand on her flesh. She was about to shrug him off when Sophie looked past them, her eyes widening. "Oh no…" she whispered.

"What's going on back here?" Dante's angry voice cut through the air like a blade.

Iris turned to face him, leaving Gregory's arm in place. "We're just having a little fun, not that it's any of your business."

He stalked over to Audra and snatched the flask from her hand. His glare rested on Gregory, who slid his arm away from Iris. "If I ever catch you giving these girls booze again, I'll rip your head off and feed it to your brother."

Gregory paled but lifted his chin. "You don't scare me."

"No?" Dante's eyes narrowed. "Then you're dumber than you look."

Iris stepped up to Dante. "Go away, you big bully."

He took hold of her arm, his grip firm. "You don't want to do this, Iris. These fellas are nothing but trouble."

She jerked away. "You are not my protector." She wasn't that frail, invalid girl anymore. She was a woman. A woman with a broken heart, thanks to Dante. Anger and humiliation burned through her, loosening her tongue, and her sense of decorum. "You have no place here. You're no more than hired help, so you need to go and leave the guests alone."

He winced and drew in a sharp breath. Iris wanted to snatch the words back, but it was too late. He gave her a look just before he stalked away, and she finally saw emotion in his dark eyes…they were filled with pain.

****

Iris barely paid attention to her favorite program, *The Aldrich Family*, playing from the radio on her bedside table. She'd only turned the radio on to listen for any news reports that might be broadcast about the war. Normally, she loved the show, but not even that could make her laugh these days. She couldn't think of anything other than Dante.

What if he died? What if her horrible words came true? No… He would survive. She believed it with all her heart. She had to believe, or she wouldn't want to live.

"Iris, darling? I brought you dinner."

Her mother's voice penetrated her fog. She hadn't even heard the door open. Hopelessness smothered her heart, her soul, and it took all her energy to lift her head from the pillow.

Eliza came to her bedside, carrying a food tray. A tempting aroma made Iris's mouth water, but she didn't have the desire, or the energy, to eat. The idea of swallowing food made her want to retch. "I'm not hungry." Her voice sounded as hollow as she felt.

"You haven't eaten in days. I must insist. You'll make yourself ill." Her mother set the tray on the bedside table and clicked the radio off.

Iris sat up quickly and tossed the pillow aside. "No, Mother, please. Leave it on."

"I want to speak with you, and I can't with that noise going on."

Panic beat at her heart, and her breath came out in shallow gasps. "I-I have to. Have to hear— Have to know if we go to war."

"Oh, sweetheart." Eliza sat on the bed next to Iris and pulled a lace hanky from her cuff. As long as Iris could remember, her mother had carried a hanky in her sleeve. She dabbed Iris's cheeks. "Why on earth have you been so despondent this past week? And why are you so worried about the war?"

Tears gushed anew. A week… It had been a week since she'd had her heart broken. A week since she'd said the most hurtful thing in the world to Dante, a boy who'd been nothing but kind to her.

"I'm a horrible person," Iris cried, pushing the hanky away. "I'll burn in hell for sure."

"Iris!" Her mother's voice was almost as shocked as her expression. "What an awful thing to say. What the bloody hell is going on with you?"

Iris flinched. Her mother was English, although her accent was faint most of the time. When she was angry, her British accent became pronounced.

Iris let out a trembling sigh and told her mother what had happened—every awful detail.

Eliza's expression softened, but worry lines crept across her forehead. "Darling, you poor, poor darling." She smoothed the hair from Iris's face, her soft hands calming and gentle. "Your Aunt Charlotte baked this special for you. You must eat." She picked up the dish and spooned out a serving, offering it to Iris as if she were still a toddler. Somehow, Iris didn't mind at all. She wished she were still a baby. And none of these grown up problems had happened.

Aunt Charlotte was the best cook in the world, but when Iris took a bite of the quiche, all she could taste was despair. She chewed and swallowed. Her mother offered another bite, but Iris shook her head. "Just tea, please."

Eliza frowned, but placed the spoon on the dish and handed Iris a tea cup patterned with tiny bluebirds. Iris sipped, the warm, sweet taste making her feel marginally better.

Her mother took Iris's free hand and held it tightly. "You must listen to me, dear. What I am going to say is important, and you must never forget it."

"Yes, Mother." Iris nodded obediently, but she wasn't certain she wanted to hear what her mother had to say. She took another drink and waited.

"First of all, I want you to know, I like Dante very much. But…" She pursed her lips, the gesture somehow making her lovely face even more beautiful. "But darling, he's common." Iris's eyes widened. She opened her mouth to argue, but Eliza held up a hand. "I know that is a horrid thing to say, but it's also quite true. His father is in prison. His mother barely kept food on the table for him and his sister. He had to start working when he was ten years old."

Iris's tears dried as anger swept through her. "Yes, and doesn't that make him admirable? And now he's joined the army to fight for our country. You might even say he's heroic."

Her mother's face turned a light shade of pink. "Of course, that makes him admirable, but… He's still common. It doesn't make him less of a person. He's a wonderful boy. And I'm so proud of him for serving our country. He's not below you, but he's not for you either, dear."

Iris pulled away from her mother's grasp and plunked the tea cup on the table so hard she was surprised it didn't shatter. "That's ridiculous. Dante would make any woman a fine husband." Pain pierced her heart. Not any woman. Her. She couldn't bear the thought of him marrying another woman. That would be worse than him dying.

A sad smile touched Eliza's face. "You think that now, but you're so young. You don't know anything about life. About love. Do you remember those dreams you had when you were ill? The monsters that came to you, tried to drag you away?"

Iris nodded, then shuddered. She'd run a high fever for weeks. The dreams had terrorized her nightly.

"Well, monsters are real, my darling. I'll never forget how hopeless I felt, how helpless. If we hadn't found medical care for you, you'd have died. Dante is a good boy, but boys like him grow up to be men who can never keep the monsters away."

Iris clenched her fists. How dare her mother say such awful things about Dante. "That's not true. He's always protected me."

"He can protect you physically. He's big and strong. But having the ability to beat someone up isn't quite the same as giving you a secure future. He can never take care of you financially. What if you have a child of your own and they get sick? You'll never know what it feels like to be helpless, to know that money can save your child, but you have none. Trust me, darling.

It's best this way. You'll fall in love with some wonderful man with the means to give you and your children the life, the security, you deserve."

Iris shook her head. "I don't want just any man. I want Dante. He's the only man I'll ever love."

Her mother laughed softly. "Don't be silly. You're too young to know what love is. You will fall in love one day with a wealthy man from a good family who can take care of you and your children."

Iris considered her mother's words. "If Daddy had been poor, would you still have married him?"

Her mother fell silent. Her mouth tightened and, for a moment, Iris thought she wasn't going to answer. Then, she let out a long breath and took Iris by the shoulders, looking her directly in the eyes. "I'd have married your father if he'd been standing on a street corner, wearing a gunny sack and holding a tin cup."

Iris was surprised when a giggle burst forth. She hadn't smiled in days, let alone laughed.

Her mother grinned. "It's true. But I want more for you. You have no idea what life can be like when you don't have money." She stared off into the distance, her golden-brown eyes darkening as if with remembered pain.

Iris had always suspected some horrible secret, some deep pain in her mother's past, but she'd never opened up about it. "Tell me, Mother." Iris took her hands. They were as cold as Philly in the winter. "What happened to you?"

Her mother shook her head, as if shaking off memories. She gave a smile, but it looked forced. "Nothing, sweetheart. Nothing at all. I just want you to be safe, happy."

Because Iris knew her mother had gone to a dark, sad place, she didn't want to burden her further. "Of course. I know you do. I will be, I promise."

"Good." Eliza stood and kissed Iris's forehead before picking up the tray. "I'll tell your Aunt Charlotte you aren't feeling well, but you thank her for the dinner."

"Yes, please. I'm sorry. I just don't feel like eating."

Her mother nodded. "And I'll say a special prayer for your Dante tonight."

Iris managed a smile. "So will I."

After Eliza left, Iris scooted off the bed and went to her dressing table. She slid open the small drawer and retrieved the seashell necklace Dante had made for her, then slipped it around her neck. Dante might be worlds away, but she could always keep a part of him near her heart. She closed her eyes against a new wave of tears and whispered, "I'll love you forever, Dante."

Chapter One

Club 501 — Boston, 1947

Soft jazz played from the bandstand of Club 501. Iris loved everything about the club, even the smells—the faint whiff of food from the kitchen, cigarette and cigar smoke, the tang of booze and the flowery scent of perfume—scents that were somehow comforting and exciting all at the same time. Above, crystal chandeliers glinted from the ceiling. The walls were adorned with gold-framed images of celebrities who'd visited the club—Iris's personal favorite being Clark Gable. Not only was he breathtakingly handsome, he was a war hero as well…like Dante. A black marble bar stretched along one entire side of the club, its back wall a series of multi-shaped mirrors.

"Mildred?" Iris leaned over and whispered to her future sister-in-law. "I believe that gentleman over there is making eyes at you."

Mildred's homely features brightened, and she swiveled her head around. "Where?"

Iris pointed in the general direction of the darkened booths along the dance floor, almost feeling guilty for her lie. "He's right over— Oh, mercy me, I don't see him now. He was quite attractive, though, and quite taken with you it seemed."

Mildred's narrow cheeks turned a light shade of

pink. “Well, isn’t that something?”

Her mother, Henrietta, harrumphed. “Stop slouching, Mildred, it’s no wonder he changed his mind. Poor posture is very unbecoming.”

Iris tightened her fingers around the stem of her glass and bit her tongue to keep from retorting. Henrietta was a beautiful woman. Although she was in her fifties, her lustrous blonde hair showed not a hint of gray, and her smooth skin was unlined. Her eyes were as green as spring grass. Mildred, unfortunately, had taken after her father. She was thin with a long, beak-like nose and unruly hair of a dull brown hue. Iris knew it was unkind, but the poor girl put her in mind of an Emu, an ugly bird she’d seen in a photo one time. Henrietta never missed an opportunity to make her daughter feel even homelier than she actually was.

Iris was fortunate that Norman—Henrietta’s son and Iris’s fiancé—resembled his mother more than his father, other than the overly large ears. They were his only physical flaw, but they gave him character and didn’t detract from his blond good looks one iota.

Iris offered a comforting smile to her soon-to-be sister-in-law. “Mildred, you’re a lovely girl. Don’t feel you need to make yourself invisible.” Iris guessed that was the reason for the girl’s slouching. Or, it could be her way of withdrawing from her mother. For that, Iris did not blame her.

Henrietta was taking a sip of tea, but Iris sensed she was about to make another scathing remark. Fortunately, Uncle Harry’s appearance at the table prevented her from doing so.

“Iris, sweetheart, how are you?”

“Wonderful, Uncle Harry.” Iris stood and Uncle

Harry wrapped her in a warm hug. Although in his forties, he was still a handsome man. Tall, dashing, with a hint of gray at his temples, Uncle Harry made women swoon. “The dinner is delicious, as always.”

He smiled. “Thank you. I’m glad you’re enjoying it.”

Henrietta gaped at him, her mouth hanging open in an unflattering expression that momentarily erased her beauty, giving Iris a warm flush of satisfaction.

Iris swept her hand toward Henrietta and then Mildred. “I’d like you to meet Henrietta Caddell and her daughter, Mildred. Ladies, Harry Dempsey.”

He bent his head and placed a kiss on the backs of each lady’s hand. “Dinner this evening is my treat.”

“Uncle Harry, there’s no need, but thank you.”

“You are most welcome.” He lingered for a few moments making small talk, then gave a quick head bow. “I must attend to other, less lovely guests. Enjoy your evening, ladies.” He winked and took his leave.

Henrietta batted her eyes rapidly. Her face, from her neck to her hairline was crimson. “Oh my.” Her words were a breathless sigh. “He’s your uncle? Your aunt is Lady Margaret?”

Iris considered letting her believe that, but the truth was almost as good. “We aren’t actually related. But my mother is best friends with Lady Margaret. I’ve known them my whole life. Their daughter, Audra, and I are best friends, along with two other girls I was practically raised with, Maddie and Sophie.” Iris didn’t know why she was babbling, except she’d finally hit on something Henrietta found interesting about her, and she wasn’t going to let the opportunity pass.

“Oh my. How lovely it must be to have such close

girlfriends." Mildred's expression was wistful. "I'm sure you do all sorts of fun things."

"We do. Yes, it's wonderful." Before Iris could think better of it, she blurted, "You should come out with us some time. The other girls will love you. You'll fit right in."

There went another lie. Mildred would absolutely not fit in. While her friends all came from wealth, they weren't snobby and pretentious like the old money families.

A beaming smile made Mildred almost pretty. "I would like that very much."

"Then, we shall plan something soon." Iris winced inwardly. The girls would utterly kill her. But if she could score points with Norman's family, she would suffer their anger. She scooped a spoonful of sorbet into her mouth. It tasted delicious. Perhaps because it was flavored with victory.

The waiter stopped at their table and bent, whispering discreetly into Iris's ear. "Miss Taggart, your company has been requested."

Iris frowned. "By whom?"

"By me."

The male voice came from behind the waiter, who was blocking Iris's view. He straightened and turned. "Sir, I asked you to wait by the—"

"It's not sir, it's Detective. And this can't wait. I need to speak with Ms. Taggart now."

That voice…something familiar tugged at a long-ago memory. Iris stood. She could now see past the waiter. A tall man stood a few feet away. He wore a rumpled dark gray suit with a white shirt and a tie that was partially undone and askew. His jacket was open, showing black suspenders beneath. His gaze caught hers, and a gasp escaped her throat. Although he looked much different—older, harder—she could never forget those midnight eyes. Her knees quivered, and she couldn't catch her breath. Then she did, and it all left her body in one big rush. "Dante? Dante Morello? Oh my God!" She skirted around the waiter, who stared at her as if she'd grown a horn and launched herself against Dante's chest. His arms came around her. Iris squeezed him tightly, barely aware of the fact that his grip was much looser than hers, his demeanor much less excited.

She leaned back and stared into his face. "It's you. It's really you. What are you doing in Boston? How long have you been out of the service?"

He set her away from him, and his gaze flickered toward the table behind her. "I didn't mean to interrupt your dinner, but I'm here on official business, I'm afraid."

Iris registered that he hadn't answered her questions, but his mention of dinner reminded her that they had an audience. She stepped away from Dante and turned to the table. Mildred's mouth was a large oval, her eyes rounded in shock. Henrietta's red lips were tweaked in a look that somehow simultaneously conveyed satisfaction and horror. Iris's face heated. She introduced him to the women and asked quietly, "What kind of official business?"

"You work at the soup kitchen, is that correct?"

"Volunteer, yes, why?"

His gaze flicked over Henrietta and Mildred, then settled back on Iris. "Can we go somewhere and talk?" He surveyed the room. "One of those empty tables near the bar? It won't take long."

"Yes, certainly." She spoke to the women. "Will you excuse us?"

Henrietta scowled. "What's this about, Iris?"

"I'm not certain. Something to do with the soup kitchen."

She sniffed. "I told you that place was trouble."

"I'm sure it's nothing. I just need to speak with him for a moment."

"I believe we're finished for the evening." Henrietta stood. "Come along, Mildred. And, Iris, thank you for a...lovely dinner." The compliment seemed forced from her puckered lips.

"You are most welcome. Maybe we can—"

"We really must go. Good evening."

They swept past, and Iris's heart sank. Whatever strides she'd made to be in Henrietta's good graces had no doubt vanished. On a positive note, Dante was here. After all these years...she couldn't believe it.

She smiled at him. "Shall we?"

He placed his hand on the small of her back and led her across the room to an empty table. She was exceedingly aware of his warm touch through the thin, soft fabric of her satin dress. Goose bumps broke out on her arms, and she flushed. How on earth was she having such a reaction to him? She'd gotten over her foolish crush years ago. And, she was engaged—and in love—with Norman. It had to be the pleasure and shock of seeing him so unexpectedly, nothing more.

He pulled her chair out for her, then sat across from her. He was as good-looking as ever, though his carefree youth was gone, replaced with an edge of something sad...and dark. But then, war would do that to a man. His mouth was set in a hard line, his face made up of severe angles. Eyes that had once twinkled with boyish charm now reflected torment, as if they'd beheld tragedies beyond comprehension.

He removed a small notepad from his inside jacket pocket and flipped it open. "Were you working at the soup kitchen last night?"

"I was. Why do you ask?"

He frowned and tensed his jaw line. "A woman was murdered. Her body was found near the railroad tracks."

"Good gracious." Iris shivered and touched her fingertips to her mouth. "Murdered?"

"We think the South End Slayer claimed another victim."

"How dreadful. But what has it to do with me?" This maniac had Iris's nerves on edge. It was bad enough he was murdering people, but he was operating near the soup kitchen where she spent a great deal of time.

"The soup kitchen is the last place she was seen alive. At…" He peered down at the notepad. "Just after nine p.m. Were you working then?"

Fear flowed through her veins. She'd been the last person to see the girl alive? She slowly nodded. "I was. I left at around ten."

He once more reached into his jacket pocket and pulled out a photograph, which he slid across the table. "Do you recognize her?"

Iris picked up the picture. The girl had light-colored hair and looked to be around twenty. She stared out of the photo without a hint of a smile. Her eyes were filled with sadness, as though she knew what her end would be. Iris laid the photo on the table and drew in a shaky breath. "I do recognize her. Mary…something."

"Mary Gaither. So, you do know her?"

"From the kitchen. She was there most every day." Sorrow gripped her throat. "She was so…sweet. Poor girl."

"Anything at all you can tell me that might help us figure out who would want to hurt her?"

"No. But if she's a victim of the slayer, he has killed four or five people, correct? I didn't think he knew his victims."

"That's correct. It's unlikely he has a connection to his victims." There was a pause. "Other than the soup kitchen."

"There's a connection to the soup kitchen?"

He sighed. "We're working on that theory. It seems all the victims so far had been seen there. But then, he targets the poor. So, I would imagine a good deal of them would be seen at the kitchen."

"Yes, I would imagine. Did you talk to the others who were working that night? I mean, why me?"

"I have officers interviewing everyone there that night."

"But you chose to speak with me?" The thought gave her a thrill of pleasure. She was over the humiliating schoolgirl crush she'd had on this man so many years ago, but it didn't mean she wasn't ecstatic to see him again. This was…Dante. The boy she'd practically grown up with. The boy who'd cared for her, fought her battles, protected her. Only, now, he was a man. An exceedingly handsome man despite the ravages the war had wrought.

He gave a brief nod. “I’m interviewing others as well. It’s my job.”

Iris tamped down her disappointment. “Of course.”

“Did you see Ms. Gaither speaking with anyone? Was she there alone or with someone else?”

“She was alone when I saw her.” Sickness coiled through her. One moment, Mary was fully alive, breathing, speaking, smiling. The next… She shuddered. “And, I talked with her.” The realization that she might have been the last one to speak with the girl hit her full force, and she almost lost her breath. Was there something she could have done to prevent what happened?

“What did you two talk about?”

“Not really anything. We exchanged a few words. I admired her pendan—” Cold swept through Iris’s body, and she gasped.

Dante narrowed his eyes. “What? What is it?”

“I—I have her necklace. The one she was wearing that night.”

His brows rose. “How do you have it?”

“She—left it for me. In my bag.”

“She just took it off and put it in your bag? You saw her?”

Iris shook her head. This made no sense at all. “No, but I assumed… I mean, how else would I have gotten it?”

“I don’t know.” A hint of suspicion entered his tone. “You tell me.”

Iris gave an incredulous laugh. “Are you suggesting I took it from her? A cheap little bauble like that?”

His mouth thinned, and his expression showed

displeasure, or maybe disgust, then he quickly masked the emotion. "No, I'm sure if you were going to steal something, you'd make sure it was valuable."

The barb stung, and Iris blinked back a rush of tears. She chose to ignore the insult. "I don't understand how it got in my bag."

"Was she wearing it when she left?"

Iris shrugged. "I didn't notice. And I didn't find it in my bag until this morning."

"And she was dead by then."

A horrifying thought occurred. "Do you think the killer left it for me?"

He was silent for a moment, then shrugged. "It's a possibility."

"But…why?"

"I don't know. I'll add that to a long list of unanswered questions. But I do know you must be careful. If this killer knows who you are…or is fixated on you somehow, you could be in danger."

Iris brought a hand to her throat. "Danger? You believe so?"

"I'm not certain, but it pays to be cautious. Maybe you shouldn't go down to the soup kitchen for a while."

"I have to. If I don't, Audra will be going alone. And Uncle Harry would not allow that."

A smile softened his stern features. "Ah, yes, Audra. Her father owns this club, I believe. It's good you're still in touch. What about the other girls, do you still see them?"

"Oh yes, we're great friends. They're all here too. Well, except Maddie. She's coming in this Wednesday, from England. We're so excited to see her. We haven't seen her since before the war."

A dark cloud passed over his face. Iris wanted to ask him about his time overseas, but his expression didn't welcome that sort of inquiry.

After a few silent moments, he spoke. "What are all of you doing in Boston?"

"Audra and Sophie and I attended Roseline. Sophie's graduating on the seventeenth. I know she'd love it if you came."

"I'll try to do that. Have you already graduated? I remember you wanted to become a nurse."

Iris nodded. "Or even a doctor." She was aware of the wistful quality to her voice. That dream was crushed, forever. The thought of telling him that her entire focus was landing a wealthy man brought another wave of nausea to her stomach. "I did go to school. I received a degree from the Woman's Medical College of Pennsylvania." That had caused her mother a great amount of consternation. But, Iris's father had convinced Eliza to let Iris go. Both her parents expected she would end up being a wife and mother, but her father wanted her to have the opportunity to attend the school of her dreams. Whether or not anything came of it. "But, I took social courses at Radcliffe, for only one semester. I won't be following up with a career. I'm actually getting married."

Nothing changed in his expression. Not a hint of disappointment, or happiness. He remained stoic. "Congratulations. Who's the lucky guy?"

"Norman Caddell. That was his mother and sister I was with earlier."

"The Caddells? The Boston Brahmin Caddells?" He gave a low whistle. "Nice job."

Her cheeks heated. It was as if he knew that

landing a rich husband had been her sole purpose in life. "I love him very much." The words sounded defensive, though she hadn't meant them to.

"I'm sure you'll be quite happy, and you'll make a wonderful wife."

But not for you. You didn't want me. I threw myself at you and you rejected me. She just barely kept from speaking the words aloud. His long ago rejection had hurt, but of course, he'd been right. She'd been a child who had no idea what love was about. She knew now. Knew about true love. And what she felt for Dante was no more than a silly crush. "Perhaps we could all get together? Me, the girls, you, and I'll bring Norman. I'm sure he'd love to meet you."

"That sounds fine." He put away his notepad and stood. "I've got more witnesses to question. I'd better go. It was nice seeing you."

"You too, Dante. Good luck. I hope you find that awful killer."

"So do I. Before he finds another victim."

Iris shuddered as his advice to be careful came back to her. Surely there was a logical explanation as to how the pendant ended up in her bag. She refused to believe she was somehow connected to a murderer.

Then she remembered the other odd items. Her heart beat so loudly, she thought the whole room could hear it. She stared wide-eyed at Dante. "I just remembered. I've found other items before this. We just assumed someone left them behind accidentally." Was it possible the killer was presenting her gifts from his victims? And if so, why her?

Dante frowned. "What items?"

"There was a…a watch. A brooch. Some kind of

military medal." That reminded her of what she'd said to Dante, before he left for a war where he could have been killed. Shame burned through her. "Dante…I wanted to apologize. For what I said the last time I saw you. That was a horrible, awful thing to do." Tears choked her voice. "I understand if you don't forgive me. I've never forgiven myself."

His lips quirked in his crooked smile, but his eyes remained emotionless. "No need to apologize. You were young and impulsive. Besides, I wasn't blown to pieces by the Germans, so no harm done."

Heat suffused her face. She didn't reply.

"Do you still have those items you mentioned?"

"No. We put them in a lost and found at the kitchen." She gave a wry grin. "And trust me, that box is cleaned out daily, whether or not the items end up with the rightful owners."

He grunted in frustration. "Okay. Thank you. I'll check with the families and friends of victims to see if the deceased owned those things." Dante stood and they said their goodbyes. Iris was left with conflicting emotions. On one hand, she was thrilled to see Dante. On the other, she was possibly being targeted by a killer.

Chapter Two

Iris stretched lazily and rolled over in her soft, comfortable bed. She enjoyed a few blissful moments between the dream world and waking before the horror of the murder came crashing back in. She let out a whimper and sat up abruptly.

"What's the matter, Iris?"

Iris started. Shelby sat at the foot of her bed, a frown marring her eyebrows. Shelby was the granddaughter of Opal, Norman's aunt with whom Iris was living until the wedding.

Iris didn't want to scare the child with what she'd learned from Dante. "Oh, nothing. I just…I had a bad dream."

"You mean about the murders?"

"How do you know about them?"

"I heard Grandmother speak to Aunt Henrietta about it. She said you were daft for traipsing down to that horrid soup kitchen, knowing a killer is on the loose."

Iris grimaced. "That's what I've been telling Audra. But she's as stubborn as an old mule."

"Why do you have to, just because Audra does?"

Iris tossed the covers back and slipped out of bed. Donning a pink dressing gown, she stifled a yawn, and a brief flash of irritation. She shouldn't have to converse before even a sip of coffee had crossed her lips. "Because, friends do things for one another, even if they don't want to. She can't go down there all alone. Besides, if I didn't go, her father would probably lock her in a dungeon to keep her from going."

Shelby's green eyes widened. "A dungeon? Her own father?"

Iris grinned. "Not really. I was exaggerating."

She smiled back, a dimple creasing her right cheek. Her silky blonde hair was pinned back with her treasured shooting star hair pins that had belonged to her mother. "Let me do your make up today."

"You know how to apply make up?"

"I've been practicing. I want to get good enough so I can go to Hollywood and do make up for movie stars like Ingrid Bergman and Gene Tierney."

Iris's heart went out to the girl. Shelby's father, Opal's son, had died when she was six. Her grandparents despised her mother—a woman they considered beneath them—and not long after their son's death, she'd disappeared. Iris never knew if she'd left of her own accord—perhaps they'd paid her off—or if something more dire had happened. But Shelby believed she'd gone off to make a fortune and that she'd be back to claim Shelby once she was able to care for her. Her latest fantasy had her mother as a Hollywood starlet, and this was no doubt her new scheme to hunt her down.

Ah, the energy and dreams of youth. With Shelby's determinedness, she'd likely accomplish her goals. "Certainly, I'll let you practice on me."

Iris went into the lavatory off her room to perform her morning ablutions. When she returned, she sat at her dressing table, and Shelby stood beside her, frowning in concentration as she applied eyeliner to Iris's lids.

"Can you tell me something?" Shelby dipped a brush in rouge and swept it over Iris's cheekbones. "I'd like to learn about sex. Grandmother refuses to discuss it with me. Did your mother explain to you?"

Iris chuckled. "No, to hear my mother speak, you'd think she was the Virgin Mary." But Iris had caught her parents, on more than one occasion, showing the passion they felt for one another. Why couldn't her mother just loosen up and talk to her about it? Well, not about her and her father, gads no, but about love and boys and kissing… She cleared her throat. "I learned about it from my friends and from older kids at the Vineyard."

"So, will you tell me then?"

"Aren't you too young to be interested in those sort of things?"

Shelby's face colored. "No, I'm not. I have the biggest crush on a boy in school. I need to know how to make him like me. And…" She gave an impish grin. "What to do if he does."

Iris chuckled, but the question concerned her. Shelby was starved for affection. Maybe that's why she was so deeply interested in finding a boy to love her. She was looking for something there that she didn't get at home. Iris hoped that wouldn't lead the girl to become involved with a ne'er do well in her search for love.

"I tell you what." Iris caught Shelby's eye in the mirror. "You'll be twelve soon. How about, after your birthday, you come back and ask me. You'll be old enough then."

Shelby's mouth twisted as if she were considering whether she should believe Iris. "Okay…but you promise?"

"I promise." Iris hoped the girl would forget about it by then, but she doubted that would happen. At least she'd put if off for the time being. She stared at her reflection in the mirror. "Oh my, you did a superb job." And it was true. She'd used subtle color on her lids to bring out the blue of her eyes and the mascara, eyeliner and lipstick was artfully applied.

"You really think so?" Shelby's eyes lit up like fourth of July sparklers.

"Absolutely. I think you're ready for Hollywood." Iris stood. "Now, let me get dressed and I'll see you downstairs for breakfast. I'm famished."

****

Opal insisted on taking meals in the formal dining room, even though there were almost always just the three of them, which made Iris feel foolish and pretentious.

Opal sat at the head of the long, elegant oak dining table, scowling at the newspaper she held. She looked very much like her brother, Cornelius, Norman's father. Unfortunately, the looks were fine on a man, but no woman should have such a manly features. As Opal flipped the page, a headline caught Iris's attention. "South End Slayer Strikes Again."

Iris put her fork down. "Excuse me, Ms. Edeson, may I borrow the newspaper when you've finished?"

"Certainly," she barked without looking at Iris. They ate in silence for a few more moments before she closed the pages and passed the paper across the table. Iris gripped the edges tightly. But her attention was riveted to the photo rather than the article. Dante…standing near the railroad tracks, a fedora perched sideways on his dark head. Even in the photo, his handsomeness radiated.

"My goodness, who is he?" Shelby's voice snapped her out of her musings.

"Oh…that's Detective Morello. He's in charge of the South End Slayer case."

"He's dreamy." The words ended on a whispered sigh. "He looks like Robert Mitchum."

Iris grinned. She could somewhat see the resemblance, though Dante didn't have that cleft in his chin.

"Iris? What on earth do you think you're doing?" Opal's strident tones whipped over Iris. "An impressionable young girl should not be exposed to such atrociousness." She thrust her arm out, hand open. "Return the paper."

Feeling like a chastised child, Iris handed it back. Shelby was awfully young, but she was quite mature. The horrors of the world were out there, and the more she knew about them, the more she could arm herself against them. But Opal was her grandmother, and it wasn't Iris's place. "I apologize. I wasn't thinking."

"Indeed." She huffed, then dug back into her egg souffle.

Iris exchanged a conspiratorial glance with Shelby. The silent message had been passed…they would discuss in more detail later. Maybe during one of their secret late night chat sessions when the house was quiet and Shelby would sneak into Iris's room and let herself be free, a young girl full of curiosity, hopes and dreams, sharing with someone who would listen. Free of the cold, uncaring grandmother whose own husband had left her and therefore she wanted no joy for others. Iris was so grateful to be engaged to a wonderful man who would never leave her alone and bitter.

****

Although it had been eight years since Iris had seen Maddie, she immediately recognized her amidst the crowd at the train station. Her pretty, girlish features had matured into womanhood, but she still had the same flawless skin and lovely dark hair—which was currently styled in a sleek, fashionable bun. Her red travel suit made her easy to spot.

"There she is," Iris said to Sophie. She lifted her arms to wave. "Maddie! Maddie, over here!" She and Sophie jostled through the crowd toward their friend. "Audra couldn't make it. She had a row with Aunt Meg. But she'll meet us for lunch. I can't believe you're really here."

Tears filled Maddie's pretty blue eyes, and Iris's throat closed with emotion. The three of them fell into one another's arms. Iris hugged her friends tightly, babbling incoherently between sobs of joy. Sophie and Maddie were doing the same and Iris couldn't make out what either of them were saying, but it didn't matter. They were together again. After all these years. Soon, all four of them would be. What a joyous occasion.

Sophie finally pulled away. "Oh, come on, we can't stay here! We can't hear ourselves at all. Audra's meeting us at the Park Plaza Grille for lunch…let's go. After we get your luggage of course."

"That sounds perfect." Iris wiped her eyes and helped Sophie with Maddie's luggage. She and Sophie each slipped an arm through Maddie's and they started out of the train station.

The streets were crowded with merchants selling everything from hot dogs to flowers. The girls had to unlink arms in order to allow other pedestrians to get by them on the sidewalk. The day was overcast and a chilly breeze nipped at Iris's skin. She wished Maddie could have been greeted with a lovely, sunny spring day. This weather was probably not much different from what she'd left behind.

"How was the journey?" Sophie asked.

"Long and dreary, but quite uneventful," Maddie sighed. "There weren't many other people on the ship, it wasn't like before the war at all."

Sophie grinned. "No handsome sailors to flirt with?"

Maddie became thoughtful for a moment, then shook her head. "The crews still haven't recovered from the war, either. It's all old men on the passenger liners now."

"How gloomy!" Iris couldn't imagine the suffering the war had caused overseas. The effects were bad enough in the U.S. She forced a bright smile. "Well, you're here now, and just wait until you see all the parties we have lined up. Uncle Harry says you have to come to the club tonight."

"He has a special dance band lined up, just for you," Sophie added. "They're English, you see. It should be fun."

"Of course. I can't wait to see the place, we've heard so much about it. I feel like I haven't been to a proper nightclub in ages." Her steps slowed as they passed a bakery, with a tempting display of confections in the window. "Or had a real cake. Sugar is still rationed, you know. I'm tasked with bringing back lots of chocolate for all my friends, and for Aunt Jess in particular."

"Mom can give you as much as you like," Sophie offered. "She'll stuff you with so many sweets you'll never want another!"

"I doubt that could ever be true. I haven't tasted a real cake since '40."

"Mercy me, that's positively tragic." Iris pulled Maddie away from the window. "Well, now you're going to have fun again. With the four of us together, this town isn't going to know what hit it." They'd reached the place where Harlon, Norman's driver, waited for them. "Here we are." Iris pointed toward the black limousine.

"What is this?" Maddie's eyes widened.

"Norman provided his car and chauffer. He wants to make sure we're safe. He's such a wonderful, thoughtful man." A shadow passed over the day as Iris's thoughts turned to the murders.

"Safe from the South End Slayer?" Maddie gave a delicate shudder as she slid into the back seat. "I've been reading the papers. How absolutely horrid. They haven't caught him yet?"

Iris shook her head. "Not yet. But I'm certain they will."

The car glided onto the street and Maddie took Iris's hand. "So, tell me all about this fiancé of yours." She turned to Sophie and patted her hand. "I want to hear all about what's going on with you as well. We have so much to catch up on."

Sophie gave a cheeky grin. "Yes, but Iris's life is more exciting. I don't have a rich fiancé and an old love back in town."

Maddie lifted her brows at Iris. "An old love? Do tell."

Iris's face heated. "Sophie's just being an imp. She's talking about Dante, who is most certainly not an old love. He is in Boston, though. He's a detective hunting for the South End Slayer."

"Hmmm…you once loved him, so I believe that makes him an old love. And," Maddie grinned wickedly. "Your face didn't light up like it is now when you spoke of Norman."

Iris shifted in her seat and looked out the window as she spoke. "That's silly. I love Norman very much. He's a perfect match for me." She flinched as her mother's words came out of her mouth. But, no, that was not why she was with Norman. She truly loved him. Her feelings for Dante were in the past. They'd just been a schoolgirl crush. Like he'd told her himself, she had been too young to know what love was.

"Have you spoken with Norman about letting you work as a nurse?"

Iris frowned. "Not yet."

Maddie harrumphed. "You've wanted to be a nurse all your life. You even went to school to get your nursing degree. Do you want to waste it?"

"No, but I'll be the wife of Norman Caddell. I can't exactly have my own career."

Maddie's expression turned thoughtful. "You know what I believe? That you can do anything you wish to do. Why should women let men dictate how we live our lives? This isn't the middle ages. Women have had the vote for nearly thirty years, for heaven's sake. In both our countries. Shouldn't we also have a vote in our own future?"

Iris sighed. Maddie was right. She was going to be a wife, not a servant. She would speak to Norman tonight.

****

"Iris, darling? Did you hear me?"

She snapped her thoughts from the question burning through her mind and smiled at her fiancé. "I'm sorry, Norman. I was wool-gathering, I'm afraid."

"Is everything all right?"

She forced her lips into a smile and hoped it wasn't as tight as it felt. Suddenly not hungry, she rested her fork on the plate. For what the Caddells had paid for this seven-course meal, the families she encountered at the soup kitchen could have eaten for an entire month. "Yes, of course. What were you saying?"

"That we have opera tickets for this Sunday."

"Wonderful." In truth, it was not wonderful. She didn't care for opera. She loved Aunt Meg's singing, and jazz and swing music. But not opera. Norman enjoyed it, though, and his family expected that Iris did as well, so she pretended she did.

Iris had faked a great deal of things since she'd first met Norman—which had been her mother's doing. When Sophie and Audra had announced they were attending college in Boston, Eliza suggested Iris come along as well. Iris's parents were acquainted with Norman's family, because Norman had been a fan of Iris's father in his boxing days and had arranged to meet him. Eliza contacted the Caddells and asked that they show Iris around the city. They'd offered their eligible bachelor son, Norman, as her escort.

Their relationship developed from there and Eliza

had been over the moon at the prospect of Norman for a son-in-law. "He'll make the perfect husband for you," her mother had said. "He's polite and wealthy, comes from family wealth so it's not likely to disappear." When Iris had said she wasn't the least bit attracted to him, Eliza had assured her that attraction…and love…could grow. Iris had reluctantly acquiesced. And now, here she was, engaged and in love with Norman Caddell.

The Caddell home was intimidating. Iris hoped hers and Norman's home would be less ostentatious. The forty-room mansion was French Chateauesque and on the front lawn were statues of gargoyles and cherubs…though Iris never understood the connection. The interior and furnishings were constructed of dark mahogany, stained glass, velvet, and marble.

"Iris, have you told Norman about running into your old…friend?" Henrietta paused just long enough to give the word *friend* an insidious connotation.

Iris had to bite down on an irritated retort. The woman was just trying to stir up trouble. "No, I didn't." She shot a look at Henrietta, who was smiling smugly.

"Who is this old friend?" Norman folded his hands together and rested his elbows on the table, staring intently at Iris.

"He-he's a boy…well, man, now, who used to be our caretaker on the Vineyard. He's now a policeman. He's on the South End Slayer case."

"You seemed quite fond of him." Henrietta picked up her wine glass and took a sip, like a cat licking cream from its whiskers. "That was quite the display."

Iris's face heated from embarrassment and anger. "He is a childhood friend who fought in the war. I never thought I'd see him again. I wasn't even certain he'd survived." The impact washed over her. She hadn't known if he were dead or alive, and now he showed up in the city where she was. Miraculous…

Norman grimaced a smile. "My, my. No wonder you were so…happy. I hope you'll introduce me to this…hero at some point."

"Certainly. He'd like to meet you as well." She cast her eyes down at her plate and forced a bite of deviled lobster into her mouth, chewing and swallowing.

Over dessert, the topic turned to other matters…the latest gossip, politics, upcoming social events. Iris nodded and commented when appropriate, but inside, she was dying for the meal to end. She was determined to present her proposal to Norman about becoming a nurse. He just *had* to listen to her.

Once dinner was over, Iris and Norman were left alone in the library. Next to the fireplace sat a lion statue, teeth bared, paws extended as if the beast were lunging at its prey. Iris had seen the piece several times, but this time, it sent a shudder through her.

"Here you are, darling." Norman's long, pale fingers extended a glass of sherry toward her.

"Thank you." She took it from him and gulped a large swallow. Now was the time to broach the subject. There was no reason why, especially before they married, that she couldn't put her nursing degree to use. The Caddells were known for their philanthropy. Surely her wanting to help people would fall in line with that. Forcing words from her frozen throat, she said, "Norman, I need to ask you something."

His blond brows lifted. "Yes?"

Iris took a deep breath. "I would like to put my

nursing degree to use. I want to help people."

"That's impossible."

"Why?"

An expression crossed Norman's face that was part amusement, part impatience. "Surely you can't be serious. The wife of a Caddell working like a commoner?" He shook his head and took a drink from his glass. "Absolutely not. Impossible."

"But I want to help people who need medical care."

He gave a derisive grin. "Medical care? From you? Leave it to someone else. Anyone can pass out bandages."

Fury trembled through her and she spoke through clenched teeth. "I can do more than pass out bandages. You are aware I have a nursing degree?"

He waved a hand dismissively. "That's irrelevant. You cannot work as a nurse, or at any other occupation, and that's final."

Disappointment deflated her. "But, Norman, please. It's been my dream since I was a child. Your family thrives on giving to the community, how would this be any different?"

He slammed his glass down on the table and crossed the room to her and took hold of her forearms in a painful grip. His angry eyes bore into her. "I do not have to explain my reasons to you. I'll not have you defying me, Iris. You are to be my wife. That should be your dream now. I won't hear another word." He gave her a shake. "Do I make myself clear?"

Shock kept her immobile, and she fought back tears. Determined not to show weakness. He'd never gotten aggressive with her. She didn't like it. Was this to be their life? Him making every decision for her and manhandling her when he didn't like what she did or said? "Yes, quite clear." She jerked against his hold. "Now, please let me go."

He stared at her for a few moments before releasing her. "I apologize for my outburst. I simply need you to understand our roles and what is expected of you."

"I understand perfectly." Iris plucked her clutch off the sofa. "I'd like to go home now." Outrage and disappointment clawed at her. How could she never have seen this side of him? How could she have thought he was Mr. Perfect?

Norman nodded. "I'll call the driver."

Iris exited the library and hurried to the front of the mansion to wait for Harlon. She couldn't stand another second in Norman's presence. Which begged the question, how would she stand his company for a lifetime?

****

He stuffed his hands in the pocket of his overcoat and leaned against the lamppost across the street from the Caddell mansion. The home was set back so far from the road, he could barely make out its silhouette in the foggy darkness. But he knew what was inside…his Bonnie…she'd come back to him from the dead. And, while he hadn't been able to claim her in her previous life, nothing would stop him from making her his now. Her mamby pamby fiancé was no match for him. He'd get rid of the jackass soon. But, for now, he was content to bide his time. Until she fully trusted him, remembered what they once had, he didn't want to free her from Norman Caddell. She might fall prey to the charms of some other buffoon. Her taste in men had changed over the years. She'd gone from a derelict, vagabond criminal to a wealthy aristocrat. She would see that the right man for her was somewhere in between. Just a normal guy who wanted to love her for the rest of her life. He was that man, and he'd prove it to her, no matter how many people had to die.

Chapter Three

Iris blew her hair off her face and wiped her damp forehead with the back of her hand. Would this day never end? Her lower back ached and her feet were killing her. She ladled chili onto the proffered plate, barely aware of the person who held it. She couldn't stop thinking about Norman's high handedness. "Passing out bandages indeed," she muttered.

"Iris!" She looked up at Audra who stood beside her serving wedges of cornbread. "Have you heard a word I've said?"

"I'm sorry. I'm just…fuming. I asked Norman about my working as a nurse, and he unequivocally refused."

Audra rolled her eyes. "I don't know why you have to be such a mouse. Stand up for yourself. Tell him, don't ask him."

"Oh certainly," Iris growled. "It's just that simple, right?" She slapped the ladle into the vat of chili so hard that bits of it flew up and burned her hand.

Audra cocked a brow. "Maybe you can use some of that aggression towards Norman. You'll frighten him so much, he'll do double back flips to keep you happy."

Iris chuckled. "You may be right."

The remainder of their shift ground to a close and by the time the last person in line was served, Iris felt like she'd faint from exhaustion. "Thank goodness…"

Her words to Audra died in her throat. Dante was walking through the front door.

"What?" Audra followed her gaze. "Oh my." She waved. "Dante! Over here."

He looked up and smiled, then made his way over to where she and Audra stood. Iris brushed back hair that had escaped her bun and took stock of her appearance—perspiration made the dress cling to her body, chili stains dotted the once-white apron. And her makeup had no doubt melted from her face. She must look a sight and smell no better than some of the street people.

She forced a nonchalant smile as Dante approached. His presence seemed to suck the air from the room and she couldn't speak. But Audra didn't have the same problem. She threw her arms around him. "I can't believe it. Iris told me you were here in Boston, about you being with the police force, but actually seeing you. Well, it's certainly a blast from the past."

"Yes, it is." He released Audra and cut a quick glance at Iris. "I'm afraid I'm here on official business. I'd like to speak with the person who runs the place."

"That would be Luther Rickers," Audra said. "I'll get him for you."

Audra disappeared and, though there were a hundred people in the room, the awkwardness of feeling like she was alone with Dante stole through her. Why were things tense between them? They'd been so close when they were younger. Had her silly, impetuous declaration driven a wedge between them? He was no doubt damaged by the war, but he'd been friendly to Audra. *Does he simply dislike me?* The thought brought a hollow ache to her chest and she found herself blinking back tears.

"Iris? Are you okay?" Dante's dark eyes studied her with concern. Maybe he didn't dislike her after all.

"Actually, I—" She was about to blurt it out, just ask him why he always seemed angry with her, when Luther's arrival interrupted her. Maybe it was for the best. If he didn't care for her, she didn't want to make a fool of herself by letting on that it mattered.

"Detective? I'm Luther Rickers." He wiped his hands on his apron and reached out to shake with Dante. "I understand you wish to speak with me?"

Dante turned his attention to Luther. "Yes, if you don't mind."

"Not at all. We can go to my office."

Dante tipped his head toward Iris, then Audra. "Ladies, nice to see you again."

They nodded back, and Iris let out a long, relieved breath when Dante disappeared behind Luther's office door.

****

"What can I help you with, Detective?"

Luther Rickers was tall and slim with a narrow face and sallow eyes of an indeterminable color. He spoke with a faint southern twang. Maybe from Texas. What had brought him all the way to Boston?

"I'm hunting the South End Slayer, and I'd like to ask you some questions."

His mouth turned down at the corners. "Yes, of course. It's just awful, what's happenin'. I'm happy to help any way I can."

"Have you noticed anyone acting suspiciously around here lately? Anyone getting worked up, violent?"

Luther's brow wrinkled in thought. "Around here, we're dealin' with people in all kinds a bad situations. Some of them ain't quite right in the head. There's bound to be flare-ups and people actin' unusual, but I can't say I've noticed anything in particular that stands out." He picked up a cigarette box and held it out. "Care for one, Detective?"

Dante took it and Luther lit it for him. "How well did you know Mary Gaither?"

Luther lit a cigarette for himself and blinked rapidly. He dabbed at his eyes with his fingers. "I didn't know the girl well, but she seemed sweet. From what I understand, she came to Boston with a boyfriend. He abandoned her and she ended up on the streets." He shook his head and sniffed. "I wonder how he feels now, knowin' he caused her death."

"Actually, the murderer caused her death," Dante told him dryly.

"Well, yes, of course, but you understand my meanin'. If he hadn't left her all alone, she might still be alive."

Dante couldn't argue with that. "We suspect the weapon used in the murders is a kitchen knife. Since the killer might be connected with the soup kitchen, I just wondered if you've noticed any knives missing? Or seen anyone here with a knife?"

Luther jerked as if he'd been given electric shock. "My God. It can't be…"

"What?"

"We have been missing some knives over the past few months. Strangest thing. Only a few of us have access to the back kitchen area where utensils are kept, but I've noticed maybe three of four knives missin'. I just replaced 'em, but it's frustratin'. We're a non-profit and receive very few donations. Any wasted expense cuts into our budget. It never occurred to me the knives might be used in the…" He closed his eyes and visibly shuddered. "….in the killins. That's disturbin' as all git out, Detective."

A chill moved over Dante's spine. "Can I get a list of everyone who has access to the back kitchen?"

"Certainly." He took a pad of paper and pen from the center of his desk and began writing. After a few moments, he tore the top sheet of paper off the pad and passed it to Dante. "That's it. Me, the few volunteers, Clarence and Gertrude, the cooks. Clarence strikes me as somewhat…lecherous around women, but I can't see him, or any of them, commitin' murders."

"No, but sometimes killers look like regular people. Evelyn Dick, the woman in Canada who killed her husband and baby. Then, of course there's Bonnie Parker. Just to look at these women, you'd never guess they were capable of murder."

Luther paled and went silent. Finally, he nodded. His voice was strangled when he spoke. "I suppose you're right. You just never know."

"Are you all right, Mr. Rickers?"

"Yes, I'm fine. I'm just horrified at what's happenin'. I worry about everyone here. Especially Audra and Iris." He smiled, and his eyes lit up. "They're such wonderful young ladies, and a godsend to the soup kitchen. Especially Iris. She's so helpful. So lovely. I can't imagine anything happenin' to her. I just hope she's not in danger."

He said Iris's name like he was caressing a lover, and Dante had a sudden urge to punch him square in his oversized nose. Dante hoped the same thing—for Iris to be safe—so why did it irritate the hell out of him that this man did? "What more can you tell me about this Clarence fellow? What's his last name? Do you think he could be dangerous?"

"His last name is Bittner." Luther shook his head. "I don't see him bein' dangerous. He's harmless, I'm sure. I help out with the cookin', so I've worked closely with him for many hours. I don't think he has much luck with women, and he likes pretty girls. He's just somewhat awkward in his approach."

"Do you keep records of work schedules? I'd like to get one for your employees and volunteers, especially Bittner."

"Certainly. I'll get that to you right away. Is there anything you can suggest? Anything I can do to help keep these people safe?"

"Maybe close down the kitchen until we find this guy."

Luther gave a patronizing smile. "Detective, sometimes the only meal these people have is what they get here. I believe they'd rather be attacked by the murderer than to starve to death. At least that would be quicker."

****

Dante poured himself a cup of coffee and settled at his small kitchen table with the case notes. Six victims and not one good suspect. All the victims had been from the poor side of town. Three women, two men. All strangled and stabbed multiple times. The murder weapons had not been found. No viable fingerprints had been lifted at the scenes. But there had to be clues. Every killer left clues. What the hell was he missing?

He took a drink of the scalding brew as he studied the notes from his interview with Rickers. He'd followed up on Bittner and hadn't found any criminal past. He'd been at the soup kitchen during two of the murders. But, if they were slightly off on the timeline, the man could still be a good suspect. Dante had a bad feeling about him. And about Rickers. There was nothing that pointed to him as a suspect, and he was a do-gooder, feeding the homeless and all. But he was also an unknown. Where was he from? How had he ended up in Boston? Was he running from something? Did he have designs on Iris?

Damn. Dante groaned and pushed back from the table and stood.

No matter how hard he tried to prevent it, his thoughts kept returning to Iris. He was attracted to her. And he hadn't expected to be. She was someone he'd protected, someone he'd cared about for years, but he hadn't expected to be attracted to her. She'd been a child the last time he'd seen her. An image of her face as she'd passionately declared her love for him rose to his mind. She'd been a child, yes, but had been beautiful even then. How would he feel now if she said those same words to him? He shook off the thought. It didn't matter. She'd never say them to him. She was engaged. And she was well past her teen-age crush. He'd lived ten lifetimes since the war. She still retained her youthful vitality. Sometimes he felt a hundred years old.

Somehow, he hadn't expected her to be all grown up. He couldn't get over what a beauty she'd become. Seeing her again was like discovering a bright light after years of darkness. His desire to protect her hadn't left, but now it was accompanied by a disturbing attraction.

He paced across the worn carpet, considering drinking something stronger than coffee. Since the war, he'd tried to lay off the alcohol. Alcohol lowered his defenses and dulled his sharpness. It allowed the memories to take hold. The miserable accommodations, the homesickness, the sounds of gunfire and explosions, the stench of death…of burning flesh. He drew in a deep breath and pinched his nose to erase the images. He was fighting another kind of war now. And the enemy was winning.

****

The faces all blended into one another, an endless procession of the haunted, the hungry. Audra hadn't shown up today, and Iris was miserable without her. At least being with her best friend was one bright spot in such a dreary place. And today, she didn't even have that. Her thoughts went to Dante. She still couldn't believe he was here. A war hero and police officer. Who would have thought it?

"Hey, hey, speed it up. People are hungry, you know."

She snapped her head up to find a woman glaring at her. She wore a dress with tattered sleeves. Her dull brown hair looked like a bird's nest sitting atop her head. Incongruously, a bright red scarf that appeared brand new was wrapped around her neck.

"Yes, I'm sorry." Iris placed a biscuit on the proffered tray. She wanted to snap at the urchin. After all, she was getting a free meal. Who did she think she was? But being rude to the poor would be wrong. They had enough unpleasantness in their lives already.

The woman moved away without a thank you, and Iris focused on serving the never-ending line of people, rather than on her aching feet and Dante Morello. A few hours later, her shift wound to a close. She couldn't wait to get out of here and head straight home for a nice hot bath. She might even sneak a glass of whiskey…

A commotion rose to her right, and a panicked voice shouted, "Help! Can someone please help?"

Iris dropped a biscuit back into the pan and skirted the table, hurrying to where a small crowd had gathered. She shoved through to find a woman on the floor, jerking spasmodically.

Iris sank to her knees beside her. It was the same woman who'd been rude to her earlier. Iris suffered a twinge of guilt at her uncharitable thoughts. "Everyone, move back and give her some space." The onlookers did as they were instructed, retreating a few steps but still gawking. "Does anyone know her name?"

Clarence, one of the cooks said, "Her name's Alma, Miss Taggart. Anythin' I can do to help?" He spoke with a hopeful, pleading tone. Clarence was always lurking, always paying too much attention to Iris and Audra. Iris was pretty certain he had an unhealthy interest in one or both of them, and it gave her the willies.

"No, thank you." Iris made her voice clipped, professional, dismissing Clarence as she focused on Alma. She rolled the woman onto her side and loosened the constricting red scarf and undid the first few buttons of her blouse. Luther had come out of the kitchen and was standing above them. "Give me your apron," Iris ordered.

Luther whipped off his apron and handed it to her.

She folded it and slipped it beneath the patient's head, wishing she had something softer. "Here you go, Alma. I've got you. You're going to be fine."

"Should we get her to the hospital?" Luther asked.

Iris didn't look up, but she heard the concern in his voice. She shook her head. "No, she's having a seizure, but it should pass. It's best not to move her right now."

Iris forced herself to remain calm, but worry pulsed through her. She'd never actually treated anyone before, and she hoped she wouldn't fail this woman. She prayed she was right about not taking her to the hospital. Prayed and waited.

In a few minutes that stretched out interminably, the woman stilled and opened her eyes, looking around as if in a daze. Saliva dripped from her slack mouth, and Iris used the edge of Luther's apron to wipe it away.

Alma's face reddened, and she came slowly, awkwardly to her feet. "I had one of them spells, didn't I?"

Iris stood with her. "Yes, you had a seizure. How are you feeling?"

She lifted a shaking hand to her forehead. "I'm a little dizzy, but I'm okay."

"Are you being treated for epilepsy?"

Her face scrunched in confusion. "For…what's that now?"

"I believe you have a condition called epilepsy. You need to see a doctor and get on some medication."

She snorted. "I can't afford no doctor. Are you outta your mind?"

Couldn't afford a doctor? Medical care was a necessity, not a luxury. But then, food was a necessity too, and they didn't have that either. These people really were suffering.

"I'm sorry." Surely the Caddells could do something for her. Norman's father was on the board at Mass General. "Let me see what I can do about getting you some help."

Alma's eyes narrowed. "Why would you do that?" Suspicion colored her tone.

Iris shrugged. "I just want to see that you get the care you need. If you'll come back to the kitchen in a few days, I should have some information for you."

Alma gave a quick nod, her expression still doubtful. She wrapped the scarf snugly around her neck, then left without a thank you.

Iris went to the sink to wash her hands, and Luther followed. He gave a low whistle. "My, that was impressive."

"I didn't do much. I just hope the poor woman will be okay."

He handed her a towel to dry her hands. "Have you had medical training?"

"I attended Women's Medical School. In Philadelphia."

"Why aren't you putting that to use? Why aren't you working as a nurse?"

She shook her head, trying not to let her disappointed show. "I'm marrying Norman. The wife of a Caddell can't have a career."

Luther pursed his lips. "It's a shame to let your skills go to waste. I have an idea. How about you set up a clinic here? These people have very few options for medical care. If you're volunteering anyway, you might as well volunteer to help where you can be put to the best use of your talents."

She didn't want to tell him she'd already asked about working as a nurse and had been refused. But a clinic…that was something different. It was just another volunteer position. And perhaps she should circumvent Norman and speak to his father—the one person who controlled Norman, since he controlled the wealth. "That's a fine idea. I'll speak with Norman's father. He's on the board at Mass General. Maybe a few doctors could volunteer their time as well." The more she spoke, the more her excitement grew. Was it possible this could actually happen? Norman might not approve of her working in the clinic, but it shouldn't matter, though, really. Like Luther said, volunteering was volunteering.

A smile spread across his narrow face. "That'd be swell. Come on, I'll walk you out. It's not safe around here for young ladies, especially after dark."

"Thank you." Iris shivered as they stepped outside, and the cool night closed in around them. Somewhere in this city, probably very nearby, was a vicious murderer. "I wonder why the South End Slayer would want to murder people down here? These people are helpless. And they can't have anything worth stealing."

Luther was silent as he hailed a cab and opened the door for Iris. "You never know what goes on in people's hearts." He shook his head. "It's a crazy old world we're livin' in. You just keep yourself safe."

She smiled and slid inside the cab. "I will, thank you. You do the same." But as the taxi wound through the darkened streets, Iris felt anything but safe.

****

A light mist fell, and an automobile rumbled by—

the lone vehicle on these deserted streets, other than his that he'd parked a block away in front of a closed drugstore.

He adjusted the bandana, keeping to the shadows as he followed the woman staggering down the sidewalk, her thin, tattered coat fluttering around her legs. She was easy to spot with the bright red scarf flapping behind her…like the cape of a matador beckoning the bull.

Slipping his hand into his coat pocket, he felt the reassuring weight of the knife tucked inside. He cast furtive glances around, not seeing a soul nearby. He picked up his pace, looking forward to the moment she'd realize he was upon her. The look of confusion, then fear. The closer he drew, the more his excitement increased.

Just before he reached her, she must have sensed his presence. She started to turn around, but before she could, he shoved her hard. She stumbled and went to the ground, whipping her head around to look behind her. She tried to scramble away on all fours, but he caught her by the front of her coat and tugged her to her feet.

Fear had her eyes widening, bugging out like Woody Woodpecker's. She'd been drunk a few moments ago. Now she was stone cold sober. "No, please, don't hurt me. What do you want?"

He snickered. As if she had anything to offer. All he wanted was for her to pay for what her kind had done to the one person in the world he'd ever cared for. His Bonnie.

He dragged her toward where he'd parked the car and pulled her into a nearby alley. She resisted, but she was weak—like most of the bums who lived on the streets. He wrapped one hand around her skinny neck and shoved her into the brick wall. He leaned close, until he was no more than a few inches from her terrified face. Waves of a rotting, sour odor washed over him, intensifying his anger. She was no better than a damned animal. "You're nothin' but the dregs of society," he whispered. "Endin' your life is a favor, to you and the rest of the world."

He watched her face as he yanked the weapon from his pocket and held it up for her to see. Watched her eyes as he plunged it into her chest. Blood spurted around his fingers in a warm rush and euphoria filled him. She went limp. He held her for a few more moments. Then he dragged her to his car. He opened the trunk and dumped her inside. staring down at her. Blood leaked from her, puddling on the plastic tarp he'd placed in his trunk. He wished Iris were here now. Would this bring back memories of old times? Would she recognize him? Remember what they'd meant to each other? He shook his head. Maybe not now. But soon, she would. And he'd finally have her. Forever.

He shut the trunk and hopped in the driver's seat, starting the '40 Ford Coupe. He drove north, heading toward the railroad tracks. He had to stick with the plan. It hadn't failed him yet.

Chapter Four

The low murmur of voices and the clinking of fine china were normally sounds Iris wouldn't even notice, but tonight, they had her teeth on edge. She was taking a big risk and it could backfire…or give her exactly what she wanted. She was dining with Norman and his parents at the Terrace Room. Before the meal ended, she was determined to ask Norman's father about the clinic. She felt broaching the topic in a public place was the right move. She mentally crossed her fingers and prayed she was right. The Caddells wouldn't want a scene, and she would hopefully not see Norman's temper flare again. She hated to acknowledge it, but the truth was, he'd scared her. If he was that quick to anger over something so minor, what might he do if she truly stepped out of line? Did she want a lifetime of walking on eggshells? Although her mother was thrilled that Iris was marrying Norman, she wouldn't be if she knew he might harm her. Iris wasn't ready to tell her yet. Her mother would tell her father. And he would surely murder Norman.

Between the second and third courses, Iris seized on a lull in the conversation. "I was just speaking to Norman a few nights ago about the need for medical attention for people in the South End." She felt Norman's tension and purposely kept her gaze on his father. "We left it open-ended, and I wondered what you thought, Mr. Caddell? I'm sure it would look good for your position on the board to assist funding a clinic to help the poor."

Mr. Caddell's face showed interest, but before he could speak, Norman cut in. "As I told you before, Iris. It's not seemly for a soon to be Caddell to toil as a common worker." His voice was tight with anger. "I don't have an issue with providing financial assistance, but I will not have my future wife working there."

To Iris's surprise, his mother came to her defense. "Now, Norman, darling. I don't see a thing wrong with Iris helping out at the clinic. At least not before you marry. After, she'll be busy giving me grandchildren and, of course, we couldn't have her working." Henrietta turned a beaming, but phony, smile on Iris. Iris was sure she'd rather have The Wicked Witch of the West bear her grandchildren, but to her credit, she seemed to accept that it would be Iris. "She already volunteers at the kitchen. I understand she attended some medical courses. Tending to people at a clinic would be a good experience for her, a way for her to stay occupied."

Iris seethed at the implication that she was a child who needed a toy so she wouldn't bother the grownups. But she forced a smile. She was getting the clinic, and that was all that mattered.

Norman looked at Iris over the rim of his scotch glass. "Would it really mean that much to you, darling?"

"Yes, oh, yes it would." Iris thought of Alma. And her own bouts with pneumonia as a child. Medical care would mean a world of difference for those poor souls.

Norman's father had been silent during the

discussion. Now, he swallowed his food and pointed a fork at Iris. "I think it's a splendid idea. Would ten thousand be enough to get it off the ground?" Stunned, Iris nodded. It was much more than she'd anticipated. "Good." He continued. "It's settled then. Perhaps we could call it something along the lines of the Caddell Humanitarian Clinic."

Of course, they'd want their name on it. No good deed goes unclaimed. While Iris was more than pleased she was getting her way, she was also ashamed, of herself and of the Caddells. They could casually toss out ten grand without a second thought, when scores of Bostonians had no idea where their next meal would come from and no place to lay their heads or seek shelter from the cold and the elements. Iris was just as guilty. While her family's money was a pittance in comparison to the Caddells', her weekly allowance was more than many of the poor would see in a lifetime.

"That would be wonderful." She tried to keep tears from her voice. She didn't want them to think she was emotionally unstable. God knew, they had enough to hold against her. But, the thought of being handed a clinic where she could give aid to the sick and injured was the best gift she'd ever received, next to God bringing Dante home safely from the war.

****

Iris spooned out green beans on the plates, moving on auto pilot. She couldn't get the thoughts of poor Mary Gaither out of her head. What kind of person was she that, when Dante brought her up, Iris barely recalled her name? But then again, she served hundreds of unfortunates each week. She couldn't be expected to know them all. No, her greater crime was her reaction to Dante. Each time he was near, her entire body heated. And she was an engaged woman. What was wrong with her? She had outgrown her childish crush…really she had. *But mercy me, Dante was a devastatingly attractive man.*

"Iris, for goodness sake, are you going to serve the stuff or preserve it for posterity?" Audra's impatient voice broke into Iris's thoughts. A homeless man waited, plate aloft, while she held a ladle filled with green beans, frozen in mid-motion like a ninny.

"I'm sorry." She dished the food onto his plate and filled the spoon with another serving for the next in line. "I was just thinking about the girl who died. The latest victim of the South End Slayer."

"Really?" Audra quirked an eyebrow. "Because judging from the smile on your face, murder was the last thing on your mind."

Iris's cheeks warmed. Had she really been smiling? She grimaced and gave a quick shake of her head. "I don't know. There has been a lot going on lately. Most of it not good. I certainly was not thinking happy thoughts."

Audra made a disbelieving grunting sound and went back to handing out slices of bread, offering her beautiful smile to go along with it.

Finally, after what seemed like days, but had actually only been four hours, their shift mercifully came to an end. Iris was bone weary, more so than usual. She and Audra removed their aprons and Audra linked her arm in Iris's, letting out a long, satisfied sigh. "Wasn't that so rewarding? I only wish Jamie had shown up." Jamie was a little boy Audra had befriended. Iris just hoped her friend wasn't getting too attached. It would only lead to heartbreak. "He and that dog of his always brighten my day." Audra glanced out the large front window. "Or night." There was no fear in her voice. Just an acceptance. But then, she wasn't the one who'd been speaking with a woman only hours—maybe minutes—before her brutal murder.

They stepped outside and brisk wind, chilly for May, slapped Iris in the face. She tightened the belt on her wrap coat. "I'm so glad this night is over."

"Well, why are you volunteering if you hate it?"

"I don't *hate* it. After all, I'm opening a clinic here. Would I do that if I hated it? I just don't like being here at night. But I can't let you come down here by yourself. Besides, I've had to do *some* kind of volunteer work." Now that the clinic was opening, she was glad she'd chosen to join Audra working at the soup kitchen, but it didn't mean she had to like being here so late. "The South Side Slayer murdered a woman who visited the soup kitchen almost every night. I spoke with her shortly before she was killed. And all the articles in the *Chronicle…*" A fist gripped Iris's throat as the darkness pressed around her. The streets were all but deserted, and it was terribly quiet. Iris shuddered. "Mercy me, Audra. This is *not* the place for proper young ladies after dark."

"You sound like my father." Iris couldn't *see* the eyeroll, but she could sense it.

"Well, your father is right." Iris hurried to keep up with Audra's rapid pace. She did not want to be left alone. "Aren't you the least bit afraid? Even after what I told you about the murdered girl?" Iris almost told her about poor Mary's pendant…and that the killer might have left it for Iris, but she didn't know for certain that was what had happened. And saying it might make it more real.

Audra huffed impatiently. “I’m careful.”

They’d just reached Washington Street where they could hail a taxi when Iris realized her hands were empty. “Damn!” Mercy me, what was wrong with her? Swearing like a sailor. “Um, sorry. Pretend I didn’t say that.”

Audra grinned and stopped. “What is it?”

“I left my bag. We’ll have to run back.”

“You go. I’ll grab us a taxi. I have that dinner with *Lady* Margaret tonight.”

Iris didn’t miss the grimness in her voice. Audra’s mother was wonderful, and Audra didn’t appreciate her at all. She was holding on to some notion that her mother had been unfaithful, had abandoned the family. It simply wasn’t true. “Don’t you think its past time being so angry with Aunt Meggie? She didn’t leave your father and you all those years ago. Well, she left for a few days, but she did come right back.”

Audra ignored her comment. “I’ll wait here. My feet are killing me.”

Great choice of words... “I wish you’d refrain from using certain phrases at this particular moment.” Iris glanced around the deserted streets.

Audra took her hand and pulled her away from the dark alley behind them, then gripped her shoulders and turned her toward the soup kitchen.

“Go. I’ll be right here, cab in hand by the time you return.”

Iris didn’t want to leave Audra by herself. Nor did she want to go back to the soup kitchen alone. She started to argue, but Audra lifted a palm to stop her protest. “Hurry. It’s getting late. I told Daddy I would make time to change my clothes.”

“Fine.” She whirled and hurried toward the soup kitchen. The quicker she got there, the quicker she’d get back to Audra. Luther was there, thank goodness. She grabbed her handbag and said goodnight to Luther for the second time.

She was almost to the spot where she’d left Audra when she heard a scream.

****

Dante’s partner, Mick Shannon, stood behind Dante, looking over his shoulder at the crime scene photos and notes on the desk. “What about that Bittner fellow? You think he’s the one?”

Dante squeezed his eyes shut for a moment, pinching the bridge of his nose between his thumb and forefinger. “I don’t know. He has a pretty solid alibi for two of the killings.”

Shannon shook his head. “This is a doozy.” He plopped down on a chair next to Dante’s desk. “I don’t know if we’ll ever catch this guy.”

“We’ll catch him,” Dante snapped, his anger more at the truth of the statement than that Mick had said it. “He’s going to make a mistake. We just have to stay vigilant.” Like he had in the trenches, always on the lookout. The war had been horrific, but at least there, you knew who the enemy was.

“Hey, Morello.” Dante looked up at the sound of his name. Willis, the desk officer, stood in his doorway. “Two dames are here to see you.”

Dante’s pulse accelerated. Iris? “Bring ‘em back.” He waited, as anxious as a boy at a school dance. His entire body deflated when Willis returned, accompanied by two women. Neither of them Iris.

"This is Detective Morello." Willis pointed to Dante, then to the women, "This is Jane Lewis and her sister, Minnie." Jane Lewis was matronly, stout with a big bosom and a plain face. Her sister was smaller, with similar features but they were somehow more attractive on her, softer. She wore a tight blouse, short skirt and tattered stockings. Her hair was in wild disarray, and tears streamed down her face. She had a hell of a shiner on her right eye, and a busted lip. Someone had knocked her around pretty good. Dante clenched his fists, disgust and anger burning through him. Jane's arms were wrapped around her sister, who leaned into her as if afraid to break contact.

Dante and Mick stood. "Please, have a seat." Dante gestured to the two chairs by his desk, sitting after the women had. Mick leaned a hip on the desk. Dante held out his cigarette case and each woman took one. He lit them for them and sat back. "So, tell me what happened." Whatever it had been, some asshole had put his hands on this woman and Dante's blood boiled. He forced himself to remain calm as he waited for the story.

Jane said, "This…fiend beat up my sister." She turned to Minnie. "Tell him."

Minnie's hand trembled as she brought the cigarette to her lips, but she didn't speak.

"Minnie, *tell* him," Jane demanded.

Her sister squeezed her eyes shut and shook her head. "He'll kill me for sure."

Jane's mouth turned down, and anger sparked in her eyes. "He almost *did* kill you. You'll never be safe from him unless he's locked up. Tell him, *now*."

Minnie took a deep drag from the cigarette and blew the smoke out her nose. "My…my pimp, Donnie…they call him Diamond Donnie…he takes real good care of me, but sometimes when I get out of line, he can get real mean. He calls it 'teachin a lesson' and boy"—she choked out a humorless laugh—"he's sure a good teacher."

"And you got out of line." Dante barely controlled his rage.

Tears flowed down her cheeks as she nodded and stared down at the desk, without seeming to really look at it, like her mind was somewhere else.

Jane sat forward and vigorously stubbed her cigarette out in the ashtray. "He *is* mean. He's a horrible violent thug. I think he might be the one killing those people…the South End Slayer."

Dante's senses prickled. "What makes you say that?"

Jane gestured to her sister. "Look at her. Only a maniac would do somethin' like that."

Dante couldn't argue. The woman looked like she'd gone a few rounds with Joe Louis. "Don't you think you should go to the hospital?"

Minnie shook her head vehemently. "I can't afford no hospital, and Donnie would find me there." She let out a wail. "He's gonna kill me for sure."

Dante tightened his hands into fists, wishing he could show the bastard what it felt like to have the shit beat out of him. "Where can I find him?"

Her good eye widened. "You're not gonna tell him I was here, that I squealed?" Her entire body began to tremble. "I'm tellin' ya, he'll kill me. You can't tell him."

Her fear was palpable. Dante rested a hand on hers. “No, I’m not going to tell him you came in. I just want to talk to him. I don’t know if I can arrest him for this right now anyway. I’ll have to gather some proof. Were there any witnesses?”

She gave a humorless laugh. “No, and even if there had been, they wouldn’t say nothin’.”

“Tell me where I can find him. And what’s his last name?”

“Hillian. Donald Hillian. He’s got a place down in the Back Bay. But he’s always out and about, slinkin’ around the streets, makin’ sure his girls are doin’ what they’s suppose ta be doin.”

Dante asked for a description and any other information she had. He’d check this fellow out thoroughly. He was definitely bad news, but was he the South End Slayer?

****

Iris ran around the corner, and Audra was barreling toward her. Iris took her into her arms and hugged her tightly. “Audra? For goodness sakes, what happened? Are you okay?”

“I-I’m f-fine.” She pulled back and ran a shaking hand over her hair. “A man… He…attacked me.”

“Oh no, oh mercy me. Did he hurt you?” Fear wormed over her skin. “Is he still around?”

Audra’s breath came in short gasps. She stared at Iris, her expression dazed.

Iris gripped her shoulders and gave her a shake. “Audra, answer me.”

“No, he’s not. He ran off. I’m fine.”

Her breathing had calmed, and her gaze was now focused. “Let’s just get out of here.”

Iris spotted a cab a few blocks away and whistled to flag it down. The vehicle rolled to a stop in front of them. Iris helped Audra into the back, then slid in beside her. She shook her head in disbelief. Audra could have been killed. “When Uncle Harry hears of this, he won’t let you come back at night. I, for one, don’t think that’s such a bad thing. It’s too dangerous. We must be out of our minds. What we need to do is call the police.” She thought of Dante. He’d know what to do. He’d find that fiend and lock him up tight. “No sane person—an unprotected woman—has any business being in this area at night, alone. It’s ludicrous. Uncle Harry will definitely put an end to—"

“Stop. Iris, just stop. We won’t tell Daddy, and we won’t call the police. I can’t stop working at the soup kitchen. I’m needed there, especially at night. Don’t you see? At the soup kitchen, I’m a regular person. I’m not Lady Margaret’s daughter.”

Iris huffed out an irritated breath. “You cannot be serious. What if that was the South End Slayer?”

“If it were, neither of us would be here to talk about it, right? Promise me you won’t tell Daddy what happened. Swear it, Iris.”

“But…but what if he’d…he’d kidnapped you?”

Audra’s chin tilted in that stubborn angle that meant she wouldn’t be swayed. “He didn’t though, did he?”

Iris shook her head in exasperation. “Audra, it’s much too dangerous. Doesn’t that mean anything to you? Coming to South End in the evening makes me nervous.”

“Then don’t come.”

“I…” Iris nearly growled. She took a long breath

and let it out slowly. There was no arguing with Audra when her mind was made up. “Fine, I won’t say a word. But if it happens again, I’m going straight to Uncle Harry. I’m promising you that too, Audra Faye Dempsey.”

Audra leaned over and wrapped her arms around Iris. “Thank you. Thank you. It will be fine. I’ll admit, I let my thoughts distract me, but it won’t happen again.”

“And we take a cab, to and from, every time we come down here. And we don’t separate, no matter what.”

“You have my solemn oath.”

“Okay, then. It’s a deal.” Iris sat back in the seat.

“Iris, can I take a quick shower at your place? Daddy will take one look at me and lock me in my room for a month. Or a year.”

Iris gave Audra’s hand a squeeze. “Of course.” Iris smiled, but inside, she was shaking. Misery me. Loyalty to Audra would surely get her murdered before it was all over.

Chapter Five

Iris brushed her hands over her skirt and shifted nervously in her chair in the doctor's lounge. The scent of chemicals, antiseptic, food and a faint underlying odor of unwashed bodies wafted to her and she inhaled deeply. While some might be put off by such smells, she was invigorated by them. There was nothing she wanted more than to work in a place like this, in the thick of it all.

She was meeting with a doctor who would be coming to the clinic once a week. Her mind kept straying to the incident with Audra. When she thought of what could have happened… She shivered and clasped her cold hands together. She must tell Dante. She'd promised Audra she wouldn't tell Uncle Harry, but she'd made no such vow regarding Dante.

The door opened and a short gentleman with a receding hairline and thick glasses stepped in. "You must be Iris Taggart?" At her nod, he went on, "I'm Doctor Gorman. Since we'll be working together, you can call me Frederick." He sat in the seat adjacent to hers at the break table, looking almost swallowed in his too-large doctor's coat. "I was impressed to learn of your idea for a free clinic. I've always considered helping the less fortunate, but I never made the move to do it. You're a brave, caring young lady."

She flushed. "Thank you. I'll admit, I never

considered the medical needs of the poor until recently, when I—" She started to tell him about Alma but bit off the words. She didn't want to sound like a braggart, so she switched courses. "When I noticed how many sick people weren't getting the treatment they needed."

"What is your precise plan?"

"I can only work there three days a week." Norman was adamant that she not spend any more time there than that. "I'll have the South Enders make appointments during the time I'm there. If I treat someone with an ailment beyond my skills, I'll make them an appointment to see you, whatever day you choose to practice at the clinic. I've gotten approval from the board to dispense medications for minor illnesses."

He smiled broadly. "Brilliant. I think you've got a fine idea there, young lady. I understand you're engaged to Norman Caddell? He must be proud of you."

She grimaced inwardly. If only that were true. "He's…pleased that everything is falling into place." That was only a slight lie.

He scowled as if thinking of something unpleasant but seemed to brush it off and spoke cheerily. "I can come down there on Wednesdays and Fridays from noon to 6 p.m. Will that work?"

"That will be marvelous." She expected he'd volunteer no more than a few hours a week. "I appreciate your generosity."

"Not at all. I'm happy to help." He stood and she took her cue and stood as well. "This city needs more enterprising young people like you." He frowned and pursed his lips. "I hope your gentleman knows how fortunate he is." He gripped her hands tightly and stared into her eyes for a few moments before saying quietly, "And I sincerely hope he treats you well."

His tone held an underlying note of doubt. Was there something about Norman he knew that she didn't? Perhaps Norman's flashes of temper had not only been reserved for her.

****

The officer behind the counter at the Boston Police Department looked up when Iris approached. "Can I help you, miss?"

She swallowed nervously. "May I speak with Detective Morello?"

His gaze roamed over her, head to toe, and curiosity sparked in his eyes. "Yeah, sure. Come on back."

He guided her into a room with several desks, some empty, some occupied by policemen. A few looked up as they passed, but the others were intent on their respective tasks. They stopped at an open office door. "Detective Morello, you got someone here to see you."

Dante sat at the desk, but he stood when he saw them. "Thank you, Willis," he said to the officer. The man left and Dante gestured her inside and closed the door. "Iris? Is everything okay?" His tie was loose beneath his black suit jacket. His hair was mussed as if he'd been running his hands through it. Dark shadows underneath his eyes indicated he hadn't been sleeping well, but they didn't deter from his good looks.

She pressed a hand over her heart to still its flutter. "Something happened I felt you should know about." Iris hadn't mentioned to Audra that she was telling

Dante about the incident. She would have surely talked her out of it.

His eyebrows drew together, and his mouth tightened. "Did someone hurt you?"

The same old protective Dante. He might have formed a barrier between them, but his desire to protect hadn't changed. "No, I'm fine, but Audra was attacked."

A dark cloud settled over his features, and Iris wasn't sure if she'd actually heard it, or just imagined he'd emitted a ferocious growl. "Who did it? Is she all right? Where is she?"

Somehow, he'd stepped closer without her realizing it, and he fired the questions at her as he'd no doubt fired rounds at the enemy in the war. "I—she's fine. It was…" Iris drew in a breath. She couldn't think with him that close, so ferocious and intense.

He took her elbow, his touch surprisingly gentle. "Let's have a seat."

Iris sat in a chair facing the desk, while he took the one behind it. "Tell me what happened." His tone was gentle, but she sensed anger simmering beneath.

She relayed the events of the previous night. "Do you think it was the slayer?" she asked breathlessly once she'd finished.

He sat frowning for several seconds. "I don't know. Audra is not his type of victim. And I'm not sure your arrival would have deterred him." His dark eyes sparked with anger. "Had it been the slayer, you'd both likely have been killed."

A cold wind rushed through her, and she gasped. Without knowing he'd moved, she found Dante standing between her and the desk. He took her hands in his big, strong warm ones and gently caressed the skin on the backs of her hands with his thumbs. "Iris? Are you okay?"

Warmth from the touch of his hands ignited electricity that traveled throughout her entire body. She lifted her gaze to his and was lost in his deep brown eyes. She couldn't respond, could barely breathe. Tension filled the room, pressing around her like a physical force. Something sparked in his expression, an intent…a desire. His gaze dropped to her mouth, and her insides trembled. Was he going to kiss her? She was aghast at the thought…because she knew she wouldn't stop him.

Summoning all her will power, she stood abruptly, but only managed to get closer to Dante, their faces mere centimeters apart. Time fell away, and she was once more that silly girl in love, and he was the handsome boy who hadn't yet been fractured by war. But this time, instead of him treating her like a child, he was looking at her like a man looks at a woman. "Dante, I…"

He frowned and seemed to shake himself as if coming out of a trance. Moving away, he put distance between them, and Iris could finally breathe. "You and Audra need to stop going to the soup kitchen, at least after dark." His voice was hoarse, agitated. "And you most certainly should not be hailing cabs that late while you're alone."

Iris cringed. "I know. You're right. Please don't tell Uncle Harry about this."

"Why not?"

"He doesn't like Audra going to the soup kitchen anyway. If he finds out about this, he'll stop her going for certain."

"Don't you think he has a right to know, for Audra's benefit?"

"Yes, but I promised Audra I wouldn't tell him. She will be miffed that I'm telling you."

His mouth twisted derisively. "So, you think a promise to a friend is more important than her safety?"

Iris squirmed in discomfort. "I can't break my promise and have Audra angry with me."

He was quiet for a moment, but his accusing glare spoke volumes. "Well, she can't be angry with you if she's dead."

His words slapped her like a physical blow. She wanted to be mad at him, but she couldn't deny the truth. If anything happened to Audra, it would be her fault.

She nodded. "Yes, you're right."

"I won't tell him, for now. Let me know if anything else happens. And be careful."

"We will. Thank you."

He narrowed his eyes. "For what?"

She didn't know for what. She just knew that, despite the odd way her insides quivered when he was near, while with him, it seemed nothing in the world could harm her. Boston began to feel like a safer place, the moment she'd known he was here.

****

Iris tugged Sophie's hand and led her toward the back of the soup kitchen.

Sophie looked around, her flame-red curls bouncing. "What on earth are we doing here?"

"I'll show you. Just a moment."

Iris stopped in front of the door that would soon be

the Caddell Humanitarian Clinic. “Right here.” She swung the door open.

Boxes of medical supplies sat on the counter and in the center of the room was an exam table which had recently been delivered. Iris proudly swept an arm around the room. “What do you think?”

Sophie’s pixie face lit up with a smile. “Oh my, it’s wonderful. This is really happening.” She pulled Iris into a tight hug. “I’m so happy for you.”

“Me too. And, of course, for the people I’ll be able to help. I was hoping you’d do me a favor. Would you paint a few pictures for the walls? Your artwork would really brighten the place up. It looks a little…sterile…right now.”

Sophie cocked her head. “Isn’t *sterile* what you want in a medical clinic?”

Iris giggled. “You know what I mean. The décor is quite bland. I’d love to have a few paintings to hang. Maybe one for the children, of clowns or puppies or something fun. And then another for the adults to enjoy. Would you please consider it?”

“I would love to paint something for the walls. I’m honored.” Sophie took Iris’s hands and looked at her solemnly. “Do you know, this is the first time I’ve seen you truly happy in I can’t tell you how long? Maybe since the night you threw yourself at Dante, before he shot you down.”

Iris scowled and tugged her hands from Sophie’s. “You started out okay, but the end was just plain mean.”

Sophie gave her signature devilish laugh. “Oh, don’t be such a baby. I was kidding. But, not about you being happy. You’re positively glowing. I’d like to paint *you* right now."

Iris smiled. "I am happy, Sophie. I feel fulfilled, like my life has a purpose. Like I finally know why I'm here on earth." She heard how her words sounded and brought a hand to her mouth, panicked. "Oh, my. That sounded just awful. I am engaged to be married to the most handsome, most wonderful man in the world. Of course, that is fulfilling too." Iris was determined to push aside the outburst from Norman. He'd been nothing but kind since. He must have been having a bad day. He truly *was* a good man. No one was perfect, after all.

Sophie snorted. "Norman is an all right fellow, but most wonderful? Most handsome? I think not. Have you taken a gander at Dante?"

The heat of a blush filled Iris's face. "Well, yes, Dante is handsome. And he's a good man. But, he's a friend. Not anyone I'd ever feel romantic about."

"Again."

"Pardon?"

"You'd never feel romantic about him again, you mean? Because you most definitely did at one time. Not that I believe you anyway. You get that same glow when you talk about him."

Iris turned away to one of the boxes and opened the flap, taking out the cotton pads, antiseptic, bandages and other items, avoiding Sophie's gaze as she worked. "I was just a child. I didn't know anything about love." It wasn't lost on her that she used the exact words Dante had thrown at her. They'd hurt terribly, but he had been right. She hadn't known anything about love. But then again, what about her reaction to his touch? She'd nearly swooned. But it hadn't been love. It had been some kind of animal urge. Something she hadn't known she was capable of feeling, and most certainly did not want to feel again. It was positively savage.

"Liar."

Iris's eyes flew to Sophie's face. Had she spoken out loud? "Liar? What…?"

"I don't for one moment believe you no longer have romantic feelings for Dante. Yes, you're engaged. But you're not married yet. A girl can always change her mind."

"Oh, mercy me. Don't be daft. Speaking of changing minds, I might change mine about letting you paint for the clinic if you don't watch that smart mouth of yours."

Sophie gave her a mischievous look. "Oh, no you won't. You know I'm a phenomenal artist. But mostly you know that I'll work for free."

Iris laughed, but it died in her throat when she stepped into the outer room and found Dante. He wore cuffed denim trousers and a charcoal gray work shirt rolled up at the sleeves. Her pulse fluttered. She was accustomed to seeing him in a suit, which somehow added some distance. But this rugged, casual look made him seem more approachable, and she had to admit…sexy.

"Dante!" Sophie threw her arms around him. "What are you doing here?"

Dante hugged Sophie, then released her and looked at Iris. "I came down to help get the clinic set up."

Iris frowned in confusion. "How did you know…?"

"Frederick Gorman is a golfing buddy of mine. He mentioned what you were doing here. I thought you could use an extra pair of hands."

Iris warmed at the expression in his eyes. For the first time, he was looking at her with respect. "I appreciate it, but I'm sure you're busy."

"Not too busy to help. I admire what you're doing. I'd love to be a part of it."

She tried to contain her excitement. Not only would she be able to open the clinic more quickly, she'd be spending time with Dante…her friend.

She grinned. "Well, how can I deny you that?"

He returned her grin. "Just tell me what to do, boss."

Sophie said, "I'd love to stay and help, but I have class. You two have fun. I'll get started on those paintings post-haste."

After Sophie left, Iris showed Dante the items to unbox. They worked in silence, but she stole surreptitious glances of him whenever she could…his handsome face in concentration as he painted the walls, his muscles bulging as he unpacked heavy machinery…. At one point, he caught her staring and lifted his brows with a grin.

She quickly looked away, concentrating on scrubbing the dust and grime from the floor, but her heart raced like she had a fever. She scrubbed so vigorously, she splashed bleach water in her eye, and the burn was intense and instant. "Ow!" She leapt to her feet, squeezing the affected eye shut.

"What is it?" Dante descended the ladder and rushed over to her.

"I-I splashed bleach in my eye."

He frowned. "Hold still." He hurried to the sink and dampened a cloth, then returned to her, gently dabbing at her eye. His warm fingers lightly gripped her chin as he worked, and she was scarcely able to breathe. The pain in her eye eased underneath his ministrations.

"Can you open your eye?" His voice was low…close…his warm breath wafting over her skin.

She nodded and opened her eye. His face was centimeters from hers. Neither moved as their eyes remained locked. His gaze moved over her face, and he ran the back of his hand over her cheek, sending shivers through her. "I'm okay," she whispered.

He gave a low growl. "I'm not." His voice was husky, and the meaning was unmistakable.

What was happening between them? She'd loved him since she was a child, and if she were truthful, she was far from over her crush. But, he'd never treated her with anything but brotherly affection. And, while she didn't have a brother, she was pretty sure they didn't look at their sisters like he was looking at her.

Her gaze dropped to his lips. Would they be firm, soft? Would they press against hers with raging passion, or tenderness? "Dante…" Mercy me. She wanted him to kiss her. Wanted it like she wanted her next breath. What kind of woman did that make her? She was *engaged…*

Dante's face tensed, and he shook his head briefly, as if to clear it. He released her and stepped back. "I'm finished with the painting." His words were a low, rough bark. "I need to head out. I can come back to help tomorrow."

Iris ran a shaking hand over her hair, swallowing and finding her voice. "No, thank you. There's not much left to do here, and you're busy with the slayer case. I won't take up any more of your time. But I'm so grateful for all you've done."

He nodded jerkily. "Happy to help."

After Dante left, she used the sink in the exam room to splash cool water on her face. She groaned in embarrassment. If he weren't so honorable, would she have let him kiss her?

She tried to think of Norman and couldn't, all she could focus on was her disappointment that Dante had held his moral ground. She dried her face and was heading back to the exam room when something red looped through the handle of one of the cabinets caught her eye. She stepped closer, and her stomach dropped. Her hand reached out as if it had a mind of its own. She told herself not to touch it, but she couldn't stop. She knew exactly what it was. Where she'd seen it.

A darker red, darker than the shade of the scarf dotted the material she gripped in her fingertips. "Alma…" she murmured. Chills washed through her. Why was the killer doing this? Why her? She immediately pushed the selfish thought aside. People were losing their lives. The fact the killer was somehow focusing on her was trivial compared to that. But, she didn't understand why? Would she eventually become a target? If so, why was he playing this sick game? Why not just kill her and get it over with?

****

Dante scraped his hands through his hair and let out an exasperated breath. What was he missing? Was this guy really that clever, that hard to nab? In the war, it was easy to know your enemies. They dressed a certain way, they spoke a certain way…they shot at you. In civilian life, it wasn't that simple. The guy next door, the baker, the postal worker, the priest, could be the enemy, could be a stone-cold killer.

Shannon hovered over him slurping coffee. Dante scowled at him. "Isn't there something useful you could be doing?"

"Sorry, boss. I wish I knew what to do." He took another slug from his cup. "I'm at a loss. You come up with anything new?"

Dante shook his head. "Nothing. I don't know why or who. All we have is the how. He's attacking the victims with a knife, at another location, then dragging their bodies to the railroad tracks for us to find. Is he trying to send some kind of message by leaving them there? Is it just a handy dumping ground?" He let out a growl. "What the hell is this bastard doing?"

At the sound of someone clearing their throat, Dante looked up. The desk officer stood in front of him, Iris a few steps behind. Dante's face burned. "Willis, couldn't you have let me know we had a visitor before bringing her back here?"

"Sorry, Detective Morello. She seemed in an awful big hurry. I didn't think—"

"Forget it," Dante snapped. Willis's expression looked as stricken as Iris's. Well, too bad. He wouldn't apologize to either of them.

Dante stood and rolled down his shirt sleeves, then slipped on his jacket, not bothering to straighten his tie. "Iris, what can I do for you?"

She held something tightly in her fists and shoved it toward him. "I-I found this."

He peered at the object—a woman's scarf, which looked as though it had been dragged through a tar pit—then lifted his brows. "And?"

She drew in a deep breath, her breasts rising with the action. He forced his gaze back to her face. "I found it at the clinic."

He shoved his hands in his pockets, waiting. He'd offer her a seat, but then she might stay all day, rambling on and on about whatever popped into her pretty head. On one hand, that sounded like the perfect way to spend his day. On the other, he had a killer to catch.

"The bastard left it there for me." She didn't even flinch at her use of the curse word. She thrust the scarf out again, and this time he took it. "Have you heard any news? Any new victims? It belongs to Alma Vernon. She's dead, isn't she?" The sentences fell on top of one another. Her eyes filled with tears and she shook her head. "Mercy me. I don't understand what's happening."

Dante tightened his fist around the scarf, battling the rage rising inside him. "How well did you know Ms. Vernon?"

"I saw her frequently at the kitchen. Then, a few days ago, she had a seizure, and I treated her."

"Morello!"

Shannon's shout drew Dante's attention away from Iris, and for a moment, he was peeved at the interruption. Although she was bearing potentially disturbing news, seeing her lovely face was a balm to his soul.

"What is it?" Dante asked.

"We got a report of another victim."

"Dammit to hell." Dante shot a look at Iris but didn't apologize for his language. He was damned well frustrated and feeling more incompetent each day. He said to Iris, "I'm sorry. I have to go. We'll talk later."

She nodded. Her lovely blue eyes swam with

unshed tears, and her lips trembled. He wanted to stay, to hold her and comfort her. It was obvious that the killer was either fixated on Iris or working his way through victims until he got to her. Either option opened a cold pit of fear in his chest.

Chapter Six

The squad car jostled over the uneven terrain of the railyard. The homeless man sitting in the back reeked of body odor and an overpowering, sour stench Dante couldn't identify—didn't want to identify. In the passenger seat, Mick Shannon had his face shoved through the open window.

Bernard sat forward. "There. She's right over there."

Dante glanced in the rear-view mirror to see Bernard pointing his grimy finger toward the tracks. Dante stopped the car. He didn't want to get any closer, in case he fouled up evidence around the crime scene. He and Shannon climbed out and Dante gulped in deep breaths of the fresh air.

Dante opened the door for Bernard and leaned his elbow along the top. "We appreciate you coming down to the precinct." Bernard had walked a mile to the station after discovering the body, which couldn't have been easy. The man had to be in his eighties. Or maybe he just looked like it due to his years on the streets. "Here in a little while, someone will take you to get some supper."

Bernard exited the car and ran a shaky hand over his stubbled face. "Reckon I could get a belt too?" His eyes held hopeless desperation. Dante had seen that expression on his fellow soldiers' faces, and he was sure his own reflected the same. Alcohol wouldn't make it go away, but it would dull it. And sometimes, that was enough. "Yeah, sure you can." Dante shut the door. "Stay here while we take a look around. We'll be with you shortly."

Dante headed toward the tracks, Shannon following close behind. It didn't take long to find the woman. She was lying on her back, eyes staring blankly at the night sky. Her dress was bunched around her pale thighs. He was tempted to tug her skirt down, to give her some decency, but he didn't want to touch anything until the pathologist arrived.

The night was quiet, except for the distant train whistle, echoing the aloneness of the dead woman abandoned by the tracks. Although the killer was long gone, Dante sensed his presence—slithery and dark like crude oil bubbling from the ground.

He squatted next to the body and let out a long sigh. In battle, he'd seen more corpses than he could count—friend and foe. But somehow this was different. Death was expected during a war. But an innocent woman slaughtered for some monster's perverse satisfaction was an abomination.

He peered into the victim's face. In the dim light, it was difficult to see much, but she appeared to be in her late forties. Once they had a positive ID, he'd be tasked with notifying whatever family she might have. Damnit to Hell. He didn't look forward to destroying their world.

If what Iris said was true, the woman was Alma Vernon. A sick feeling weighted him down at the thought of Iris's proximity to the victims…and therefore the killer. If anything happened to her…

He brought his attention back to the victim. He couldn't let thoughts of Iris distract him from his job. Like the others, the woman's throat had been slashed. Blood had dried on her neck and on the ground beside her. Not much, though. "She was murdered in a different location and brought here." He spoke to Shannon over his shoulder.

"You can tell that?" His partner's voice held a note of awe. The guy had the misguided notion that, because Dante had been in the war, because he'd been awarded a few medals, he was some kind of hero. He had no idea how far from the truth that was.

"Not enough blood here. With a gash like that, there'd be a river of it." Dante frowned and rubbed his forefinger on the scar along his jaw line. Why did he leave them by the railroad tracks? Was he trying to make a statement of some kind or was it just a convenient dumping ground?

Rain scented the air. They'd have to work the scene quickly, before the coming storm washed away critical evidence.

Dante stood. "Let's take a look around."

He and Shannon walked around the area, shining their flashlights searching for a clue…something the killer left behind. He hadn't left anything at the other crime scenes, but they could get lucky. This made the sixth victim in that many months. If they didn't get lucky soon, there'd be more.

A car pulled up and Dante waited as the pathologist exited and came toward him. In the distance, the mournful wail of a train whistle sounded.

The killer had been careful not to leave any clues. But Dante would just as carefully hunt the bastard down. And put an end to him.

****

"You're slaughtering me!" Iris cried in mock exasperation. She and Shelby were playing their favorite card game, Mau-Mau. When they'd first begun playing months ago, Iris had let her win. Now the little imp was so good, she frequently beat Iris fairly.

"Miss Taggart." Martin, the butler stepped into the room. "I apologize for interrupting."

Iris let out an exaggerated sigh. "That's quite all right. Little miss Shelby here is on the verge of winning. You saved me."

Shelby giggled and held up the single card in her hand. "I have one card left, and Iris has six."

Martin didn't appear to be impressed. He inclined his head. "A police detective is asking for you, miss."

Iris's heart fluttered. It had to be Dante. Whether it was good news or bad, she didn't know. But she did know she was about to see him again. She put a hand on her heart to still it. "I'll be back shortly," she told Shelby.

Dante stood in the foyer, worrying his hat through his fingers.

"Detective Morello." She kept it formal, for appearances. Martin was always lurking. "Please, come into the library."

He followed her inside and they took seats across from one another. She left the door open for propriety's sake. "Would you like tea? Coffee?"

"No, thank you."

She didn't ring for refreshments since he didn't want any, but her mouth was so dry she could have drunk an entire pot of either. She linked her fingers together and rested them on her lap. "What can I do for you?"

His expression was grim, and he seemed hesitant to speak. After a few moments, he said, "We found Miss Vernon's body."

Dread tightened her stomach, and tears clogged her throat. She knew it was coming, but it didn't make it easier. "Oh my, how awful."

Dante dropped his head and let out a breath. "For God's sake, Iris. What's going on?"

She wiped at her eyes. "I have no idea. But it's terrifying."

"When was the last time you spoke to Ms. Vernon?"

"That day she had the episode. It was Tuesday."

"Have you seen her at the soup kitchen since?"

Iris thought back. "Not that I recall."

"What can you tell me about Clarence Bittner? I understand he's somewhat of a lech."

She frowned. "He is. He makes me uncomfortable, the way he stares and some of the things he says. You don't think he's the killer, do you?"

Dante shrugged. "Just checking out all potential suspects. I don't like what I'm hearing about this guy." He asked her a few more questions, but she couldn't provide anything useful. "I'm concerned about the connections between you and the victims. I'm going to request officers be stationed outside. And I'll come by and keep watch when I can."

Iris was touched by his concern. "I don't think Opal will approve of a policeman staking out the house."

"I don't care what she approves of. Your safety is

my priority."

"I appreciate that, but I don't believe she will allow it."

"And I'm not asking permission. Unless you'd like to come stay with me so I can keep an eye on you."

Heat flushed through her body. Living with Dante? In close proximity with his overwhelming, masculine presence? She could imagine Norman's reaction. "That wouldn't be seemly."

"Neither is getting murdered."

She shuddered. The word never had as much meaning to her as it did now. "Go ahead and have the officers guard the house. I'll deal with Opal."

He stood, and she did as well. "I'll have someone out soon. And I'm always a phone call away."

"Thank you, Dante." She reached out to shake his hand, and he closed both of his warm ones over hers. A frisson of electricity traveled through her at his touch.

He stared at her intently, his obsidian eyes seeming to drink her in. "I'll do anything to keep you safe."

For one crazy second, she was tempted to step into his arms, feel them close tightly around her, press her body to his…

She shook off the urge and reluctantly pulled her hand from his grasp, immediately missing his touch. Giving him a small smile, she whispered, "I know you will, Dante .You always have."

****

Dante had been searching for Donald Hillian for days and had finally found him. The pimp was in a café on Washington Street at a table by himself. He looked up when Dante approached. His expression immediate showed irritation. "What can I do for you, Detective?"

His voice was scratchy, like he had laryngitis.

"You know who I am?" Dante slid into the booth across from him without waiting for an invitation.

"I read the papers." He waved his hand, as if to show off the diamond ring on his pinky finger. He was pudgy, with stained teeth and pockmarked cheeks. His hair was slicked down and combed to the side in an obvious effort to disguise a receding hairline.

"I'm surprised you find time to read, with all your other activities."

"Such as?"

"Roughing up women, for one."

His mouth tightened, and color flooded his face. "That's a nasty rumor, and a bald faced lie."

"Come now, Donnie." Dante smirked. "We both know that's not true. Unfortunately, I have no proof, at the moment, so I can't haul you in. But I'll be keeping an eye on you."

"I'm honored."

"Where were you night before last?" Dante didn't want to spring all the dates of the murders on him, he didn't want the bastard to know he suspected him. He'd chip away a little at a time, so he didn't have a chance to concoct an alibi for all the killings.

Hillian's brows drew together as if he were thinking hard. "I believe I was at church. I'm a choir boy, after all."

Dante didn't let his irritation show, but this fellow rubbed him the wrong way. And even if he wasn't good for the South End slayings, Dante was determined to put him down for his other crimes. "Yeah, you are at that. I'm gonna need you to give me a straight answer. Otherwise, I'll assume you're purposely hiding something. And I'm gonna haul your ass in and lock you up. So you better start talking. And this time, the truth."

Hillian scowled and pursed his lips like a petulant child. "I was at home."

"Were you with anyone?"

Hillian shook his head. "All by my lonesome."

Dante retrieved a photo of the Alma Vernon from his pocket and held it out for Hillian to see. "Do you know this woman?"

Hillian squinted at the photo then sat back. "Never seen her in my life. What happened? She get herself killed?"

Dante didn't respond. He studied the man for signs he was lying but didn't spot any. Of course, people without a conscience could lie like a politician and never blink an eye or twitch a muscle. He asked a few more questions and advised Hillian not to leave town…not that he would. It seemed his business was booming in Boston and the scum wouldn't want to give that up.

Dante stood, anxious to get away. Just being near the slimy asshole made him feel like he needed a shower.

****

The ballroom of the Fairmont Copley Plaza hotel was brimming with elegantly dressed, wealthy Bostonians who'd turned out in droves for the charity event of the season—an auction to sell possessions donated by the wealthy. The donors put on airs of making a great sacrifice by turning loose of their valuables but replacing those objects would not even dent their fat pockets.

Iris glanced around, her eyes finding Dante across the room. The captain and his detectives had been invited, as the police force was one of the entities that would benefit from the proceeds.

Dante wore a black tuxedo with satin lapels, a white shirt with a royal blue bow tie. His glossy black hair was combed neatly, but a stray curl hung over his forehead. Her fingers itched to brush it back, to slide her hands through his hair…

She swallowed the dryness in her throat and looked away, gulping from her champagne glass. When she turned back, Dante was heading toward her, and in moments, he was standing directly in front of her, his nearness playing havoc with her senses.

"You look…beautiful," he said softly, taking in her mauve silk evening gown embellished with lace roses.

"Thank you. And you look quite dashing."

He grinned and tipped his glass to her. "Where is the lucky fiancé?"

She gestured with her champagne flute to where Norman stood by the bar, chatting with his cronies. "Probably devising some grand financial deal. His mind is constantly on business."

"Well, he's a fool for not keeping his mind on you."

Her face flushed. What was with this new, flirtatious Dante? He lifted the glass of amber liquid to his mouth and drained it. And she understood. He was slightly tipsy. She smiled at the idea of Mr. In Control Morello being inebriated. "And you would never be so foolish, is that correct?"

His eyes captured hers, and she couldn't have looked away if the room caught on fire. "If I had a woman like you, I'd keep her right by my side day…" His voice dropped to a husky whisper. "…and night."

She couldn't prevent a gasp escaping. She was shocked at his boldness…but not appalled, not offended. No, something very different was going on inside her body…a warm flush seeped through her, heating her skin from hairline to toe. "I—I…" She couldn't speak over the lump in her throat. Her stomach tightened. "Will you excuse me?"

His firm lips crooked in a grin. "Of course."

She hurried away, resisting the urge to fan her face. She could feel Dante's gaze on her, even though her back was to him. She stopped at the bar and rested her palms on the smooth wood, taking deep breaths. "A champagne. Please," she told the bartender.

He handed it to her, and she took a long sip. Norman approached, and she gave him a bright smile. "Hello, darling. So pleased you could join me."

"I'm sorry I've been neglecting you. No more. I'm yours for the evening." His gaze raked her body, and she was chagrined to realize she felt nothing…not a hint of the scorching heat she felt when Dante was near. This couldn't be. She was going to marry this man. Her traitorous thoughts about Dante must be squelched. Norman was the man she loved. She probably only had that reaction to Dante because he was newly back in her life. A war hero and detective. How could she not be impressed? It was nothing more.

Sweeping her gaze over the room…not searching for Dante, just…looking…she spotted Norman's father accompanied by a man she didn't recognize. They were headed toward her and Norman. Mr. Caddell's expression was thunderous. What on earth…?

They halted in front of Iris, and Mr. Caddell brandished a manila envelope.

Norman said, “Father, what is the meaning of this?”

His father leveled a steady, angry stare on Iris. “Your little fiancée here has been keeping some pretty juicy secrets.”

Iris frowned. “What…what do you mean? What’s this about?”

His mouth formed into a snarl, and he opened the envelope, retrieving a stack of papers and thrusting them toward her. “It’s about your mother being a whore.”

Chapter Seven

Iris jerked back as if he'd dealt her a physical blow. "How dare you? My mother is a lady, an angel." Tears shook her voice. "You take that back!" She sounded childish, but she felt like a child. A lost, scared child.

She hadn't seen Dante approach, but suddenly he was there. "Iris? Is everything okay?" Concern hovered in his dark eyes.

"He—he's saying…" She sniffled. She couldn't go on.

"Father," Norman sounded as dazed as she felt. "Where did you get such wild ideas?"

Mr. Caddell held the papers out to Norman. "Read this. It's all right there. At your mother's insistence, I hired a private detective to investigate her. Her mother was a prostitute who worked for a man named Oscar Cummings. As it turned out, Cummings was killing girls who worked for him. He nearly killed Iris's mother, but Vincent Taggart arrived and saved the day."

His words chilled her soul like the breath of a cold wind. "No…she would never…" It couldn't be… Her mother a prostitute? It was ridiculous, impossible, preposterous. But something about it felt so…true.

Norman scanned the papers, then lifted his head and looked at Iris. "My God, you filthy, lying bitch."

"Hey—" Dante stepped forward.

Iris barely saw Norman's hand move, but he slapped her face so hard, she reeled back and fell against the bar. Her face stung like a thousand needles pierced her cheek, and tears sprang to her eyes.

Dante rushed to her side. "Iris, are you okay?"

Stunned, she pressed a hand to her battered cheek and slowly nodded. He gently moved her hand and checked her injury. Fury blazed in his ebony eyes.

He whirled and launched into Norman, taking him to the ground. Dante punched him, over and over. Norman's head snapped back and forth, slamming against the hardwood floor with each strike. The other party-goers realized what was going on, and voices soared along with the sounds of bodies jostling to get closer to the action.

"Someone stop this maniac." Norman's father's voice rose over the hubbub.

A handful of men, the captain included, converged on Dante. It took several attempts, but they finally pulled him away. Norman lay bleeding and whimpering, curled in a fetal position.

Dante was breathing hard, jerking against the men who held him. He glared down at Norman. "If you ever touch her again, there is no place on earth you can hide that I won't find you."

Iris—even through her bewildered humiliation—couldn't control a surge of delight. Her strong, brave, soldier had defended her honor, had come to her rescue as he had so many times before. And in that moment, she wanted nothing more than to throw herself in his arms, to kiss him, with all the pent-up yearning she'd held back so long. She had been lying to herself, making excuses for her reaction to Dante. But the truth was, she loved him. Always had. Her schoolgirl crush had blossomed into the deep love of a woman for a man. Sadly, although he cared for her too, he didn't return that love. But he was still her hero.

The men—with great effort—dragged Dante out the door. His gaze never left Iris. She blinked back tears. She wouldn't show any further emotion in front of this crowd of arrogant, phony…assholes. There, she'd cursed. *Assholes*.

Norman had come to his feet. "Get out," he growled, his long, slim fingers nursing his bloody face.

She stared at him and, for the first time, saw him for what he really was—what they all were. A man who despised the poor but allowed his fiancée to serve them at the soup kitchen for the benefit of his social standing. And his father, who wouldn't think of showing his son the slightest bit of affection but would go to the ends of the earth to ensure he succeeded, even attempting to destroy his future wife. And his mother who served on multitude of charitable committees, but was cruelly, exceedingly uncharitable to her own daughter. Iris would have ended up just like them. But since her mother was a prostitute, she was deemed unfit to become a part of their hypocritical, snobby circle. Such delicious irony. She chuckled, then erupted into full-blown laughter.

"What's so damn funny?" Norman bit out.

"You, Norman Caddell, almost married the daughter of a whore." She looked around the room at the faces, some shocked, some disgusted, some angry…and a few surprisingly sympathetic. "I suppose that would have been a topic to liven up the excruciating boredom of your parties."

Iris picked up her champagne flute—which had miraculously remained intact on top of the bar—and downed the contents in one gulp. "Good evening." She inclined her head in what she hoped was a regal nod and, chin up, sauntered out the door. She couldn't wait to get away…to go home.

A thought slammed into her mind, and panic set in. 'Home' was the dwelling belonging to Opal. She would no longer be welcome there. Just like the people she pitied at the soup kitchen, she was now—at least temporarily—homeless.

****

Dante was not surprised when Captain Davenport called him into his office on Monday morning.

Dante started to sit, but Davenport jerked the cigar out of his mouth and shook his head. "Nope, no siree. Don't even bother to sit. I want this as miserable on you as can be."

Dante held his hands out. "Okay, I'm standing. What now?"

He glared and stuck the cigar back in his mouth, talking around it. "What the hell's wrong with you? Did you take a mortar to the head over there?"

Dante didn't reply. He let the captain rant.

"What were you thinking, beating up one of the Boston Brahman?" The captain ran a hand through his thick gray hair and huffed out a breath. "Do you have any idea how powerful they are?"

"He struck a woman." And not just any woman, Iris…

"I don't care if he ate a baby, you can't coldcock a Caddell."

"If I had to do it all over again, I would do the

same thing. Only this time, I might kill him."

The room fell silent, except for the ticking of the clock on the captain's wall. "That's what I thought. And honestly, just between you and me, can't say I blame you. You know, me and the boys had no choice but to pull you off of the bastard. But I can tell you, we took our sweet time getting over there. But my ass is on the line." He snatched the cigar from his mouth and stubbed it in the ash tray. "You're outta here, Morello, I gotta let you go."

Dante had been expecting it, but hearing it still made him go cold inside. He'd been a cop in the army, he was a cop in civilian life. He didn't know how to be anything else.

He rested his hands on the desk and leaned forward. "But, Captain, there's a murderer out there. It's my case. I gotta stop him." He heard himself begging and didn't like it, but he'd kiss the captain's big round ass if it meant he could stay on. "I just got a lead. I think this will go somewhere."

The captain shook his head. "Someone else will have to follow up. Give me your gun and your badge."

Dante stared at him for a moment, then straightened. He retrieved his gun from its holster and placed it on the desktop. It landed with the thud of dirt hitting a coffin. His badge followed, spinning then coming to rest beside the .45.

Dante moved to the door. Without turning around, he said quietly, "I can't stop." He didn't know why he'd shared the admission. But he was talking more to himself than to the captain. Badge or no badge, he wouldn't rest until the son of a bitch was stopped. Iris was in the killer's crosshairs. And Dante would protect her with his last breath.

"Yeah, I figured that." The captain's words were as quiet as Dante's. They were also filled with an underlying meaning.

Dante looked back at him.

"Sometimes, files go missing around here. It's the damnedest thing. Sure would be a shame if the South End Slayer files came up missing. Say, tomorrow morning around 6 a.m. before the shift change."

Dante grinned. "Yeah." He settled his hat on his head and opened the door. "That'd be a damned shame."

****

Iris drank from the glass and grimaced. She was on her second whiskey, and the booze was starting to numb her.

The morning after the debacle with Norman, she'd been roughly awoken by Opal and promptly ejected from her home. Iris had expected as much. She wouldn't have stayed there anyway. She wanted to be far away from anyone with Caddell blood…except Shelby. The poor little thing had cried her eyes out as she clung to Iris, begging Opal to let her stay.

Tears rose to Iris's throat and she gulped more of the Four Roses. Her parents learned of the fiasco and put her up in the Omni Parker House hotel. She hadn't wanted to take their offer, but neither did she relish the idea of sleeping in the streets. She hadn't discussed what had happened over the phone. They would be here soon for Sophie's graduation and Iris would demand answers then.

Rage bubbled inside her. How *dare* her mother do such a horrible thing, then act like miss high and mighty, insisting her daughter not settle for anything less than marriage to a wealthy man? Eliza's words from years ago came back to her. How *dare* she say Dante was beneath them? She was a common whore yet Dante was beneath them? She let out a laugh that was a half sob.

"Miss, are you okay? Can I call someone for you?" The bartender was polite enough not to say that it wasn't seemly for a woman to drink at a bar alone. But Iris knew he was thinking it. She decided to put his mind at ease.

"No, no. Don't worry. It's perfectly acceptable that I'm at a bar, alone, unchaperoned, drinking. See, it's only natural. I'm the daughter of a whore."

His face whitened, and she felt a twinge of remorse, but she didn't have time for such nonsense as apologies and sparing people's feelings. She had a lot of drinking left to do. She gulped the whiskey, draining the glass. Warmth traveled through her, and she was finally starting to feel…nothing. Nothing except relaxed. And fuzzy.

She ordered another. The bartender hesitated, then filled a glass and slid it to her.

Iris turned in her seat to view the dance floor, watching the couples swaying together. They all looked so happy… Maybe she should find a man and take him to the dance floor…let him hold her close, body to body. Let him take what he wanted, because, that was the way Taggart women behaved. She blinked back tears that had been threatening all evening.

A strange sensation washed over her. Something in the air changed. Tingles skittered along her flesh and she knew, before he spoke, that Dante was near, and she turned to see him standing beside her.

"Mind if I sit?" His low voice rumbled through her and she wanted to cry. She immediately felt less alone, less abandoned. Safer.

She kept her voice as even as she could, not wanting to betray her emotions. "Sit, if you want, but this is the broken, adrift and alone section. You won't fit in." She could hear the slur in her words and hoped he couldn't.

He slid onto the stool next to her and ordered a whiskey. The bartender looked exceedingly relieved that Iris was no longer his problem. "Yeah," Dante said as the whiskey was placed in front of him. "I fit in just fine."

"Oh yes, the war." Her tone suggested 'that same ole' thing' but it wasn't how she meant it. Once again, she couldn't find it in herself to apologize.

"Everything isn't about the war."

"What, then? What has Mr. Superhero Detective in a funk?" Her voice hardened as she looked at him. "You didn't also find out your mother was a whore, did you?"

"No. I lost my job."

"You lost your job? Who'll catch the South End Slayer?"

A long sigh left him. "I wondered the same thing, but when you get down to it, I haven't done it either." He shrugged. "Might as well let someone else take a crack at it."

If Dante couldn't catch him, no one could. How many more would die at his hands?

She didn't want to think about that tonight. Didn't want to think about anything. Except the here and now.

Except Dante. “Let’s dance,” she blurted.

He lifted his brows. “Wouldn’t that be scandalous?”

She grimaced a smile. “When you find out your mother’s a prostitute and your fiancé humiliates you in front of God and the world, you don’t have much to worry about in the scandal department.” She slipped off the barstool and stumbled. Dante shot out a hand to right her. His touch was warm. Something sizzled through her body, and her eyes met his. Even in the dim bar, she could see his dark gaze spark. Something passed between them. Something she wanted to explore further. “Dance with me,” she said huskily.

Billie Holliday’s throaty, passionate voice belted out “Lover Man” as Dante stood and took Iris’s hand, leading her to the dance floor. He pulled her into his arms, and she rested her head on his chest and gave a long, satisfied sigh. Being held by him was so much better than she’d imagined.

Everywhere their bodies touched felt like electric fire. Desire burned through her, blocking out all thought. She wanted him. So desperately. She lifted her head from his chest and put her lips close to his ear. “I want to kiss you, really kiss you. With everything I’m feeling right now.”

He groaned and she felt a shudder run through his body. “I…you’re drunk,” he said hoarsely. “You don’t know what you’re saying.”

She tilted her head back to look into his face. “I do. I am drunk, but I know what I want. I’d want it drunk, sober, tonight, tomorrow. Forever. I’ve always wanted you, Dante. You know that, right?”

He sucked in a sharp breath. “What I know is, you

need to get home. Alone, and safely tucked in bed."

"Okay." She let a teasing note enter her voice. "But you can't stop me from thinking about you, while I'm lying in bed, I'll imagine what it would be like to feel your lips on mine, our bodies pressing tightly together—" She stopped abruptly, as if she'd been doused in a bucket of cold water. Where had that come from? She sounded like her mother. She pulled away from him, humiliation sweeping through her. "I'm sorry."

He frowned. "Iris? Are you okay?"

She shook her head. "I want to go home." She was suddenly sober. And filled with regret. Dante had made it clear years ago that he wasn't interested. And she was throwing herself at him like a harlot. "I-I need to call a taxi."

"No. I'll take you home." She couldn't identify his tone…what he was thinking. She barely knew what *she* was thinking.

Dante attempted to engage her in conversation on the ride to the hotel, but she barely responded. It was more than humiliation. She was terrified of what she'd become. They pulled in front of the Omni, and he came around to open the door, then walked her to her room.

Unable to look at Dante, she kept her gaze averted as she thanked him and said goodnight. She started to go inside, but he halted her with a hand on her arm.

He turned her to face him, gently took her chin, and tilted her face up. "What's wrong?" He searched her face, his expression bewildered. "Are you angry with me?"

"Oh no, Dante. Never." Tears choked her voice. "I'm angry with myself. I don't know what came over me, and I'm sorry for pushing myself on you." Her voice hiccupped into a sob. "Maybe I'm just like my mother."

Anger flashed in his dark eyes. "You did nothing wrong."

She gave a self-deprecating laugh. "Oh, but I did. I was ready to hop into bed with you."

"That doesn't make you a prostitute. If one of the men in the bar had offered you a twenty, would you kiss him, would you let him hold you and remove your clothes, would you have sex with him?"

His words both titillated and shocked her. "Mercy me, of course not."

He released her chin and tugged her against him. She gasped as their bodies came together. His lips hovered over hers, so close, they almost touched. "I'm not going to pay you a dime." He pulled her closer until their hips fit snugly together. Hardness in his groin sent heat rushing through her. Dizziness made her head swim. She was afraid she might faint. Not even the whiskeys she'd downed had made her feel so flushed and hot and wanton. And needy. "Can I kiss you?" he murmured.

His lips were so close to hers, he almost *was* kissing her. But they weren't close enough, not nearly close enough. "Yes," she moaned, realizing it sounded a little like begging.

"Even if I don't pay you?"

She nodded vigorously and tilted her head back so his lips could have their way. "Yes, yes, please, you can." She'd never in her life wanted anything more.

He looked at her for a moment, then released her, leaving her cold, bereft, and utterly confused. "Wh…"

She blinked at him. “What are you doing?”

“Proving you are nothing like a prostitute.”

With that, he walked away. If she had the strength, she’d chase after him and beat him over the head with her handbag. But her legs were rubber, and she couldn’t move. She stared at his retreating back and, somehow, in spite of her anger and disappointment, she began to laugh.

Chapter Eight

Iris's parents arrived the day before Sophie's graduation. They were also staying at the Omni, and Iris took the elevator to their suite. As she ascended to their floor, she wrung her hands nervously, practicing in her mind what she would say to them. As the elevator doors slid open, she lifted her chin and squared her shoulders. She was ready now.

Her mother opened the door to her, and Iris couldn't help but feel a wave of joyous nostalgia at seeing her parents. Her father, tall and strong and handsome, his blond hair starting to show signs of gray and her mother, still beautiful with her golden eyes, creamy skin and shiny dark hair. She didn't look at all like a prostitute.

"Iris, darling." Her mother pulled her into a hug, but Iris remained stiff, unyielding. She wanted to sink into her mother's warm embrace and bawl her eyes out, like she'd done as a child, letting her sweet comfort chase away all the bad in the world. But that wouldn't work this time. Her mother *was* the bad.

When Eliza released her, Iris hugged her father. His expression was grim, where her mother's was crestfallen.

Iris crossed her arms tightly over her chest and glared at Eliza. "I can't believe you…what you did. What you were." Her body shook, and she fought back tears. "You lied to me. My whole life was a lie."

Eliza flinched, and tears coursed down her cheeks. "I'm so sorry you had to learn that way."

Iris grunted a humorless laugh. "Oh? Is there a better way to learn your mother prostituted herself for money?"

Eliza jerked back, then deflated like a punctured balloon and sank into a nearby armchair.

"Iris!" her father barked. His face was a thundercloud of anger. "Don't speak to your mother that way."

Iris swallowed back tears. Her father seldom raised his voice to her. "What about what *she* did? Do you have any idea what I've been through because of her? How do you think it felt when my fiancé's father announced to a room full of people that I am the daughter of a prostitute?" Her rising fury gave her momentum. She paced, gesturing with her arms, her voice shaking. "Then, my fiancé, the man that she insisted I marry, talks to me like I'm a piece of filth and assaults me." She was sobbing now, the remembered humiliation and betrayal piercing her heart like a blade.

"Oh, sweet love." Eliza stood and took Iris in her arms, stopping her frantic movements. "I'm so sorry. So deeply sorry. I never meant for you to find out."

Iris wanted nothing more than to sink into her mother's comforting embrace, but she wouldn't allow it. Her mother didn't deserve to comfort her. Didn't deserve her forgiveness. She jerked away and shook her head. "Of course you didn't want me to find out. If I hadn't, you could have gone on with your prim and proper act, insisting that I be a lady, snag a wealthy man. When I could have been like you and lay on my back to make a living."

"Iris—" Her father stepped toward her, but her mother intervened.

"Vince, please, give us a moment alone."

He hesitated, looking from one to the other, then gave a nod. He put his hands on Iris's shoulders, and his features softened. "I am sorry, pumpkin. I could kill that bastard for laying a hand on you. But, please, go easy on your mother. You don't know what she's been through."

Iris didn't answer. He placed a kiss on her forehead. "I'll take a walk. Be back soon."

He left and, when the door shut behind him, Eliza sank into the armchair and began speaking. "I don't want to share all the sordid details with you. I've spent years putting all of that behind me. But, you deserve an explanation." She drew in a deep breath and let it out slowly. "When I was in England, I worked as a kitchen maid. The Earl I worked for decided he…desired me. He tried to force himself on me, and I managed to fight back. I hit him with a vase, and he went down. I thought I'd killed him, so I fled. I met Charlotte, Margaret and Jessica on a ship to America. When we arrived, I had no money. I met a man who offered to employ me as a party host." Her pretty face tightened with anger. "What I didn't realize was, he actually intended for me to be a…a prostitute. When I refused, he threatened me. I'd signed a contract, and he told me I'd go to prison if I didn't follow through. I was young, naïve, desperate. As it turned out, the bastard was also a killer. He'd murdered two women who tried to leave him. One of them was your father's childhood friend. He came to New York to find her, and that's how we met. He ended up…" She closed her eyes and shuddered. "Your father ended up killing the man, who was trying to kill me. It was a horrible, horrible incident, but it brought me and your father together. I hated myself. Hated what I did. Every moment made me want to die. It was only a few times. And I only did it to survive. Don't you see, that's why I've pushed you to find someone to take care of you, so you'd have a secure and stable life, so you wouldn't have to do the horrible things I did."

Iris was shocked…appalled…and so very sorry at what her mother had gone through. She imagined the young, frightened girl. Desperate, terrified. Trapped. Unwanted sympathy rose, but she squelched it. She snorted in disgust. "Oh yes, well, great plan, Mother. I did find a rich man to take care of me…and look at me now. I'm left with nothing."

Eliza shook her head. "You don't have nothing. You have all you need."

"Oh? And what do I have? I don't have a career, a man, anything." She shook her head. "It's ironic that *you* found someone to love you, someone wonderful. I can't believe that Daddy married you, knowing what you were."

Eliza smiled wistfully. "Your father is a great man. He loved me in spite of what I'd done. That's the kind of man I want for you, whether they have money or wealth or stability, love is all that matters."

Iris lifted her brows. "Why the sudden change of heart when you've drilled into me my entire life that I had to marry someone wealthy?"

"I was wrong. Norman Caddell may be wealthy, but he's no better than a roach. I understand you being upset with me, but please don't let your bitterness ruin your life. You're a strong, smart woman. You don't need a man, but I hope you find someone to love, someone wonderful who deserves a wonderful person like you."

Iris felt herself softening, found it more difficult to hang onto her anger. She'd missed her mother so. Even with all that had happened, all she'd learned about Eliza, just being with her brought comfort. But she wasn't ready to completely let go of her resentment. "And what am I supposed to do? Live with you and Father until some man comes along and takes care of me?"

Eliza smiled. "What about a job as a nurse? I was opposed to your father allowing you to attend nursing school, but now I'm so glad he did. You can have a career where you don't have to depend on a man to take care of you. You'll never have to degrade yourself to survive."

A frisson of excitement worked its way through Iris. She did have her degree. She could get an actual position as a nurse. A paid position. Although, she would still want to volunteer to give aid to the poor. If she'd learned nothing else, she'd learned that there were people out there who needed help. And that helping the less fortunate made her feel better than anything else ever had…except maybe Dante's touch… She squeezed her eyes shut briefly and forced the thought from her mind. She and Dante were not to be. And she'd better get used to that. Or she'd never move on. "I would love nothing more than to put my nursing degree to use."

Eliza took Iris's hands in hers and squeezed gently.

"Your father and I will support you no matter what. We truly only want you to be happy. I just had the wrong idea of what would make you happy." She released Iris to brush away her tears. "I hope someday you can forgive me. And understand I didn't know what else do to at the time."

Iris wasn't ready to let her mother off the hook, but the horror of what she'd gone through made her sympathize and even understand how she could have been drawn into the predicament she was in. But, she should have been honest with Iris. Should not have pushed her to find a rich man, which led to the fiasco. But she was glad they'd had the talk. And she knew she'd forgive her…someday. She allowed Eliza to hug her. And when she whispered, "I love you," Iris found herself whispering it back.

****

For Sophie's graduation party that night, Club 501 was decorated in sparkling tiny lights, with roses on each table and a large sign reading, *Congratulations, Sophie* strung along the stage. Uncle Harry and Aunt Meg had gone all out.

The actual graduation that day had gone by in a blur. Iris tried hard to focus. She was proud of her friend and wanted to savor her big moment. But her mind wouldn't stay off of the shambles her life had become. She shook off the gloomy thoughts. Today was about Sophie. Iris would put all the miserable things out of her mind and enjoy the evening's celebration, surrounded by friends and family…even those who'd betrayed her.

But someone was missing, and worry nagged at Iris. Audra was nowhere to be seen. She should have been here an hour ago. Iris chewed her bottom lip, her anxiety rising with each moment that passed. What if something had happened to her friend? What if the South End Slayer… Panic rose to her throat. She should have told Uncle Harry about Audra being attacked. If she had, he'd have been able to keep an eye on her. If something had happened to Audra, it would be Iris's fault.

She spotted Maddie, who waved and headed her way. They hugged and complimented one another's gowns, then Maddie glanced over Iris's shoulder and made a tsking sound. "Oh my, Sophie's got her sketchpad out. At her party." She took Iris's hand. "Let's go."

They wound through the crowd until they reached Sophie. Maddie tapped her shoulder. "What are you doing? This is your graduation party, and you are going to celebrate."

"Yes," Iris backed Maddie up. "This party is in your honor."

Sophie looked morose. "I don't feel like celebrating."

"What's the matter?" Iris and Maddie said at the same time, then took places on the settee on either side of Sophie.

"The last few weeks have been hell. I'm afraid my parents are going to ship me to London."

Iris hated that her friend was down, but honestly, there were worse things in the world…like a murderer on the loose. Who may have done something to their friend… No, she was being ridiculous. Nothing had happened to Audra. She forced sympathy into her voice. "Why?"

"That's not so terrible. I'll be there." Maddie sounded put out with Sophie.

"I'm sorry, Maddie. It's just that I wasn't prepared to go to London. My life and career are here. I've just made such a mess of things."

"That's okay." Maddie patted Sophie's shoulder. "Let it out. But you really shouldn't fuss so. I've already invited Audra to visit London. We could really make a party of it."

Iris was growing impatient. She loved her friends but, really, sometimes they made such a to do over nothing. And she had more important things to worry about. She couldn't rest until she knew what was keeping Audra. She stood. "Audra. Have either one of you seen her?"

They glanced around, and Sophie shrugged. "Not yet."

"Misery me. She promised she wouldn't take too long. Something must have happened." Iris spotted Uncle Harry and Aung Meg on the other side of the room. Without saying a word to Maddie and Sophie, she headed toward them. The band played Frank Sinatra's "Five Minutes More," and the music seemed to beat into Iris's brain…something's wrong…something's wrong…

Now near tears, she rushed up to them. Aunt Meg frowned when she saw Iris's face. "Iris, my dear, whatever's the matter?"

"I—" She took a deep breath and blurted it out. "I'm worried about Audra. She's late, and I'm afraid something's happened to her. It wouldn't be the first time. Last week, when we were leaving the soup kitchen, she was attacked."

Uncle Harry's curious expression immediately switched to anger. "She was what?"

"A-attacked. I left my handbag, and she was outside alone and when I returned, a man was grabbing her, but she fought him off, and he ran."

His jaw clenched, and his words were clipped. "And you're just now telling me about it?"

Tears sprang to Iris's eyes, and she nodded miserably. "Audra made me swear not to. But now she's missing. I-I'm just frightened it may have happened again."

"Iris?"

Iris whirled at the sound of Audra's voice behind her. She was so relieved her friend was okay, she wasn't even upset that Audra was looking at her as if she wanted to strangle her.

Behind her, Uncle Harry spoke in a voice filled with a rage she'd never heard from him. "Audra Faye? You mind telling me where you've been?"

Iris rushed to Audra and took her hands. "I'm sorry, Audra. I was so worried. You should have been here an hour ago. And, after the last time …"

Audra didn't reply, but the look on her face—fury, pain and determination—spoke volumes. She tugged her hands from Iris's, turned and fled out the front door. Her parents called after her, but she didn't stop. Iris put her hands to her face and shook her head in misery. Add another loss to her growing list—this one the most painful of all.

****

His footsteps echoed in the silence of the deserted streets. He needed a kill. Desperately. He wasn't sure how much longer he could wait to tell his Bonnie he knew who she was. They'd danced around it too long. Sometimes, he caught a knowing look in her pretty blue eyes. As if she was waiting for him to make the move, to bring the secret out into the open. His body tensed with the agony of holding back. *Soon, my sweet, Bonnie, soon...*

For now, he knew how to release some of the tension. At the corner, two women of the evening stood, talking and casting glances around, no doubt looking for a john. Must be a slow night. He wouldn't make his move while the two of them were together. He'd gotten by so far with keeping his targets to one at a time. No reason to change the plan now. If they didn't part soon, he'd find someone else. There was always someone else.

A figure caught his attention, heading to the door of a motel. He knew that man. He chuckled, louder than planned. The hookers spotted him, their faces alighting with interest and hope. Little did they know, that hope was misplaced. If he focused his attention on them, it wouldn't be the results they wanted. But they were lucky. Tonight, they'd be spared. He'd just thought of another way to release his anxiety.

He ambled to the door of the motel, staying several paces back from his quarry. The man didn't know him, but he still didn't want to get too close.

Inside, the man walked purposefully down the hallway and stopped in front of a room, then tapped on the door. It opened in seconds, and the rat slipped inside.

He waited for several moments, giving the rat and his lady friend time to get involved in their...activities so they'd be distracted, more vulnerable. When enough time had passed, he tied the bandana around his face, approached the door where moans of ecstasy floated through the wood, and knocked lightly. “Management, I need to speak with you urgently.”

The door opened, and a thin young man wearing nothing but a grungy pair of underwear stood looking at him, eyebrows raised. Surprise made him hesitate as his mind computed this new information…not a lady friend after all. His quarry had different leanings. Before the prostitute could process that his visitor was not the manager after all, he shoved the door all the way open, causing the whore to stumble back.

On the bed, the rat lay with his hands and feet tied to the bedposts. He wore underwear as well…women’s underwear. A laugh escaped. This was much better than he expected. In that moment, he made a decision. The rat would not die tonight. But he would likely wish he had.

“What…what is the meaning of this?” the rat sputtered. His voice held fear and indignation. “Who are you and what do you want?”

“I think you know who I am. And I think you know what’s about to happen.” He pointed a finger at the whore, who remained on the floor, trembling and sobbing, arms wrapped around his knees. “You sit there and keep your mouth shut. You make one move, and I’ll be madder ‘n all git out. And you don’t want to know what happens then.”

The whore nodded over and over, his narrow face twisted in terror, tears streaming down his cheeks.

He approached the bed and slammed his fist into the rat’s face. A cry of pain rose. “What…no…what are you doing…why?” The words were interspersed between blows, then came the begging. A red haze clouded his vision as he pummeled the rat, but among the anger was elation…none of his kills had ever felt this satisfying. *Kills…* The word penetrated his consciousness, and he abruptly stopped before he killed the man. If it wasn't too late already…

He shook his head, snapping himself out of his fog. Sobbing and wailing filled the air, from both. Good, good, good. Not dead. But badly hurt. He was bleeding from every visible orifice.

Knocking sounded on the door. "Hello? Hey, is everything okay?"

He pointed a finger at the hysterical man on the floor. "Consider yourself lucky, you're the only whore I've come across who's survived the encounter."

The man opened the door and shoved past the confused desk clerk. He turned back, letting his stare rest on the clerk, then the whore. "Wait ten minutes before calling the police. Leave him tied up. If you untie him, I'll know. And I'll come back and kill you both. Tell the coppers he's a gift from the slayer."

He fled the motel, nearly rubbing his hands in glee. The police would come soon, along with the newspapers. The rat was trapped and would pay a hefty price.

Chapter Nine

Dante stopped his car on the street and entered the South Inn Motel, his pulse thrumming with excitement. It seemed the South End Slayer had struck again but, this time, the victim survived. Mick had arrived before him and was with the man now. His injuries were not life threatening, so they had themselves a witness.

An overweight older guy stood behind the desk, wearing a dazed expression. On the other side of the counter, a younger, smaller man with a thin blanket wrapped around his shoulders was smoking a cigarette and trembling violently.

They both looked up when Dante entered. "Detective Morello," Dante said. "Tell me what happened."

The big man, the desk clerk, Dante presumed, gave him a bewildered stare then pointed down the hallway. "There's a fellow in room 15. He's beat up real bad. An officer is in there with him."

"Beat up?" Dante's hope deflated. That was not the slayer's MO. He tilted his head toward the hallway. "Lead the way."

"If it's all the same, I'd rather not." The clerk pointed. "It's down the hall and to your right. The South End Slayer might come back any time to finish the job."

Dante raised his brows. "You're sure the South

End Slayer did this?"

The other guy spoke for the first time, squeaking out the words. "Y-yes, it was him."

"And who are you?" Dante asked.

His face reddened. "I was with the man who got beat up…he…hired me for the evening."

Dante tried to cover his shock. He'd never encountered a male prostitute. "You guys stay right here. I'll send my partner out to finish up taking your statements."

The hall smelled of urine and sweat and other odors Dante didn't want to think about. The door to room 15 was ajar, and Dante stepped inside. The odor was stronger inside the room…fresher.

A man lay on the bed, his wrists and feet secured with rope to the bed posts. He was naked, except for a pair of women's panties. Dante had seen a lot of crazy things in his life, but this threw him. The victim's face was battered, but a jolt of recognition shot through Dante. Norman Caddell…sobbing and writhing on the bed. "Help me, help me, oh God, help me." His gaze focused on Dante, and his eyes narrowed. "Help me, I said. I need a doctor. Why are you just standing there? And, for God's sake, untie me!"

Dante just barely suppressed a smile. He couldn't say he was sorry to see Caddell in this predicament. "Sure, sure, just calm down. We'll get you cut loose and call an ambulance."

"No, you stupid dolt. Call my private physician, Hank Mersing. I can't have the publicity of an ambulance."

Dante pushed his hat back on his head and grinned at Mick. "Call an ambulance for Mr. Caddell."

"What? No! You moron, I said no ambulance."

"I'm very sorry Mr. Caddell, it's protocol. We have to put your safety first and we need to get you to the hospital." None of that was true. Dante tried to keep the smile off his face. He tried not to feel satisfied at seeing the pompous, twisted asshole like this, but was unsuccessful. He deserved this and more.

His battered face scrunched in anger. "Untie me, asshole. Now!"

Dante stepped closer to the bed and looked down at him. "Cool your heels. I will. I just have some questions first." Dante glanced around the room, then back to Caddell. "Also, I'm waiting for our crime scene photographer."

Caddell's eyes widened in horror. "You'll not have me photographed. This will not stand."

"It's protocol," Dante said again. Normally, it would be protocol to have the victim receive medical attention first and foremost. But it was obvious Caddell was fine. His injuries were not life threatening, just painful. And his situation wasn't dangerous, just humiliating. "Now, tell me what happened. Start from the time you procured the prostitute."

He scowled, and his face reddened. "I don't have to talk to you, not without my attorney."

"You're not a suspect, you're a victim. Different rules apply. And, if you want to be untied anytime soon, you'll answer my questions. Pronto."

He huffed. "Fine. I'll talk. But you'll hear from my lawyer about the way you're treating me."

Dante smiled. "Oh, I'm sure I will. We'll both hear from several people about this incident."

Caddell growled in rage. "You can't tell anyone. It

will ruin me."

"Something like this is not going to stay out of the papers."

He began sobbing again. "You can't…I can't have this…my parents…"

"Right now, you need to be concerned with telling me what happened."

He took a deep, shaky breath. "Fine. I arrived at 8 p.m. for my…meeting. About ten minutes later, the door crashes open. This…this *maniac* bursts into the room. He threatens to kill the guy if he moves. And then, he just attacks me. Starts punching me. He tells the guy to call the cops after he's gone, to wait ten minutes and not to come back in the room, or he'll know, and he'll come back and kill him. He says he's the South End Slayer." Tears streamed down his face, and the trembling increased. "Good God, the South End Slayer. I could have been murdered."

Dante wasn't convinced the slayer had done this. He usually didn't leave his victims alive. A sound at the door made him turn. Bo, the photographer, had arrived. He took in the scene and his eyes widened, then a big grin spread over his face. "Holy mackerel. You're Norman Caddell." He chuckled. "Nice undies."

Norman strained against his bindings and cursed.

"Go ahead and get the photos," Dante said to Bo. "I need to get this fellow untied and to the hospital." As if on cue, an ambulance siren sounded from nearby.

Bo snapped several photos, while Norman cringed and closed his eyes. "These are just for the police, right?" he asked.

It was common for crime scene photographers to sell their photos to the newspapers. Dante usually hated that practice, but this time, the thought filled him with satisfaction. He didn't bother to respond to Caddell's question.

Once the ambulance had left with Caddell, Dante went back to the lobby where Mick was still speaking with the desk clerk and the prostitute. Mick looked up when Dante approached. He stepped away from the witnesses and waved Dante over out of earshot. "I got their statements. I think I got all we can get from them. I also got a bit of news. The station called here, and I spoke with Willis. Your main suspect, Donald Hillian, couldn't have done this."

"Why not?"

"He's just been found dead."

Dante lifted his brows. "How?"

"Don't have a lot of detail, but it appears he kidnapped a woman and a kid. Someone found 'em and went after Hillian, who ended up dead. So, either he wasn't the slayer, or the slayer didn't do this."

Either was possible. Dante wasn't sad the asshole was dead, but he sure had a mess on his hands. If the slayer had done this, why wouldn't he have killed the prostitute? Or Caddell? Maybe tonight's attacker was just someone who had it out for Caddell. There had to be a long list of people who did.

Was Iris safe now that Hillian was dead? Or was there someone still out there who was obsessed with her? She'd be safer if she went back to Philly. Even as he told himself that, the thought of her leaving punched a canyon-sized hole in his chest.

****

Iris ignored the stares and whispers of the other diners at the Parker House Grill. She took a bite of her eggs benedict but was suddenly without an appetite. She felt like a monkey in a zoo. She could have remained in her room, but she wouldn't hide. After all, she was possibly being stalked by a murderer—gossip certainly couldn't harm her. She sipped her coffee, the weight of the past week settling over her. She missed Shelby. The girl's tears when Iris left had nearly broken Iris's heart. She was the only person in that entire family who'd truly loved Iris…and who Iris had truly loved. She could see that now. She'd never loved Norman. She'd expected to be heartbroken after the breakup but once she got past the humiliation and shock, all she felt was relief.

She unfolded *The Boston Post* and let out a gasp of shock. On the front page was a photo…a man lying on a bed wearing women's undergarments. Even before she read the headline, she recognized her ex-fiancé.

What on earth? She read the article and couldn't squelch a giggle. This would positively *ruin* the Caddells' reputation. There was a ring of poetic justice to it, and she felt a malicious satisfaction. Had the South End Slayer done this? The reporter indicated he had. But it was under investigation so there was no proof yet. Her glee was tempered with fear. The devil was still out there…and every victim, Norman included, seemed to relate to her.

An odd sensation brushed over her skin, like the atmosphere in the room had changed. She looked toward the door, and her breath caught. Dante stood at the front of the restaurant, scanning the room. His gaze landed on her, and she put a hand to her stomach to still the butterflies as he headed to her table.

In moments, he was at her side, his handsome face

shadowed by dark stubble. He looked tired, and she wanted to run her fingers through his disheveled hair and kiss away the frown line between his eyes. "Dante. What are you doing here?"

"I have some news. A lot has happened, and I didn't want you to read about it in the papers." He indicated the chair across from her. "May I sit?"

She felt immediately better with Dante here. The others could stare all they wanted. "Yes, of course."

A waitress stopped at the table. "May I get you something, sir?"

"Black coffee, please." After she left, Dante looked at Iris, his expression concerned.

"What is it? What's happened?" She pointed at the newspaper. "Are you here about this?"

His eyes flickered to the paper then back to her. "Yes, but there's more. Audra was attacked, kidnapped."

Iris's hand flew to her mouth and tears knotted her throat. "Oh no, oh mercy me. By the South End Slayer?"

He shook his head. "It appears not. The man who took her was one of my suspects. My main suspect, actually, Donald Hillian. But, he was killed by Leo Frisk, who helped rescue Audra."

Iris's mind whirled. Audra hadn't told her a thing about it. Was she truly that angry that she wouldn't share such a monumental event? "Are you sure she's okay? What about Jamie?"

"They're all fine. Leo, Audra, Jamie. And his little dog too."

Iris managed a grin at the *Wizard of Oz* reference. Dante smiled back, and her anxiety eased. "So, go on.

How do you know he wasn't the slayer?"

"I don't know for certain. But I have reason to believe the slayer is the one who attacked Caddell."

"If you didn't catch his attacker, what makes you think it was the slayer?"

"I can't reveal too many details of the investigation, but some of the witness statements lead us to believe it's a possibility."

Iris shuddered. "I can't believe the…*fiend* is still out there."

"Yeah. I can't either. I'm worried about you staying here on your own. If your parents knew the slayer has been targeting you—"

"They mustn't know." Iris cut him off. The irony that she was doing the same thing Audra had done—lying to her parents and perhaps putting herself in danger—wasn't lost on her. "I will be going back to Philly soon, once I wrap up things at the clinic. I'll tell them then."

A shadow passed over his face. "I think that's best. That you get out of the city where you'll be safe."

She tried not to be hurt that he was so eager to be rid of her. She nodded. "Yes, that would be best."

He held her gaze for a moment, his expression conveying sadness. Maybe he didn't want her to leave. Maybe he only wanted her safe…like he always had.

He broke eye contact and stood. "I need to go. The chief hired me back and we're upping our investigation. We're assembling the entire force to launch a massive effort to catch the slayer."

She stood as well and placed a hand on his arm. "I know you'll catch him. You'll stop him from killing anyone else."

He looked at her hand on his arm. "I wish I had your confidence." He smiled grimly. "How about I walk you to your room and see you safely inside, behind locked doors?"

"Yes, that would be nice. Thank you."

He escorted her to the elevator and when the door closed, leaving them alone in the small space, Iris's heart raced like the front runner at the Kentucky Derby. Her entire body tensed, and she was hyper aware of him…so close…so masculine.

They didn't speak during the ride to her floor. She wondered what he was thinking. About the killer? Or was he thinking the same thing she was, that this might be the last time they were together? The thought brought an ache deep within her soul. How could she lose Dante, again, so soon after finding him?

The elevator stopped, and the doors slid open. They exited and walked to her room. She stopped in front of her door and turned to find Dante so close she could feel his breath on her forehead. She brought her eyes up to his and swallowed loudly. "Thank you, for seeing me up."

"I should come in, just to check your room." His voice was tight. "Make sure you're safe."

She nodded and opened the door. Dante stepped inside behind her and flipped on a light. She waited by the front door as he went from room to room. Her tension increased when he disappeared into her bedroom. She tried to recall if she'd left any unmentionables lying about. The thought of Dante seeing them was so…intimate, yet titillating.

He came out and nodded. "Everything's fine."

"Thank you."

"Right. Well, I guess I'll be going now." But he didn't move. He stood, motionless, his dark eyes roaming over her face, as if committing it to memory.

"I...I'll miss you," she whispered, placing a hand on his chest.

His hand came up to grip hers, and she thought he was going to remove it, but instead, he held it tightly, his gaze sweeping over her face, lingering on her lips.

Heat suffused her, igniting her flesh. She took in a short breath and ran her tongue over her lips.

He let out a small groan and stepped closer, taking her face in his hands. He brushed his lips over hers, a light, gentle touch.

Tingles raced through her body. She was inexperienced, but instinct led her, and she stood on tiptoes, slipping her arms around his neck and pressing her mouth against his. Her heart swelled and nearly exploded as she kissed him with all the pent up feelings she'd carried for six years. She loved him. Had never stopped loving him.

Dante moaned against her lips, and his hands dropped to her lower back, pressing her tightly to him. She flushed as she came into contact with his hardness. A thrill that was part fear part elation swept through her.

He deepened the kiss, his tongue tangling with hers, and she was sure she would have sunk to the floor if his strong arms hadn't been holding her up.

With a growl, he wrenched his mouth from hers. "Oh God, Iris. I can't...I don't know what I was thinking."

He released her and stepped away. She wrapped her arms around her body, suddenly cold, and feeling foolish. "Dante, what's wrong? I love you. I never stopped. And I know you feel something for me. I'm no longer engaged. Why can't we be together?"

He shook his head and squeezed his eyes shut. When he opened, them, they were filled with regret. "I can't. I have nothing to offer you. You're used to the finer things in life, and you need to find a man who can give you what Caddell could." He crooked a grin. "Well, minus the rage and perverted proclivities."

She didn't smile. Anger bubbled up inside her. "I'm tired of everyone telling me what I need, what I want." Her voice rose with each word. "You may not want me, but you can't tell me what kind of man I should find. You know what? Maybe I don't need a man at all. I certainly made a bad choice with Norman, and it appears I've done the same with you." She drew in a deep breath, hanging onto her anger so she wouldn't break down in tears. "So, thank you very much for the advice, but I don't need it. And, you may go now. Thanks for all you've done. Good luck catching the killer. I probably won't see you before I leave for Philadelphia. So, farewell and have a good life."

He flinched, and a muscle jumped in his jaw. He seemed about to say something, then snapped his mouth closed and gave a curt nod. "Goodnight then. Have a safe trip home."

She inclined her head in what she hoped was a regal dismissal. Inside, she was trembling, her heart was crumbling, and the sobs were building. She waited until the door closed behind him before allowing the dam to burst.

****

Iris frowned in confusion as the taxi dropped her off at the soup kitchen. Several people stood outside. Why weren't they going in?

Clarence stepped from the crowd and approached her. "Have you seen Luther?"

"No. Not since a few days ago. He's not here?"

"Nope. And we can't get in to feed these people."

Worry trickled through her. Had something happened to Luther? She fumbled in her bag. "I have a key. Luther gave me one so I could access the clinic when the kitchen is closed."

She unlocked the door and Clarence and the others filed inside. "I'm sorry, folks." Iris said to the group. "As you can see, we opened a little late, but the food will be ready soon."

There were a few grumbles but they settled at tables to wait.

Iris bit her lip. Audra wasn't here, and they were short on volunteers. But she had to check on Luther. She followed Clarence into the kitchen. "Do you know where Luther lives?"

"Sure do. Me and some of the fellas go over there for poker once in a while."

"Please give me his address. I'm going to check on him. I'll try to be back before it's time to serve."

"How about I take you?" His gaze slid over her. "A pretty filly like you shouldn't be runnin' around all alone." He smiled his lecherous smile, and she shuddered. There was definitely something off about him and she'd certainly not be alone with him. Especially if…

Had Clarence done something to Luther? Was he the slayer? No, he was a creep, but he couldn't be the slayer. And why would he want to hurt Luther? Of course, why would anyone be doing what this sick person was doing? She huffed in frustration. So many questions she had no answers to. For now, her concern was Luther. "No, thank you. Someone needs to stay here and get the food ready. Plus, if Luther shows up, or if we hear news about him, you'll need to be here to take care of things."

He scowled but acquiesced and gave her the address. She hailed a taxi and tried to remain calm on the way to Luther's. There must be a logical explanation. He wasn't hurt…or dead.

The taxi pulled up to a modest two-story home with a neat lawn. Luther's car was in the driveway. She knocked on the door. No response. She knocked louder. Still nothing. She tried the doorknob, surprised to find it unlocked. She pushed it open and stepped inside. "Luther? Are you here?"

The house was quiet…an empty kind of quiet. She was sure no one was here…no one living, that is. She shuddered and moved farther into the house, calling Luther's name. The house was clean and neat. But utterly still.

Anxiety took hold as she moved from room to room. She climbed the stairs and stopped in front of an open doorway. She stepped inside, then halted abruptly, a gasp escaping her. The room was devoid of furniture, other than a desk on which several newspapers and a pair of large scissors lay. The walls were papered with articles on the South End Slayer case.

On shaky legs, she moved closer. Among the articles were photos of her…and of Bonnie Parker. Iris recognized the outlaw from photos she'd seen in newspapers. What on earth…? A cold chill skittered through her. Could Luther be the South End Slayer? Surely not. Perhaps he was just interested in the case because of the connection to the soup kitchen. But why were there photos of her? And of Bonnie Parker?

Footsteps sounded behind her and, before she could turn around, she heard Luther's voice. "Bonnie?"

Chapter Ten

Iris whirled to find Luther standing just inside the room. Her vocal cords froze, and she could only stare in bewilderment. While he was normally neatly groomed, now he looked as though he'd battled a windstorm. His hair was messy, his clothing wrinkled, and something that appeared to be blood dotted his forehead.

Iris finally found her voice. "Did you…did you call me Bonnie?"

He moved farther into the room. His eyes glittered with an odd excitement, and his smile was almost…feral…like a rabid cougar who'd come upon a wounded deer. She shuddered. "You are my Bonnie." He spoke softly, reverently. "All this time, I've waited until the moment was right. And here it is. My Bonnie has come back to me."

Mercy me. He thought she was Bonnie Parker. "Luther…what's wrong with you? You know I'm not Bonnie. I'm Iris."

He continued slowly toward her. She backed up. "No. We don't have to pretend anymore. It's all been leading up to this moment. We're finally free to be together."

Sickness coiled in her stomach. "I am not Bonnie." She made her voice firm but couldn't control the note of panic that lay beneath it.

Luther halted with a frown. "Maybe you don't

know. Is that possible?"

She'd continued backing until she was against the wall, the paper taped to it crinkling against her spine. Luther stood only inches in front of her. He placed a hand to the side of her face, and she recoiled. "Luther…you're scaring me." What was happening? He'd lost his mind. He must be the slayer. And now, she was trapped with him.

"I don't want to scare you. I only want to love you. Like I wanted to all those years ago, but Clyde stood in our way."

This was insane, and his touch made her nauseous. She slapped his hand away. "I am not Bonnie, and this is ridiculous." She started to step around him, but he grabbed her arm and pulled her to him. Anger flared in his pale eyes. "You're not going anywhere." The softness left his tone, and now it vibrated with anger. "What the hell kind of game are you playin'?

Tears sprang to her eyes. She tried to pull free, but his grip was like steel. "I'm not playing a game. I don't know what you're talking about."

He narrowed his eyes, studying her face. "If you're not Bonnie…" Rage and confusion contorted his features. "Then what have I been doing all of this for?"

"A-all of what." Her heart pounded so loudly, she could barely hear her own words. A sick feeling clogged her chest, and she knew what he meant. "It was you. You've been killing people. Why?"

"I did it for you. For Bonnie. If you're not her…then it's all been a lie, and it's over." Tears filled his eyes, and he shook his head. "There's no point to any of this." His hold eased but he didn't release her. "I have no reason to live…" His wild gaze settled on her face. "No reason to let you live."

Fear gripped her. He was completely crazy. And dangerous. She had to appease him until she figured a way out of this. She brought her free hand to her forehead and hoped she possessed at least a modicum of acting skills. "Oh my…my head…I'm so confused. I can't think…" She blinked and looked into his eyes. "You're right." Her voice dropped to a whisper. "I am Bonnie."

He frowned, his gaze wary. "But you just said you weren't."

"I know. My memory…it's fuzzy. It comes and goes, and when I'm anxious…" She forced a note of happiness into her voice. "I was nervous. I—it's been so long. And I've wanted this moment to happen but now that it's here, I'm afraid."

His expression softened. "What are you afraid of? If you're my Bonnie, you have nothing to fear. I'd never hurt you."

"I know. You've always cared for me. Haven't you?" Based on the extent he'd gone to in her honor, she assumed that was true. Had he been part of the Barrow gang or someone from Bonnie Parker's childhood? She lifted a hand and massaged her temple. "After all that's happened, I'm a little fuzzy. The ambush, the shooting…that was traumatic as you can imagine."

His face caved in sympathy. "I know. I'm so sorry I couldn't save you from that, my darling." He pulled her to him, and she let him. The feel of his body against hers brought a lump of revulsion to her throat, but she swallowed it back. "I had no idea Ivan Methvin had betrayed you. If you'd have left Clyde like I asked you to, it never would have happened. I knew that no good rattlesnake was going to get you killed."

So, he *was* part of the criminal gang. "I know. You were right. I should have listened to you. I'm sorry. Can you forgive me?"

He pulled back and smiled down at her. "I did the moment you walked into the soup kitchen, and I recognized that it was really you."

This was utterly *insane*. Icy chills raced down her spine. "How did you know it was me?"

"You still have them same eyes, like a blue sky after a squalor. You got her deep down strength though sometimes, you're like a scared filly, same as Bonnie. The second I laid eyes on you, there was this connection. I'd begged the universe to bring you back to me. And it did."

Heavens above, the man was stark raving mad. She had to figure out a way to get away from him. She almost wished she *were* Bonnie Parker. The outlaw would probably be carrying a gun and would blow a hole right through him. For now, she had to keep him talking. "I don't understand, though. Why did you kill those people? We always only killed out of necessity." She'd read that about the Barrow Gang, though some accounts had contradicted the claim and painted a much nastier picture of the outlaws.

His face darkened. "Because I couldn't kill Clyde."

"I—I don't understand."

"These people are just like him. He was a vagabond too, livin' on the streets like an animal when he was growin' up. Each time I took one of their lives, I thought of him and all he'd done to you. It was so…" His eyes glazed over like he was reliving a joyous memory. "…so satisfyin'. Plum euphoric."

Her gut twisted. He'd killed because of her. Or, because of who he thought she was. Guilt wormed through her, but she pushed it aside. She hadn't knowingly made him think of Bonnie, nor had she had anything to do with the murders. She had to stay focused and get out of this. She shuddered. She still couldn't believe *Luther* was the South End Slayer. But then, she hadn't really known him at all. He was a devil. And she'd gotten close to him, shared her thoughts and feelings and cared about him.

She paced away, needing to distance herself from his malevolence…needing to think. Needing to buy time and hopefully work her way to the scissors. She pointed to his forehead. "What happened to you? Where have you been? I came here looking for you when you didn't show up at the kitchen."

He touched his forehead with his fingertips. "Oh, this. I was out last night, and I had a scuffle, but I got away. Got into my car and…I think I must have passed out."

A scuffle? Was he attacking someone? She hoped he hadn't committed another murder. She hoped the state he was in meant the person had gotten the best of him and escaped. "But your car was in the driveway."

He smiled. "I have another. A secret vehicle I use for my…hunts. I park it in the back and keep it out of sight."

"Well…I'm glad you're okay."

"I can't believe this." He closed the distance between them. "You and me, together now. We can leave Boston and start over somewhere. But first, we have to get rid of Morello."

Her heart clenched. "Get rid of Dante? Why?"

Darkness settled over his features. "The bastard is after me. And, he's got designs on you."

She gave what she hoped was a nonchalant laugh. "Designs on me? Not at all. He's just a childhood friend. We don't have to harm him. We can just leave. Leave all of this behind. We'll go somewhere that he'll never find you." She was bluffing, stalling for time. But the truth was, if it meant saving Dante, she'd run off with Luther in a heartbeat.

****

Dante scrubbed his hands over his face and ground his teeth. He'd been over the notes, the case, the photos, hundreds of times and not a damn thing led to a good suspect. He'd liked Hillian for it. And he'd considered Caddell as well. They were both now out of the running. That left him Bittner and Rickers. He had nothing concrete on either. The slayer could be someone who hadn't even crossed his radar. "Son of a bitch," he growled. While he was chasing his tail, the killer could be out there now, murdering another innocent victim.

He took a slug from his coffee cup and focused once more on the interview Shannon had conducted with the prostitute and the motel clerk. This was the closest they'd been to the slayer…if the guy who'd done this had been him. And Dante had a gut feeling it had.

This time, when he read the report, a phrase jumped out at him that he'd previously overlooked. The perpetrator had told them that if they made one wrong move, he'd be '*madder n' all git out.*' His gut tightened. He knew exactly where he'd heard that phrase.

He leapt to his feet and rushed out the door, jumping into his car and driving like he was on fire to the soup kitchen. He burst through the doors, looking for Iris, but didn't see her. His heart raced with fear. He found Bittner in the back. "Where's Luther?"

The cook frowned at him. "I don't rightly know. He didn't show up. Iris went to fetch him."

"Iris…?" Cold terror gripped his heart. "Where does he live?" When Bittner didn't respond immediately, Dante gripped a handful of his shirt and shook him. "Where does Luther live?"

"Jiminy, all right, all right. You don't have to go nuts. He lives over on Newton." He gave the address.

Dante released him and ran, his heart trying to climb through his throat. He jumped into his car and sped toward Rickers'. He prayed he wasn't too late. And prayed for the bastard's soul if he was.

Chapter Eleven

Iris had maneuvered closer to the desk…almost there. She kept her voice light and hoped she was convincing Luther she was willing to be with him, that she was Bonnie. “If you want, we can kill him. But, I say we don’t bother. Why waste time when we can just leave? I’ll go to the hotel and grab some things and meet you back here.”

Luther’s brows drew together. “No. You don’t need nothin’. I’m not lettin’ you outta my sight. But we’re not leavin’ town until that rattlesnake is dead.”

“Okay, sure. But we can’t kill him at the station. How will we get to him?” She’d backed her way to the desk. The scissors were almost within reach. When she got them, she had to aim well and strike quickly and with all her might. She only had one chance at this. She leaned with her hands behind her on the desk, wiggling her fingers back until she felt the handle of the scissors. Now, to entice Luther closer. “I’m just so…” She forced a delicate shudder. “So excited and scared at the same time.” She gave him a beseeching look. “Tell me it’s all going to be okay.”

He sighed and stepped forward, taking her arms in his hands. “Of course, darling. I promise you, we’ll get out of here and—”

A creaking sound—like footsteps on the wood floor—came from downstairs. Iris gaped at Luther.

Who was here? Could it be Dante? No. He had no idea where she was. But maybe he was onto Luther?

Luther cocked his head. He'd heard it too. He abruptly released her and turned away, reaching inside his jacket pocket. Horror slammed into her when she saw the gun in his hand. Panicked, she snatched up the scissors and lunged forward, jamming them into the back of his neck.

He screamed and dropped to the floor, losing his hold on the gun. She turned to run, but he caught her ankle, dragging her down with him. She landed hard on the floor, losing her breath.

"Iris?" Dante yelled. Footsteps thundered up the stairs.

"Dante!" she sobbed. "He's got a gun!"

"You bitch," Luther snarled in pain-filled rage. "I'll kill you both."

She looked back. Luther held onto her with one hand, scrambling for the gun with the other. He was bleeding profusely, the scissors jutting from his back. With surprising strength, he latched tighter onto Iris's leg and yanked her to him, then wrapped his arms around her and struggled to a standing position, pulling her with him.

Dante appeared in the doorway. His gaze quickly took in the situation, and fury came over his features. "Let her go, Rickers."

Luther stumbled back, his hold like a vise, using her as a shield. "You won't shoot me," he huffed out. "Not while I've got her. Drop it, or I'll jump out the window and take her with me." As he spoke, he backed them both toward the window. "I mean it, Morello, drop the fucking gun!"

Iris trembled with fear and anger. Luther had already taken so much. So many lives. If Dante relinquished his weapon, they'd both die. "Don't do it," she choked out. "Kill him." But she knew Dante couldn't take a shot, not without risking hitting her as well.

She met Dante's gaze, hoping he could see her love for him. A love that had never died. Had only grown with the passing years. She'd do anything for him. Anything to protect him, just as he'd protected her all these years.

Making a split decision, hoping like hades it was the right one, she shoved backward with all her strength. Luther grunted in surprise. She rammed him against the wall as hard as she could, attempting to drive the scissors deeper. From his pained cry, she was sure she had. But he still didn't let go. He emitted a howl of agonizing rage and jerked her down to the floor with him as he fell.

"Iris!" Dante's panicked shout filled her ears.

Luther scooted with her gripped in his arms, while she fought with all her might. But, even with him injured and bleeding, she was no match for his strength. He was angling for the gun. And he was getting close. With one last burst of strength, she twisted her body as hard as she could, letting out a cry of relief when Luther's grip loosened.

She scrambled to her feet, her eyes seeking out Dante. He aimed his gun at Luther, but at that same moment, Luther reached his. A shot rang out, and Iris screamed.

****

Dante's arm went limp, and he squeezed his eyes

shut. He was back in the trenches, the boom of machine-gun fire and mortaring pounding the air. The screaming, the thick mud that smelled of sulfur, sweat, and death. From far away, came the voice of an angel. “Dante? Are you okay? Look at me! Open your eyes.”

Iris…his Iris. He blinked his eyes open and scanned the room. The scent of blood permeated the air. Luther lay sprawled on the floor, sightless eyes staring upward. A dark stain puddled around him.

Dante tore his gaze away, and it landed on Iris. She was trembling. Tears streamed down her cheeks. Her lovely eyes were glittering pools of aqua. He slid his gun back in its holster and opened his arms. Iris fell into them, and nothing in his life had ever felt sweeter, more perfect…more right. “I love you,” he murmured against her hair. “I thought you were…” A groan left his throat, and he pulled back, cupping her face in his hands and letting his eyes drink her in. “You are the most important thing in the world to me, and I thought I’d lost you. I love you, Iris,” he repeated, meaning it with every molecule of his heart and soul.

A smile lit her face, and her eyes shimmered with unshed tears. “It’s about time you came to your senses.”

He grinned and bent his head, capturing her sweet lips with his, barely thinking about the dead monster lying a few feet away.

****

Iris held onto Shelby while the girl sobbed into her shoulder. “There, there,” she soothed. She pulled back and gently wiped tears from Shelby’s cheeks. “Don’t cry. You’ll get your eyes all red and your pretty face splotchy. And, look at this, we’re wrinkling our lovely dresses.”

Shelby sniffed. "But, I can't bear the thought of you leaving. You're the only person in Boston I care about. The only one I can talk to."

"We'll stay in touch, I promise. And I'm always just a phone call away."

Shelby nodded and wiped her eyes, but she didn't seem mollified. "This is the worst party ever. Why do people have a party for someone who's going away? They should have a wake."

Iris chuckled. "That's actually not a bad point." Iris looked past Shelby's shoulder. Opal approached, arms crossed, her manly features set in a disapproving expression. Iris was surprised Opal had come, that she had allowed Shelby to come. Though, Shelby was pretty strong-willed and had probably bombarded the woman until she'd given in.

"Come along." Opal took Shelby's hand. "It's getting late. We must be going." Shelby reluctantly allowed herself to be dragged away, giving Iris a small smile and wave.

"Iris?"

Iris turned at the voice, her heart leaping with joy to find Audra standing behind her. Her handsome beau, Leo, stood next to her. Iris hadn't spoken to her since the night of graduation, when Audra had been so furious with her.

"Oh, Audra. You came."

"Of course I did." She sniffed and a sob caught in her throat. "I'm sorry I've been so stubborn. I know you were only trying to look out for me. Can you forgive me?"

In spite of Iris's heartbreak at leaving Boston, joy filled her soul. She had her friend back. "Yes, I forgive you. I'm sorry too."

They embraced tightly, and Iris grinned. Her dress would surely be ruined before the evening was over. They pulled apart, but Audra kept hold of her hands. "I can't believe you're leaving. I'll miss you so. We all will. And, how can you leave Dante? He loves you."

She grimaced. "I'm not so sure about that." Yes, he'd told her he did. But she hadn't heard a thing from him since. Not a word, even though he knew she was going back to Philly.

Audra cut a look at Leo. "Trust me, men can be stubborn."

Leo laughed. "As can women. Convincing this one to stay was a Herculean task." He slipped his arm around Audra, who literally glowed with happiness. Iris was glad for her friend but she couldn't prevent a tiny bit of envy from sneaking in. Her three friends had all found the loves of their lives. Was Iris destined to be alone forever?

Audra looked over Iris's shoulder. "Speak of the devil," she said softly.

Iris turned, her heart leaping to her throat when she saw Dante striding toward them. In moments, he was standing at her elbow, so close, she could feel the heat from his body.

"Good evening." He greeted them, giving Audra a hug and shaking Leo's hand. "How's it feel to be a hero? Good job on taking Hillian out."

Leo shook his head. "Hero? I don't think so. I'd say it was a lot of luck and some help from Audra here, along with a huge dose of determination to save the woman I love."

Dante's eyes went to Iris. "I can definitely

understand that."

She clasped her fingers tightly together but didn't speak.

Dante turned back to Leo. "Maybe you should think about joining the force, the way you handled yourself."

Leo shook his head with a smile. "No, thank you. The most dangerous things I plan to encounter are stray balls at Red Sox games and Audra's temper."

Audra jabbed him in the ribs. "Watch it, buster."

Iris laughed. "Maybe you and Audra could come to Philadelphia sometime and take in a game. The Red Sox will be there playing the Athletics on May twenty-seventh." Her dad had taken her to many games as a child. They were Phillies fans over the Athletics, but they supported both teams.

"That would be wonderful," Audra said. She looked between Iris and Dante, a twinkle entering her eyes. "Leo, I'm parched. Let's go find something to drink."

As soon as they were gone, Dante said to Iris, "Can I speak with you? Alone?"

Nerves jangled inside her. "Certainly." He led her outside. The sky was a blanket of blackness dotted with stars. Wispy clouds floated in front of the half moon. The moon looked just as it did on the night she confessed her love for Dante for the first time. So much had happened since then, but her love had never wavered…it had only grown. She'd been crushed at the time, but now she knew what true heartbreak felt like. She took a deep breath of the cool night air and let it out slowly. She'd not be breathing Boston air much longer, and the thought made her heart heavy.

She turned her attention to Dante, who stood next to her, so close their arms nearly brushed. She moved back a step so she could think clearly. "What did you want to talk to me about?"

He didn't speak for a few moments, just stared at her. His dark eyes seemed to penetrate her soul. "You're still leaving Boston?"

"Yes. I go back to Philly tomorrow."

"Now that you're no longer in danger, I wish you'd stay. The clinic needs you."

The clinic…not him. Of course, that made sense. He'd said he loved her in the spur of the moment, when they'd both almost lost their lives. And she hadn't heard from him in the two days since. "The soup kitchen will surely close with no one to run it, and then where will the clinic be?"

"The kitchen isn't closing. Clarence is running it for now, but he doesn't want to continue. He'd rather just be the cook. My mother is moving here, and she'll run the soup kitchen."

Iris lifted her brows, surprised and pleased at the news. "Truly?" The thought of the poor and hungry not losing their place lifted her spirits. Funny how a month ago, she could barely tolerate them, now the thought of them starving or being hurt broke her heart. "Oh, Dante, that's wonderful. But I still have to go. I imagine someone from the hospital will help out with the clinic. Dr. Gorman was quite enthused at the idea. Volunteering at the clinic doesn't pay the bills. In Philly, I can live with my parents until I find a steady job. The clinic doesn't really need me."

He stepped closer, his mouth set in a grimace. His ebony eyes glittered in the reflection of the moonlight.

"Maybe it doesn't need you." His voice was rough with emotion. "But I do. Doesn't it mean anything to you that I love you? You claim to love me. Why would you leave me?"

She pressed a hand to her stomach to still the butterflies. "I-I wasn't sure. I haven't heard from you since that…thing…with Luther."

"I know. I'm sorry. I've been busy wrapping up the case. That doesn't mean I haven't been thinking about you every second."

"I just thought…I thought you said you loved me in a moment of panic, because I was nearly killed. I didn't know if you meant it. If you're actually *in love* with me. I know you care for me. We've known each other for so many years. And—"

"Stop!" His angry voice cut through her words. His expression was positively thunderous. "Don't minimize my feelings for you. I told you I love you, and I meant it. Completely, wholly, truly and forever. I love you. I don't say that unless I mean it. I've fought it these past months, but the truth is, you're my heart, my soul. The moment I saw you here that first time, all grown up and so beautiful, I was lost. The fact that you were marrying another man tore a hole in my heart the size of Fenway Park. And then, as time went by. I only grew to love you more. I saw a caring side of you I never knew existed. And, even though you were targeted by a vicious killer, you didn't let that stop you." He grinned. "And you were a little hellion when you fought Luther off."

His words fell on her like a gentle summer rain. She couldn't believe he loved her…couldn't believe the depth of his feelings for her. She had so much to say, but she couldn't speak. Her throat was closed with a knot of tears and if she spoke, they might never stop flowing.

He lifted his hand and brushed his knuckles gently down her cheek. His touch made her shiver, and she longed to lean into him. "Please say you'll stay. Please say you'll marry me. If you want a career as a nurse, I'll support that. If you want to work at the clinic, I'll support that. If you want to stay home and do nothing but warm my bed and give me children, I'll support that. Just, please, don't leave me." A sheen of moisture hovered in his eyes. "I've faced death many times…fought in a war…but I've never been more scared of anything than I am of losing you."

She laughed, but it came out a sob. "I don't think I've ever heard you say that many words."

He smiled. "That's because you've never seen me so desperate." He hooked an arm around her waist and tugged her to him. "Please, Iris. Please say you'll marry me." His gaze dropped to her mouth, and she let her eyes drift shut, wanting to feel his lips against hers.

She managed to whisper, "Yes," and then he kissed her. And she kissed him back as that same moon smiled down on them.

A word about the author…

Alicia Dean lives in Edmond, Oklahoma. She has three grown children and a huge network of supportive friends and family. She writes mostly contemporary suspense and paranormal, but has also written in other genres, including a few vintage historicals.

She is a freelance editor in addition to being an editor for The Wild Rose Press.

Other than reading and writing, her passions are Elvis Presley, MLB, NFL (she usually works in a mention of one or all three into her stories) and watching her favorite televisions shows like Vampire Diaries, Justified, Sons of Anarchy, Haven, New Girl, The Mindy Project, and Dexter (even though it has sadly ended, she will forever be a fan). Some of her favorite authors are Michael Connelly, Dennis Lehane, Lee Child, Lisa Gardner, Sharon Sala, Jordan Dane, Ridley Pearson, Joseph Finder, and Jonathan Kellerman…to name a few.

Please follow Alicia on Twitter: @Alicia_Dean_ and visit her website: AliciaDean.com, or feel free to drop her a line at: AliciaMDean@aol.com.

Thank you for purchasing
this publication of The Wild Rose Press, Inc.

For questions or more information
contact us at
info@thewildrosepress.com.

The Wild Rose Press, Inc.
www.thewildrosepress.com

www.ingramcontent.com/pod-product-compliance
Lightning Source LLC
Chambersburg PA
CBHW051537260626
47170CB00003B/971
9781509236800